5

110

T-9

2015-4

2017-1

L 7/17

11-19 (10)

# Hell on Wheels

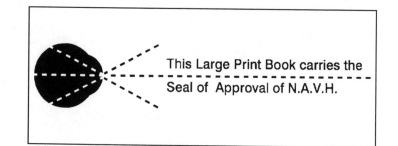

This Large Print Book carries the
Seal of Approval of N.A.V.H.

AN ODELIA GREY MYSTERY

# HELL ON WHEELS

# SUE ANN JAFFARIAN

**THORNDIKE PRESS**
*A part of Gale, Cengage Learning*

GALE
CENGAGE Learning·

Farmington Hills, Mich • San Francisco • New York • Waterville, Maine
Meriden, Conn • Mason, Ohio • Chicago

# GALE
## CENGAGE Learning

**LIBRARY OF CONGRESS CATALOGING-IN-PUBLICATION DATA**

Jaffarian, Sue Ann, 1952–
  Hell on wheels : an Odelia Grey mystery / by Sue Ann Jaffarian. — Large print edition.
    pages ; cm. — (Thorndike Press large print mystery)
    ISBN 978-1-4104-7374-5 (hardcover) — ISBN 1-4104-7374-0 (hardcover)
    1. Grey, Odelia (Fictitious character)—Fiction. 2. Women detectives—California—Fiction. 3. Overweight women—Fiction. 4. Legal assistants—Fiction. 5. Quadriplegics—Fiction. 6. Murder—Fiction. 7. Large type books.
I. Title.
PS3610.A359H45 2015
813'.6—dc23
                                                                                    2014040238

Published in 2015 by arrangement with Midnight Ink, an imprint of Llewellyn Publications, Woodbury, MN 55125-2989, USA

Printed in Mexico
1 2 3 4 5 6 7 19 18 17 16 15

For Heide van den Akker.
Thanks for being such a great friend.

# ONE

The crash was not a surprise. I saw it coming, steeling myself for the inevitable sound of metal hitting metal at a high, reckless speed. The final impact rattled my teeth and took my breath away. It always did.

Shouts and mild profanity filled the thick air, yelled with both anger and excitement. Next to me, on my left, my husband, Greg Stevens, was pumping his fist high as he cheered. His favorite team, the Laguna Lunatics, was ahead.

It's called murderball.

The official name is quad rugby. It's a game played by quadriplegics in wheelchairs on a regulation basketball court. It's also an official Paralympic sport. The object of the game is to get the ball past the other team's goal. It's fast, brutal, and exciting. Using special wheelchairs that look like modified *Mad Max* bumper cars, players slam into each other with no thought of injury. Sometimes they tip and the occupants, usually secured by a safety belt, go down with them onto the hardwood floor. Think sacks of flour from a tipped hand truck and you get the picture.

My name is Odelia Patience Grey, and until I met Greg, I didn't even know the sport of quad rugby existed. Now every November we pilgrimage down to Balboa Park in San Diego for the Best of the West tournament. Greg would love to play. Even if he hadn't told me so many times, I can see it in his eyes. They light up like high beams on a dark road whenever we attend the tournament or go to any of the regular games and practices.

My husband is an excellent athlete. He plays basketball, golf, and tennis; he surfs and sails, and he has taken self-defense courses. He doesn't let being in a wheelchair stop him from doing anything he wants to do. He even jumped from an airplane on his last birthday. It was something he'd always wanted to do, and I reluctantly had given it to him as a gift. I went to watch and get it on video, but the whole time my heart was in my throat, along with my breakfast.

But quad rugby is something Greg can't do. It's a sport only open to quadriplegics

— men and women who have impairment to some degree in all four of their limbs. Greg is a paraplegic, with full use of his hands and arms. Who knew that the one sport he's dying to try would be something he's too able-bodied to play?

Greg has lots of friends who play quad rugby. A few of them — players with more mobility in their upper extremities — also play on some of the wheelchair basketball teams in Greg's league.

The Municipal Gymnasium at Balboa Park was like most any gym found anywhere in the world. It's a huge no-frills building reminiscent of an airplane hangar and large enough to hold two full-size basketball courts, with a generous middle section for bleachers facing both courts and a wide open space for mingling. The floors are hardwood, the walls scarred, and the air a mix of sweat, wood polish, and rubber that no cleaning product or room freshener could ever abolish. Defeat, competition, and triumph filled the room like the Ghosts of Christmas Past, Present, and Future.

We were watching the Laguna Lunatics take on the Fresno Flash. Our friend Richard Henderson, better known as Rocky, played for the Lunatics. His wife, Miranda, sat next to me on the bleachers to my right.

Two years ago after a tournament, she'd confessed to me that she hated quad rugby. She'd been drunk at the time. We were in the ladies' room at the hotel where several of the players, along with their families and friends, had been celebrating the end of the tournament and the Lunatics' win. I had been holding Miranda's hair while she knelt on the dubious floor in one of the stalls and puked. She all but pinkie swore me to secrecy after — not about the vomiting but about her feelings toward the game her husband loved second only to her. But she need not have worried. I'm a firm believer in the sanctity of the ladies' room. If someone trusts you enough to hold her hair while she pukes, then you'd better not screw her over by divulging any secrets she spills along with her dinner, even if some of that dinner splashes onto your new blue shoes that you didn't buy on sale. It's like a priest hearing confession, but messier. I didn't even tell Greg.

*Crash!* Kevin Spelling, a California golden boy with curly blond locks, wide shoulders, and upper arms thick as redwoods, smashed into an opposing player. He flashed a toothy grin of perfect white teeth as the ball came loose and was regained by the Lunatics. He'd been injured in a surfing accident when he was barely twenty-one and was now in his early thirties.

A few rows behind us, Samantha Franco jumped to her feet and screamed with enthusiasm as her husband, Jeremy — one of the new players on the Lunatics — took the ball down the court for the score.

Almost as soon as the ball was back in play, the jarring sound of collision filled the air, battling with the shouts and crashes coming from the other court for attention, as if the noise was a competition. Each crash rattled my teeth. I could only imagine what it felt like on the court. Another crash, and next to me Miranda jumped to her feet. On the court in front of us, Rocky was on the floor. Strapped into his tank of a wheelchair, he floundered on his back like a flipped sea turtle. A whistle sounded, and the game stopped. The coach of the Lunatics, Able Warren, and his assistant, his college-aged nephew Ian, ran onto the court from the sidelines. Ian was holding a very large piece of cardboard, like a large appliance box that had been dismantled and flattened. They stuck the cardboard under the wheelchair, wedging it under the small back wheels used for spinning and quick turns, and righted Rocky. The crowd cheered. As soon as he was stable, the cardboard was removed and the whistle blew to resume play. The whole exercise took about ten seconds. A NASCAR pit crew could take lessons.

Seeing Rocky upright again, Miranda plopped back down on the bench. "I'll never get used to that." Her face was stony with worry. "Never."

I reached an arm around Miranda and gave her a quick motherly hug. She was young, not even out of her twenties, and on the flighty side. Rocky was in his late thirties. Being in my mid-fifties, I was closer in age to the parents of many players than to their significant others. Even Greg, at ten years my junior, was long in the tooth next to most of the players.

"Don't worry," I told her. "A little fall is not going to hurt him. Considering what Rocky and these other players have been through, this is nothing. They're made of steel."

Which was true, considering how many of the players had undergone multiple surgeries following the various accidents and injuries that had placed them in the chairs in the first place. Some of the players had lost limbs to illnesses, like one star player who played without all four limbs. Using rubber sleeves on the stumps of his arms, which had been amputated just above the elbow, he could smoke most of the players as he headed down the court. He could catch the ball and even throw it a short distance with accuracy. Any scrapes and bumps received playing quad rugby were child's play compared to what these people had already been through. Even Greg had gone through hell and back in his rehabilitation after injuring his spine during a bad fall while in his early teens. When we first started dating, I had been concerned about him injuring himself further, but in time I had learned to go with the flow — or at least not to voice my worry. Miranda hadn't quite gotten there yet even though she and Rocky had been married several years.

It was almost as if these men and women, after being thrown against the wall and physically broken, were looking fate in the eye with all the brass and balls they could muster and yelling, "Is that the best you've got?" They were courageous, with an ain't-got-nothing-to-lose cockiness that most people could never command — certainly not me.

When the game was over, Greg and I caught up with Rocky and some of the other players in the middle of the gymnasium. Miranda wasn't there. She was probably in the ladies' room, hopefully just to pee and not vomit. Using my smartphone, I took several photos of Greg with the players, Rocky with his team, and the gym crowd in general.

Today was Sunday, the last day of the tournament. At the end of the last round, it was down to just four teams. Two would play for third and fourth place, two for first and second. The Lunatics had won their game, putting them in the finals for first or second place.

We were standing around chatting in a large, boisterous group when my phone rang. The ringtone was that of an old-fashioned phone — the ringtone I'd assigned to my mother. In fact, both Greg and I had that sound set on our phones for Mom. For his mother we both had the tinkling of bells. At the sound Greg turned his attention to me, curious about the call. I shrugged in his direction and excused myself, stepping just outside the gym to hear better.

"Hi Mom, everything okay?"

Mom was staying at our house to look after things while we were in San Diego. Usually we would bring our golden retriever, Wainwright, with us to the tournament. Many of the players had dogs, and many were goldens. Wainwright loved the canine camaraderie. But this year Greg and I had decided to leave Wainwright at home with our cat, Muffin, and treat ourselves to a longer weekend and a romantic hotel on the beach. Even with the crisp air of November, we loved the beach and made our home in Seal Beach in north Orange County.

My mother, Grace Littlejohn, had moved from New Hampshire to California this past year and made the perfect house and pet sitter. She'd bought a condo in a nearby retirement community that was far enough away for us to lead separate lives.

"Everything's fine here," my mother confirmed in her clipped voice, "but Steele called and said he needs to talk to you. He said he tried your cell but it wasn't working."

Michael Steele is my boss, a real pain in the ass who had studied the fine art of arrogance along with the law. We both work for a firm called Templin and Tobin, better known as T&T, in their Orange County office. I serve as their corporate paralegal. Steele is the managing partner of the office. Mike Steele calls everyone he works with by their last name, so I'm Grey, and I call him Steele. It's like we're in the military or part of a sports team. My mother calls him Steele also, much to his amusement.

"My phone is working just fine, Mom. I just didn't answer it when he called."

"He said he tried Greg's phone too."

"Greg and I are out of town, having a mini vacation. Steele knows that. We are both ignoring him."

"Well," Mom said, drawing out the short word into a three-syllable extravaganza of disapproval. "Steele is your boss, and you wouldn't want to get fired if something went wrong."

I sighed. "Don't worry, Mom. Steele is not going to fire me, and I doubt he has an emergency. But tell you what: if he calls again — and he will — tell him I'll call him back tonight when we get to our hotel. Is everything else okay at the house?"

While I chatted on the phone, I saw a man in a wheelchair making his way from the far end of the parking lot to the gymnasium. He was dressed in the uniform of the Ventura Vipers — the team that would play the Lunatics in the playoff for first place. It seemed odd that he'd be out here instead of getting ready to play, but I didn't have the time or the brain cells to think much more about it with Mom talking on the other end.

"Everything is just fine and dandy," she reported. "Wainwright and I walked down to the beach a little while ago. Oh, and you're almost out of treats, both dog and kitty."

"Yeah, I forgot them when I went shopping, but they'll live until we get home. Besides, you tend to spoil them rotten with treats."

I knew that last comment would fall on deaf ears. Mom loved Muffin and Wainwright almost as much as she loved her real grandchildren by my half brother Clark. She'd grown attached to our old cat, Seamus, last November on her visit, and when he passed away she took it very hard and started spoiling our other two fur babies as a way of overcompensating for the loss. She's been talking about getting a cat of her own, and both Greg and I think it would be a great idea. For Christmas we might take Mom around to the pet adoption places and let her pick one out.

Mom was yammering again about Steele, reminding me not to forget to call him, but I was only half listening. I wanted to get back and settle in for the big game. "Don't worry, Mom, I'll get in touch with Steele when I can. I have to get back now."

As I stashed my phone back into my bag, I turned and collided with the man I'd seen crossing the parking lot, nearly landing my two hundred twenty pounds in the poor guy's lap. As if he didn't already have enough injuries.

Quickly, I righted myself. "I am so sorry," I told him in an embarrassed rush. "I should pay more attention to where I'm going."

"That's okay, pretty lady."

Using one curved hand and arm, he secured some sports bottles nestled in his lap. Using his other arm, he tried to steady me as best he could. He was handsome and well built — an Asian with coal-black eyes, shiny black hair, and a smile just crooked enough to be rakish instead of odd. And the way he looked at me told me he knew he was the total package and I should be honored to be in his presence. I guessed him to be in his mid-thirties. He was sitting in a regular wheelchair, not a rugby one. I'd seen the Vipers play before but didn't recognize this guy.

"Name's Peter Tanaka." He looked me up and down, appraising the goods. "And I love me some chubby cougar."

"I'm Odelia." I flashed my left hand in his direction, showing off my impressive diamond ring and wedding band. "And I'm married."

He shrugged. "Most of the good ones are." He maneuvered even closer and gave me a smoldering look. "But you haven't lived until you've had a gimp. Trust me. We know how to treat a lady."

"Back off, Tanaka," came an angry and familiar voice. "She already has a gimp in her life, and I treat her very well."

Greg rolled up and forced his chair between Peter Tanaka and me. I stepped back to make room. Peter didn't budge an inch. Around us, people who'd come outside to catch some fresh air between games stopped to watch the confrontation.

"Well, if it isn't Greg Stevens. It's been a long time." Peter glanced at me. "So this is your lady?"

"Damn straight," Greg growled. "This is my wife."

Again Peter's eyes scanned me like I was canned goods at a checkout. "You always had good taste in women, Stevens. I'll give you that."

Next to me Greg was breathing in and out in long, steady breaths. It was what he did when he was trying to control his temper. A lot of people count to ten; my hubby takes long, deep breaths like the kind you do for the doctor when he's checking your lungs for bronchitis.

"You still playing in the basketball league?" Peter asked Greg. "Or have you retired by now? Maybe doing a little coaching on the side just to keep your hand in the game? Most washed-up players do that."

"Don't you have a game to get ready for, Tanaka?" Greg asked between breaths.

"That I do," Peter admitted. "Though I doubt we'll need to warm up much to wipe the floor with the Lunatics." He rolled his chair back and turned it in the direction of the gym entrance.

Greg positioned his chair to watch him leave. I was behind him, keeping my eye on the knots forming in Greg's neck and shoulders, clearly visible through the fabric of his shirt. I know Greg is a bit jealous and very protective of me, but the way his body was tensed and ready for a fight told me his animosity toward Peter Tanaka was more than that.

Peter headed back into the gym, but not without a parting shot. Giving me a killer smile, he said, "You ever get tired of this old man, Odelia, you can find me on Face-book. Like I said, I like cougars."

I was so glad I was standing behind Greg because at that moment he surged forward, ready to give Peter Tanaka a beating. My husband, while he tried and mostly suc-ceeded at keeping his temper in check, could and would throw a few punches if provoked. I grabbed the back of his chair and hung on, throwing one arm over his shoulder and across his chest. It stopped him in his tracks. I bent down, my mouth close to Greg's ear. "He's not worth it, honey."

Greg's deep breathing started up again, but at least he didn't try to shake me off and go after the guy — not that I wouldn't have enjoyed slapping the insufferable SOB myself.

# Two

"Was that Grace on the phone, sweetheart?" Greg asked as soon as his blood pressure had returned to normal.

"Yes. Steele has been trying to call both of us, and he called the house when we didn't answer."

Greg pulled his phone out of the breast pocket of his shirt and looked at the list of recent calls. "Yeah, I saw that Mike called. You know what it's about?"

I shook my head. "Only that he told Mom it's urgent we call him back, though I can't imagine what it is. He knows we're out of town this weekend. That's probably the problem — we're having a nice weekend and he can't stand it."

Greg laughed for the first time since coming out of the gym. "I doubt it's that. He's probably at the office working and can't find something he needs. Why don't you give him a quick call just so he doesn't have a stroke?"

"You know darn well there are no quick calls where Steele's concerned." I positioned my mouth into a pout. "If I call him, there's a good chance he'll try to convince me to return tonight and come into work early tomorrow."

"But we're staying here tonight," Greg reminded me, as if I needed it. "And spending tomorrow relaxing at the beach."

I raised an eyebrow in his direction. "You've got my vote for that."

Greg looked at his phone again, then madly started sending a text.

"What are you doing?"

"Texting Steele. I'm telling him we're tied up tonight with friends and will get back to him tomorrow morning. He'll take it better coming from me."

"I told Mom if he calls again to tell him we'd call later tonight, after we got back to the hotel."

"No can do," Greg said. "After the game we're having dinner with everyone." My husband looked up from his phone and grinned. "After we get back to the hotel, I have plans of my own."

"Are you sure we have to go out to dinner?" I winked at him. "I hear the hotel has great room service."

"Don't tempt me. But I promised Rocky, whether they win or lose, we'd dine with the Lunatics tonight. He also said he has something he needs to discuss with me after the game."

I sighed with disappointment.

"Don't be so glum," Greg told me. "I'll make it up to you, I promise." Now it was his turn to wink, and he did it with panache.

"Hold that pose," I told him. Pulling out my phone, I snapped another photo of my handsome hubby. Inspecting the photo and not happy with it, I said, "Move over there, to the left of the entrance. I think the light's better." He rolled his wheelchair into the spot I directed, and I took a couple more. Looking at these, I gave them a thumbs up.

Together we headed back into the gym. It was only a few minutes before the start of the final game, and we didn't want to miss a minute of the action.

"By the way, honey," I said to Greg as we moved through the main aisle to find Miranda. "Who is that Peter Tanaka character? Seems like you dislike him for more than making a pass at me. I don't recall seeing him before."

"He's bad news," Greg snapped, tensing up again. "He used to play for the Lunatics a while back. I heard he'd been playing in

Canada for the past few years. Too bad he didn't stay there."

I took a seat at the end of a row off the middle aisle, close to where we'd been sitting for the last game. Greg lined his chair up next to me. On the floor, players were rolling along in their wheelchairs, circling and turning, warming up for the game. Rocky had his game face on, clearly concentrating on what he needed to do for the next twenty to thirty minutes. On the other end of the court, Peter Tanaka, now sitting in his rugby wheelchair, was warming up with his team, but unlike Rocky and his teammates, he was joking around. Miranda showed up. I stood, letting her pass to take the seat next to me on the inside. She looked like she'd been crying.

"You okay?" I asked, touching her arm. She nodded in response but pulled away from me.

Right before the whistle blew to start the game, I made a mental note to talk to her later. She was obviously distressed about something. I also wanted to know more about Peter Tanaka. There was a juicy story there, I just knew it. I'd ask Greg after his plans for us at the hotel or maybe even at breakfast tomorrow.

Early on in the game, the play got rough.

It was for first place in the tournament, and the players were giving their all. Mona Seidman, one of the few female players in the league, was giving as good as she got right along with the men. She'd been injured in a snowboarding accident, and she'd even been an Olympian in the sport. She played for the Lunatics and was a favorite with the crowd. Mona was making her way down the court with the ball when Peter Tanaka rammed her from the side with such force that it tipped her chair over. The action stopped while the pit crew for the Lunatics ran onto the court and righted her. From the sidelines, Cory Seidman, her husband, paced and shouted, clearly concerned for his wife. Peter rolled by him and blew Cory a kiss. For a minute I thought Cory was going to launch himself at the player, and he probably would have if the people standing next to him hadn't held him back.

Seems like my husband wasn't the only anti-fan of Tanaka's.

If the first quarter was rough, the second quarter was rougher. During the period of play, Tanaka went after Kevin Spelling with such repeated viciousness that Spelling dumped the ball a couple of times and started brawling with Tanaka, causing him to be penalized.

Halftime did nothing to dampen the emotions of the players. By the time the fourth and final quarter started, the game was brutal and the score tied. The ball was moved up and down the court with speed and agility and plenty of metal crashing into metal. In the thick of it were Rocky and Peter. Next to me, Miranda gripped my arm for support.

"I hate this game," she said under her breath to no one.

Throughout the game, Peter Tanaka went after everyone with vicious abandon, causing several players' chairs to flip. The referees warned him several times and he acquired a couple of penalties, which he accepted like trophies. The coach of the Vipers had taken him out in the third quarter to cool him down. By the fourth he was out of control and seemed to be having the time of his life taunting the other players while they struggled to play a fair game in the face of his recklessness. In all the years I'd been watching the sport with Greg, I'd never seen such a malicious player. He skirted on the edge of the rules, managing just barely to stay within them, receiving fewer penalties than he probably deserved and forcing otherwise honorable players to play like thugs in response. Mixed with the crowd's cheers were an equal number of boos. No wonder Greg disliked Peter Tanaka. Greg embraced fair play and good sportsmanship like I embrace Ben and Jerry's ice cream and Thin Mints.

Rocky, who was the captain of the Lunatics, encouraged his players to neutralize Peter Tanaka as much as possible, but by the beginning of the fourth quarter he was personally waging war on the nasty player. Peter, with glee in his eyes, took up the challenge. The two teams took turns taking the point lead, and it looked like the win would go down to the wire.

Then something happened to change the game.

Quad rugby players are classified according to their functionality, with a ranking system from 0.5 to 3.5 points. The higher the ranking, the more movement a player has in his or her limbs; the lower the ranking, the lower the mobility. At any one time a team cannot have players on the court totaling in excess of 8 ranking points. Both Peter and Rocky were ranked at 3.5 with good, though still limited, use of their hands and arms. Even without Rocky's decision to stop Peter's reign of terror on the court, they would have been matched up against each other.

Peter had the ball and Rocky had him penned in, using his chair and his extended arms to block Peter from advancing or passing the ball. For good measure, every now and then Rocky would take a swipe at the ball, trying to dislodge it from Peter's grasp and steal it away. Just when it seemed hopeless for Peter to move the ball in any manner without losing it, he bent forward toward Rocky and said something. It was low, only between them, and said with a wide smirk — sports trash talk, most likely.

Rocky scowled and said something back. Peter said something again and glanced toward the stands. Next to me, I felt Miranda stiffen. Rocky didn't waver in his coverage of the ball. He stayed firm, keeping his eyes on the ball and Peter, but his face was flushed. Once again Peter said something to Rocky, and this time Rocky did glance back at the stands to look at his wife. In that split second Peter was able to sneak the ball past Rocky and pass it to another Viper, who took it down the court for the score. This all happened in just seconds in front of a roaring crowd, even though it felt like slow-moving minutes with the two men on the court alone.

With the point loss, the Lunatics called a time-out to regroup. The point had put the

Vipers ahead by one, but there was still four minutes left to play in the game — plenty of time to make up the score and then some. But during the time-out Rocky didn't go to his team's bench to rest and get something to drink. Instead, he rolled over to the bleachers.

We were on the second level, with only one line of spectators seated between us and Rocky. Miranda was still on her feet when Rocky faced her. "Is it true, Miranda?" Rocky asked the question with a stone-cold face and without clarification, confident she'd know what he was asking.

Instead of answering, Miranda pushed past me, stepping on my feet as she passed. Getting to the end of the row, she stepped down to the floor. Greg scooted his chair out of the way and held out a hand to assist her to the ground. I thought she was going to comfort her husband, but when her feet hit the floor, she pushed her way through the crowd in the opposite direction.

"Is it true?" Rocky howled in her direction. But he received no answer, only her retreating back.

Coach Warren jogged over to Rocky and tried to get him to join the team, but Rocky shook him off. Greg moved forward to talk to his friend, but Rocky waved him off without a word. He finally turned his rugby chair around and stared at the far side, at the bench of the Vipers. He watched Peter Tanaka drink from a water bottle and joke with his teammates, oblivious to the conflict he'd started.

Greg returned to my side, his face cloudy with concern. "Why don't you go find Miranda? Whatever is going on, I'm sure she could use a friend right now."

I nodded in full agreement. Greg was helping me down from the bleachers when the whistle blew to restart the game. A few seconds later, pandemonium broke out on the court. The ball had been passed to Peter, who was near the sidelines in front of the bleachers to our left. Rocky had followed the ball, but instead of playing defense, he threw a punch at Peter as soon as he'd gotten close enough. The people on the bleachers got to their feet and started yelling. Those on the ground, both standing and in wheelchairs, surged forward almost onto the court. I stepped back up on the bleachers to get a better view.

On the court, Rocky had Peter Tanaka's Viper shirt grasped in his curled hand. He had pulled Peter close and was punching him in the face with his elbow and forearm, using whatever he had to pummel the

31

obnoxious player, who was fighting back. Then suddenly Peter stopped fighting, and his arms dropped limply at his side.

Both coaches were trying to intervene, but Rocky's rage was over the edge as he continued to punch Peter, who was no longer trying to defend himself. In trying to pull the players and their chairs apart, Peter's wheelchair tipped over. Rocky seized the moment. Unfastening his own safety belt, he heaved his body out of his chair and onto the floor next to Peter, where he continued the battering. Around us cell phones were whipped out as people recorded the fracas. The official photographer for the event was busy taking her own photos. I kept my phone tucked away. This wasn't exciting; this was scary and not the norm.

While quad rugby is a rugged, rough sport and players are allowed to use their chairs as battering rams, one of the cardinal rules is no physical contact. Usually a player receives a penalty for this lapse, but in this case I was sure the consequences to Rocky and even his team would be more serious.

Rocky Henderson was usually a cool-headed player and a good team leader. What could Peter have said to make him go ballistic and physical? That question wasn't just on my lips; I'm sure it was in the minds of almost everyone who'd seen the exchange. And what about Miranda? What did it have to do with her? The first thing that popped into my mind was that she'd been cheating on Rocky, and Peter had been the bearer of the news or at least of a rumor. Maybe he was even the other guy.

The noise in the gymnasium had reached a deafening level. Even the two teams playing on the other court for third and fourth place and their spectators had left their game to see what all the commotion was about.

Joining the coaches of the Vipers and the Lunatics in breaking up the brawl were the referees. With great effort, they managed to get Rocky off of Peter. Once they got him back in his rugby chair, they moved him away from Peter and to the Lunatic bench. The front of his jersey was spattered with blood. On the sidelines, his teammates gathered around him. Some seemed supportive. Others appeared angry over Rocky putting the team and the final game in jeopardy. They could only wait to see what the referees would do to the team as a result of the fight.

Peter Tanaka remained on the floor. His coach and the referees gathered around him. Two security guards rushed in. The on-site medical care came running with a first-aid kit to assess his injuries, but the cardboard wedge stayed on the sidelines. There was no attempt to get him back up and rolling. Instead, like removing a shell from a snail, they slipped him out of the reinforced wheelchair. From where I was sitting, it looked like Peter had vomited after he fell. An acrid odor floated on the air toward the bleachers.

I slipped off the bleachers onto the floor just behind Greg, who had rolled forward for a front-row seat. I leaned down. "I'm going to go find Miranda now."

"Good idea," he replied, not taking his eyes off the drama on the court. I placed a hand on his shoulder, and for a moment he covered my hand with his and squeezed, finally looking back at me with tender eyes. We had a lot of little gestures like that between us. They meant no matter the madness around us, we were our own solid team.

As I turned away to begin my search for Miranda, Greg reached out and grabbed my hand, this time with urgency. "Odelia, wait. Something's wrong."

I took my place behind his wheelchair again, placed my hands on his shoulders, and turned my eyes to the court. The crowd, also sensing something important, had hushed as the minutes ticked by and Peter Tanaka did not get up.

The air in the gym grew still and muggy, like a summer night right before a bad storm. Over three hundred people held their collective breath. One of the security guards was talking into a cell phone, keeping his voice low, while another security guard stood between the court and the crowd. The idea of his scrawny rent-a-cop body stopping the crowd should it decide to surge forward was a joke. Lucky for him, the people watching were respectful and concerned and kept their distance.

*He's dead,* I told myself. *Peter Tanaka is dead.* But I dared not say it aloud. I squeezed Greg's shoulders, trying to convey my thoughts. In response, he twisted his head up and around until he caught my eye. He raised his eyebrows, letting me know he had reached the same conclusion.

The Viper coach was on his knees next to Peter. He pointed a finger at Rocky and shouted in Spanish, *"Asesino. Asesino!"*

*Murderer.*

One of the referees left the scene and went over to the Lunatic's bench. He whispered something to Rocky and Coach Warren. Rocky exploded again, but this time in anguish, not anger. "No! No! No!" Rocky's guttural cry echoed against the high ceiling to its steel beams and ricocheted down to bounce off the hardwood floor. "It's not true!" He started for Peter's body, but his coaches and the referee stopped him. "It can't be true!"

Except for Rocky's cries, silence hung heavy over the gym, split only by the scream of sirens approaching the building.

"We have to do something to help Rocky," I told Greg.

Greg patted my hand. "We will, but let's see what shakes out first."

I looked over at the Lunatic's bench where Rocky was sobbing and being comforted by Coach Warren and Ian. I'm sure if he'd not been in a wheelchair, Rocky Henderson would have fallen to his knees and begged Peter Tanaka to get up.

Police rushed into the building and took charge. Behind them came paramedics. The crowd, just a few minutes before filled with cheer and encouragement, fell into a low buzz of hushed, anxious chatter.

# THREE

"Go find Miranda," Greg said to me.

I fought my way through the crowd and headed for the door. At the door I was stopped by a female officer. "Where are you going?" she asked.

"I need to find one of the player's wives. She left a few minutes ago."

"No one is to leave the building," she told me. "You can find your friend later."

"But this is important," I stressed. "She's the wife of one of the injured players."

"Then we'll find her. Please go back inside and wait with everyone else."

Before turning to leave I scanned the parking lot, looking for any sign of Miranda Henderson. For the tournament, the park had set up extra disabled parking spaces in the front of the building. I looked for Rocky's van. When we had arrived this morning, I'd noticed the dark blue van parked in one of the front spots. It was now gone.

Inside the gym, the police were pushing the crowd back, away from the court. They were herding them to the other side of the gymnasium and asking everyone to be patient and quiet. They did the same with the Lunatics and the Vipers but cut them off from the crowd to another section, keeping the two teams apart. Several of the Viper players were outraged at the turn of events. They were rallying their team into an almost mob-like mentality, asking for Rocky's blood in return for their fallen teammate until threats from the police calmed them down.

Rocky was alone, cut off from the crowd and players, with only Coach Warren by his side.

I found Greg talking with Cory Seidman and a few of the other people associated with the Lunatics. As soon as I approached, he said to the others, "I sent Odelia out to look for Miranda." He turned to me. "Any luck?"

With a shake of my head, I said, "The police wouldn't let me leave, but I did notice that Rocky's van is gone."

"What was that all about?" asked Samantha Franco.

"My guess," said Cory, "is that Miranda

has been playing around with Tanaka."

It was the same thing that had gone through my head when Rocky had faced off with his wife.

"He's notorious for hitting on the wives and girlfriends of other players," continued Cory, his voice full of anger.

"And not just in this sport," added Greg.

*You always had good taste in women, Stevens. I'll give you that.* Greg's animosity toward Peter Tanaka was becoming clear.

"But I still can't imagine that Rocky beat him to death," said Greg. "He was getting in some pretty good blows, but hard enough to kill Tanaka?"

"Could be Peter hit his head when he fell to the floor," I suggested, wanting it to be anything but Rocky's punches that caused the death.

"That's a pretty good theory," said Cory. "Let's hope it is something like that."

Greg and I had been questioned by police before on numerous occasions and knew the drill. By the time the police spoke to each and every person in the gym, or at least took down everyone's name and contact information, it would be pretty late. People would not be let out of the gym or allowed into it until the head cop was satisfied everyone had been accounted for. We had

39

been hanging around about thirty minutes when a young cop came over to where the bunch of us were hanging out, waiting to be questioned. Many of us not in wheelchairs had slid to the floor to wait with some comfort.

"Who's Greg and Odelia?"

After exchanging glances, Greg and I half raised our hands simultaneously.

"Come with me, please," the officer said.

I stood up, and we followed the cop over to where the police were holding Rocky. He'd transferred himself to his regular wheelchair and was getting ready for his trip to the police station. He looked like crap. Blood had dried around his nose where Peter had landed his own blows before collapsing. His eyes were dark, his face pale. As soon as we got there, he said, "You have to find Miranda."

"I looked for her," I told him. "She's gone, and so is your van."

"What happened, Rocky?" Greg asked him. "What did Peter say to you to start this?"

Rocky looked at the cops guarding him, then back at Greg. "Another time. Just find Miranda and tell her what happened. She may help; then again, she may not. I'll call my lawyer when I get to the station. Would you do me a favor and find my brother and tell him what's going on? He'll take care of any bail I might need — at least he'd better. You got the number?"

"I do." Greg held out a hand to Rocky, but one of the cops stopped them from any physical contact.

I started to say something, but another cop stepped in and handcuffed Rocky's hands in front of him.

"Is that really necessary?" Greg snapped. "He's a quadriplegic."

The cop who fastened the cuffs gave Greg a half smirk. "Yeah, a quad who just killed someone with those *useless* hands." Another officer got behind Rocky's chair and started pushing him toward the entrance, with the other officer walking by his side.

Rocky didn't look at anyone as he made his departure — not at his teammates huddled and waiting their turn for questioning, not at us, not at the crowd of retained spectators, not even at the body of Peter Tanaka as it lay on the hardwood floor being processed by the authorities. Everyone was silent as the captain of one of the star quad rugby teams was pushed out of the gymnasium where just a short while before he had been cheered on in the pursuit of a championship.

Since we were already in the circle of police activity, we were approached next for questioning. We were handled separately. A bald, middle-aged detective with horn-rimmed glasses and a pronounced slouch showed me to a folding chair not far from the main entrance. He introduced himself as Detective Bill Martinez.

"You and your husband are good friends with Henderson and his wife?" he asked after taking down all my particulars.

"We get together once in a while, both down here and up in Orange County. My husband also plays wheelchair sports."

"But not quad rugby?"

"No, he has full use of his hands and arms, so he can't play. He mostly plays basketball."

"Doesn't Henderson also play wheelchair basketball?"

"Yes, sometimes. But he's not in a regular league like Greg," I answered. "Some of the quads with more upper limb mobility play both."

"So that means Richard Henderson has good use and control of his hands and arms?"

*Crap. I walked right into that.* "He is still a quadriplegic, Detective, with a lot of physical limitations. So is Peter Tanaka."

"You mean *was*, don't you? So *was* Peter Tanaka."

"Look," I said, leaning forward. "I'm not saying Peter deserved to die, but he was a real jerk, and right before Rocky went after him he said something to Rocky about his wife."

"About Miranda Henderson?"

"Yes. And it must have been quite inflammatory because Rocky confronted her and she left. That's when he went after Peter. And right before all that happened, Miranda had been crying."

"Someone told me they saw your husband having harsh words with the deceased earlier today."

I took a deep breath, very thankful I'd stopped Greg from carrying the interaction further. "Peter made a pass at me, and my husband intervened and told him to back off. That's all it was."

"So you knew the deceased?"

"No. It was the first time I'd met him. Greg told me Peter had been playing quad rugby in Canada for a few years."

"So he knew him?"

"I think so, but it was from several years ago."

Detective Martinez asked me several more basic questions before asking me to describe what I'd seen during the fight. I told him everything I could remember. At the end, he handed me his card and said, "Call me if you remember anything else or if you find Miranda Henderson."

# FOUR

We'd taken my car to San Diego because it was easier to park than Greg's van, even though in the past year he'd downsized from a full-size behemoth of a van to a sporty modified Honda Odyssey in a cool metallic silver. As soon as we were both tucked away and heading back to our hotel, we exchanged notes on our interviews. They had gone pretty much the same, even down to being questioned about Greg's run-in with Peter.

"Who do you think saw that?" I asked Greg.

"There were several people milling around just outside the entrance at the time. Could have been anyone."

"Why do you think anyone mentioned it?" Annoyed that Greg's name had been brought into the investigation, I gripped the steering wheel tighter.

My husband glanced over at me. "Now

don't go getting all huffy about it. Whoever told the police was probably trying to point out how antagonistic Tanaka was. After all, he provoked Rocky, and if that's proved, it could go easier on him."

"At the most it should be manslaughter. There is no way that was premeditated."

"I totally agree. But I'd love to know exactly what Peter said to Rocky about Miranda." Greg stared out the windshield while he gave it more thought. I'm sure if I peeked into his left ear I would have seen gears moving.

"Do you think Peter was sleeping with Miranda like Cory suggested?"

Greg waited a long time before answering. "Knowing Tanaka, I think it's a very good possibility."

Over the years, Greg and I had shared information about our various relationships and heartbreaks. I couldn't remember any that involved a problem with another guy, but that didn't mean it had happened, just that Greg didn't mention it.

"Which of your old girlfriends did he hit on?" I finally ventured.

Greg's jaw tightened. He stared straight ahead and said nothing.

Sometimes — not often — I know when to keep my mouth shut. This was one of those times. I continued driving until we were at our hotel. Valets opened both of our doors. The one on Greg's side pulled his wheelchair from the back seat and set it up for him. By the time Greg had transferred himself to his chair, I was by his side. Obviously, plans for dinner with the team were not going to happen. Those players who had been released by the time we had were definitely not in a social mood. And everyone was too stunned to talk about what had happened in a group setting, though I was sure there would be a lot of whispering and speculation behind closed doors tonight.

"Should we go to the hotel restaurant," I asked Greg as we entered the hotel lobby, "or order room service?"

Without answering, he went straight to the elevator. We rode up to our floor in silence. When we got into the room, Greg went to the patio sliding doors and opened them, rolling outside into the cool sea breeze. I put down my purse and joined him, taking a seat on a chaise longue. It was already dark out, and the beach couldn't be seen except for the few yards caught in the lights lining the hotel property. Beyond that the dark waves, their backs shimmering with snatches of moonlight, rolled in to spend themselves on the sand. We could hear the ocean clearly. Its rhythmic ebb and flow was the heartbeat of our silence.

"It was Linda Atwater," Greg finally said.

It took me a minute to place her in my memory of Greg's past girlfriends. "You mean the girl you dated a few years before you met me — the one you almost married?"

"Yes."

"But I thought you said she moved away to attend grad school."

My husband turned to me, his eyes sad. "And that's the truth, but not all of it." He looked back to the sea. "At one point we were talking about getting married, then she stopped talking about it and avoided the subject when I mentioned it. I thought she was mad because I hadn't formally asked her yet. I was going to do it right, with a big romantic gesture. I'd already started shopping for her ring." Greg turned and faced me. "One night over dinner she confessed that she'd been seeing Peter Tanaka behind my back."

"How well did you know him then?"

"Quite well. He was very young and brash and making a splash on and off the courts. He'd met Linda when I brought her to one of the rugby matches. The night she confessed, she also told me she was leaving

48

California and going to Canada with Tanaka. He was becoming more and more unwelcome around here for his conduct on the court, and none of the teams would have him anymore. He received an invitation to play for a team in Montreal and asked Linda to go with him."

"Greg, I'm so sorry." Truth be told, I wasn't sorry Linda Atwater had dumped Greg. If she hadn't, we might not have met. But I was sorry for his obvious pain.

He reached out and took my hand. "I'm not. If that hadn't happened, I would never have met you."

*Geez — add mind reader to his other talents.*

I squeezed his hand back. "True, but it's still something that hurt you. It makes me want to slap her while thanking her at the same time." I dug through my memory for a second. "I didn't see Peter with anyone today."

"No," answered Greg, his eyes growing dark. "They were gone about a year, maybe a little more, when I heard he had dumped Linda. She returned to California and eventually contacted me, not to get back together but to apologize for what she'd done. Soon after, she left for grad school in the East, like I told you. She wanted to start over."

"And that's the last you heard of her?"

He shook his head. "I ran into her mother a few years after she left. She told me Linda had finished school and gotten married. She lives outside Philly, I think."

He gave my hand one last squeeze and let go. "So, how about that room service?"

I got up and retrieved the room service menu. Greg followed me inside. "So it's not far-fetched that Peter was seeing Miranda?" I scanned the menu, but my mind wasn't on dinner.

"Not far-fetched at all. He seemed to go out of his way to steal women from other quads and paraplegic athletes, like it's part of the sport. He'd done it a couple of times to other players before he took up with Linda."

"For sport," I repeated, processing that information. "To men on his own team or on opposing teams?"

"Never his own teammates."

"So it was like a strategy to get inside their heads?"

"Maybe." Seeing me making no progress on our dinner, Greg took the menu from me. "Or maybe it was just to prove his virility off the court as well as on."

"Seems to me his bad sportsmanship wasn't just reserved for the games."

"Nope," Greg said. "He's a dirty player all around." He put down the menu and looked me square in the eye. "I'm not saying Peter Tanaka deserved to die for being an ass, but I'm not sorry he's dead. I'm only sorry, deeply sorry, that Rocky got caught up in it. We have to help him."

As soon as he said those words, Greg pulled his cell phone out of his pocket. "I forgot — Rocky wanted me to call his brother."

"Yes, I noticed Lance wasn't at the tournament. He usually is, isn't he?"

Greg nodded as he looked through his contacts list for Lance Henderson's information. "Yeah, but Rocky said he had to work this weekend."

Greg made the call, reaching only voice mail. He left a message for Lance to call him. I tried calling Miranda and also only reached voice mail. I told her what had happened and asked her to call me or Detective Martinez as soon as possible. I left both of our numbers and Greg's. We then ordered dinner, but when it arrived we only picked at it, our minds trumping our hunger as we went over what had happened right in front of us.

It wasn't the first time I'd seen someone die or be killed right in front of me. It's not

51

like I keep track of it, but I think it's close to a half dozen people whom I've seen gasp their last breath. And, sadly, the number of dead bodies I've seen is far more than that. I seem to attract them like cat hair to a sofa or like Velcro to . . . well . . . most anything. I know women who keep track of how many sexual partners they've had. I've never understood that. Was there a magic number where if they reached it, they stopped having sex? Or was it a matter of secret and sometimes not-so-secret pride of conquest, like jocks in a locker room? In my case, it's dead bodies that pile up like cords of wood in my brain. Seth Washington, friend and husband of my best friend, Zee, had dubbed me Corpse Magnet several years back, and the nickname has clung to me like a sticky booger.

Several years ago, I even pulled the trigger of a gun that ended someone's life. In doing so, I'd saved another person from death. But even though it was not considered murder, it changed my life forever. For the first six months there wasn't a day I didn't think about it. I'd walked around in a dense fog of depression and cried without warning. I'd even gone into therapy for a short while to deal with the overwhelming sense of guilt. Now I only think about it occasionally, like on the anniversary of the event or whenever I see another dead body. Seeing Peter Tanaka's corpse on the floor of the gym had brought it all back. Tonight I'll beat it down until it's no longer in the forefront of my mind. It takes much less time and effort to do it now, but the knowledge that I'm a killer will remain, buried deep, like a fungal infection that lives under toenails, just waiting for a weak-willed moment to pounce and make me feel like shit again.

Two hours later, neither of us had heard from Lance or Miranda yet, so when my cell phone rang, both Greg and I jumped eagerly. But it wasn't Miranda returning my call. Instead, it was Devon Frye, a Newport Beach detective and a good friend.

"Hey, Dev," I said.

"I hear you and Greg are in San Diego."

"Yes, we are. We'll be coming home tomorrow." I wondered if Dev had heard about the murder at the tournament and was wondering if we were in the thick of it, since we always do seem to be involved with murder. Finding dead bodies and becoming embroiled in nasty situations seems to be the lot of a Corpse Magnet. It's more my curse than Greg's, but he's often along for the ride. "Why? Is there a problem?"

53

On the other end, Dev hemmed and hawed. "Yes and no. Have you been getting calls from Mike Steele?"

"Yes, both Greg and I have today, but we've been too busy to answer. I think Greg texted him that we'd call him tonight."

"Don't bother; I've taken care of it."

"You?" Panic started to rise, starting in my shoes and moving upward like a sharp pain. "What's happened to Steele, Dev? Is he okay?"

My words put Greg on alert. He asked me to put the phone on speaker.

"Dev, you're on speaker, and Greg's here. So what's up with Steele?"

"He'll be fine. He just had a little scrape with the law in Perris."

"Paris, France?" I searched my brain but couldn't remember Steele having international travel plans on his calendar.

Dev laughed, his gravelly voice rolling over the chuckle like rocks in a tumbler. "No, Perris, California. It's a small town off the 215 Freeway."

"I know where it is. I just didn't think Steele did." I paused, then said, "So Steele called you when he couldn't get us?"

"Yeah, and good thing. I have a buddy who works with the sheriff's department out that way. With his help, I was able to convince the owner of the bar not to press charges in return for full restitution."

"Charges? What in the hell happened?" asked Greg.

"I'll let Mike fill you in on the details, but here's the overview: it seems our fine Mr. Steele got intoxicated at a bar in Perris frequented by unsavory characters. He somehow managed to start a brawl, get his tailored ass kicked, and was almost thrown in jail."

Greg and I stared at each other, speechless as mimes.

"Odelia, you still there?"

"Yes, Dev," I said after a long moment, "we're here. I'm not surprised Steele started a fight. All he has to do is open his snobbish mouth to do that. I'm in shock that he was even there in the first place. Do you know why?"

"No clue, but from what I've pieced together, he called you before the fight and me after he was detained."

"And where is the illustrious Michael Steele, Esquire, now?" asked Greg.

"At his place in Laguna Beach, probably passed out from the pain pills the doc gave him."

"Pain pills?" I barely got the words out.

"He was worked over good by the boys at

the bar. I took him to urgent care, and they said he should be fine with several days of rest. But his pretty face isn't so pretty right now."

My mind was spinning like a top. "This isn't like Steele, Dev. No matter how obnoxious he can be, it's not like him to get drunk and start a fight. And why Perris?"

"Again, no clue. He couldn't talk much through his swollen mouth. I'm guessing he's going to need some dental work."

"Jesus," said Greg, running a hand through his hair. "When it rains, it pours."

Dev cleared his throat. "I heard there was a homicide at the rugby tournament in Balboa Park today. You two aren't involved in that, are you?"

I twitched my nose in annoyance, not at the question but because I really didn't want to answer. "If you're asking if we found the body, the answer is no, nor did we cause the death. But it's why we haven't called Steele back yet."

"So what happened?" asked Dev with interest.

Greg filled Dev in on everything that had happened at the gym.

"I know Bill Martinez," Dev said when Greg was finished. "Let me give him a call and see what gives. Your friend probably won't be arraigned until tomorrow or even Tuesday. Meanwhile, you two stay out of it."

"No guarantees there, Dev," Greg said, getting closer to the phone. "Rocky Henderson is a good friend, and I can't imagine the blows he landed were enough to kill Tanaka."

"The right blow in the right place can take down a man easily, Greg. You know that."

"Rocky is a good guy," I added, "and Tanaka clearly provoked him. Everyone watching saw that."

"Still no reason to kill a man, Odelia." Dev paused. "But like I said, I'll give Bill a call, and you two finish up your trip and head home. Got that?"

"But," I said, "we promised Rocky we'd find his wife. No harm in that, is there?"

"There's always potential harm when you get involved, Odelia," Dev replied, his voice devoid of humor. "Mostly to yourself. I do know, however, that the San Diego police put out a BOLO on the wife's vehicle; that's how I know about the murder. Stay out of it, both of you. Let the cops do their job." A dry chuckle came from the phone. "Then again, look who I'm talking to."

"Well," I said reluctantly, "we do need to get home tomorrow. My mother is watching the house, and we both need to be at work on Tuesday."

"Maybe, Odelia," Greg said, "we should stop off at Mike's place on the way home and see how he's doing."

"Now that," Dev said, "sounds like a dandy idea."

"Unless," I added, "Steele pulls himself together and goes into the office tomorrow."

Another rocky chuckle came from Dev's side of the call. "Trust me, Odelia. Mike Steele isn't going anywhere tomorrow or for a few days. And when you do see him, tell him he owes me. Big time."

When the call ended, Greg and I stared at each other in a stupor. "What in the world is going on?" I finally said. "You, Rocky, and now Steele all brawling on the same day. Is there some kind of special full moon going on? Something only guys can feel?"

"I was not brawling," Greg corrected.

"But you would have if I hadn't stopped you. You know you were about to throw a punch at Tanaka yourself today."

"But I didn't, did I?"

"Only because I stopped you," I repeated. I stared at Greg, latching my eyes onto his. He was the first to look away because he knew I was right. Sometimes — not often — I am right in this relationship.

Picking up my phone, I started texting.

"What are you doing?" Greg asked, kicking back the last of a beer he'd snagged from the mini bar.

"Texting Steele that we heard from Dev and didn't want to bother him with a call tonight. I'm telling him to call us tomorrow when he gets up." I sent the message.

"Should you tell him we might stop by or should we surprise him?"

"Steele isn't big on surprises."

"True," Greg agreed. "And he might be embarrassed by what happened."

Now it was my turn to laugh. "Steele is embarrassed about nothing, especially in front of me. Haven't you learned that by now? Still, I should give him a chance to say yes or no to our visit." I started texting again, this time letting Steele know we'd like to stop by on our way home.

"Mike Steele embarrassed by his actions," I said, more to myself than to Greg as my fingers punched out the message. "What a joke. But at least he didn't kill anyone or get killed himself."

# FIVE

Instead of spending a leisurely Monday as we had originally planned, we checked out of the hotel right after a quick breakfast. Okay, I'll admit, it was a late breakfast. Greg had heard from Lance late the night before, but I still hadn't heard from Miranda. We'd both heard, however, from Steele. He had sent both Greg and me texts saying it was okay for us to stop by and could we bring him a few things. The list included orange juice, ice cream, bananas, and milk, all with specific organic high-end brand names.

"Notice anything about that list?" Greg asked as we headed north on the 5 Freeway.

"That it's missing booze?" I suggested.

Greg laughed. "I'm sure Steele has plenty of that at his place. Doesn't he even have a small wine cellar?"

"Yeah, he does." I thought about the list. "Do you mean that we're going to have to go to Whole Foods to get this stuff instead

60

of a regular grocery store?"

"No, but that's a good observation." Greg looked out the windshield, then at me. "All the foods on that list are soft. Not a piece of meat or crunchy vegetable anywhere on it."

I looked over at Greg, my eyes wide with understanding. "So you think Dev wasn't kidding when he said Steele might need some dental work?"

"I don't think Dev was kidding about anything. Not even about Steele owing him big time."

I thought again about the list. "Frankly, honey, if we have to drive to Beverly Hills to get this stuff, we'll do it. I feel so darn guilty right now about not answering Steele's calls."

"Me too, sweetheart, but we can't beat ourselves up over it. In all the years you've worked for Mike, I think this is the first time one of his calls to you on a day off wasn't some kind of BS. It's the classic boy crying wolf. This time the wolves were real."

"True, but I still feel rotten. He's not just my boss, he's our friend, and we might have been able to stop what happened."

"Doubtful. From the time of his calls, there wasn't enough time for us to get to Perris from San Diego to intervene." Greg reached over and patted my knee. "Really, sweetheart, there wasn't, and we were in the middle of our own drama."

I glanced over at Greg, shooting him a raised brow. "So you don't feel the least bit guilty about this?"

"I didn't say that."

Steele's large two-bedroom luxury condo was in Laguna Beach in a gated complex right on the beach. After being buzzed through the security gate, we parked and made our way to the elevator. Steele's place was on the top floor, affording him the best view. When he opened his door, I nearly dropped the bag of groceries I was carrying. By my side, Greg didn't seem all that surprised. A guy thing, I guess.

"Not a word, Grey," were the first words Steele uttered when he noticed my shock. The words were expelled slowly and with obvious pain through swollen lips, like a dying breath.

With my free hand, I made the gesture of zipping my lips. Only then did he back up and allow me to cross his threshold.

When Steele helped Greg tip back enough to clear the low step up into the condo, I saw him wince. Frankly, Steele didn't look strong enough to wipe his own butt, let alone help Greg, but I'd known him long enough to know that if I said something about it, he'd keep Greg and evict me.

Taking the groceries into the kitchen, I put the cold stuff in his fridge and left the dry goods on the counter, since I wasn't sure where they should go and they needed to be where Steele could find them. Then I joined the men in Steele's den.

The main floor of Steele's condo was made up of a den, living room, and dining room. Off the dining room was a state-of-the-art kitchen with a small breakfast nook, and off the kitchen was a half bath and utility room. Upstairs was a large guest bedroom and bath, along with a huge master suite and bathroom that could easily rival a very expensive hotel suite. Steele mostly used his guest bedroom for a home office.

All the downstairs rooms had recently been remodeled and redecorated, an event that drove us all crazy at the office and I'm sure drove the decorator and contractor to drink heavily. Before the remodel, the condo had been beautiful; now it was stunning. The den, living room, and dining room flowed effortlessly from one into another but could be divided into separate rooms with the closure of double doors. One wall in the den was nearly covered by a flat screen TV that with the flick of a remote could be hidden by a panel covered with artwork. Even his leather recliner, in which Steele was now ensconced with his feet up, didn't look like a recliner when it was upright. He'd successfully created the perfect man cave, one that disappeared when a more formal space was required. Even the den's built-in wet bar was designed to look like paneling and stately book shelves.

Greg and Steele were watching a sports show on the TV, happy as clams at high tide, while I fidgeted, biting the inside of my lip to keep from demanding what had happened to Steele's face and why he had had to call Dev. If Greg was curious, he didn't show it. Instead, he tipped back a beer in manly camaraderie. If Greg hung out here too long, he'd be demanding his own man cave and billboard-sized TV.

I plunked myself on the sofa next to Steele's chair and stared at him. Between the sofa and the chair was a small table. On it were his iPad, cell phone, a couple of remotes, and a box of tissue — his command central. I was determined to make him talk first before I busted a gut along with the invisible zipper on my mouth.

"You want a beer, Grey?" Steele mumbled. "Help yourself." He waved a hand toward the paneled wall. I noticed Steele wasn't drinking beer. He was sipping from a straw stuck in a bottle of what I recognized as one of his favorite protein drinks.

I got up and headed for the wet bar, pressing on one panel after another until I sprung open the hidden mini fridge. Instead of a beer I grabbed a Diet Coke and returned to my seat and my quiet campaign to get to the bottom of things.

A commercial came on — an ad for a newscast later that day. A somber, lithe blond holding a microphone was standing in front of the gymnasium at Balboa Park. "What caused one disabled athlete to beat another to death? That's the question being asked in San Diego today. More on this tragic story on our five o'clock newscast." Next came a commercial for Oreos — the one where the adorable toddler tries to get his cookie into his sippy cup.

Aiming the remote at the TV, Steele muted the sound. "So, what can you tell me about that?" he asked, slurring his words. The question was tossed out like a soft volleyball serve with no intended recipient.

"It's a chocolate cookie with a cream center," I told him. "Best dunked in cold milk."

"Smart ass," Steele replied. "The murder.

I'd bet my car you two were there."

"And what can you tell us about what happened to you?" I asked, breaking my vow to remain quiet on the subject.

"You first," Steele said, fixing a blackened eye on me. The other eye was still whole and unharmed, but I know he aimed the ugly one at me on purpose. Between the eye, the wide bandage over his swollen nose, and his fat lip, Steele looked like he'd just had a play date at Fight Club. The old gray sweats he was wearing only added to the ambience. I was tempted to snap a photo with my phone and post it to Facebook. Maybe I could use that as a threat to get him to talk?

Greg broke the standoff by rolling closer to us. "He was a friend of ours."

"I'm sorry," Steele mumbled.

"Not the dead guy," Greg clarified, "although I knew him too. But the guy who gave the beating."

At hearing the word *beating,* Steele flinched.

"Rocky and his wife are friends of ours," I chimed in.

"Tanaka — that's the dead guy — totally provoked Rocky," Greg continued.

Again I saw Steele flinch. I wasn't sure if it was a stab of pain or the memory of his actions the day before.

"Now Rocky," explained Greg, "is in jail, charged with murder."

"And his wife is nowhere to be found," I added.

Greg took the next few minutes to give Steele an account of what happened, including his close encounter with Peter Tanaka before the game and Rocky's confrontation of Miranda. Steele listened, his good eye gleaming with concentration in spite of any pain medication he might have taken.

"Dev Frye is going to call the detective on the case and see if he can learn anything new," Greg told him, ending the story.

"Dev's a good man." Steele turned to look out the large sliding glass door at the ocean beyond. "I owe him a huge debt."

"Yeah," I said. "He wanted us to remind you of that."

Steele turned his attention back to us. On his puffy lips was a half smile.

I reached out and put a hand on my boss's forearm. "I'm sorry we didn't answer your calls, Steele. We were just so tied up and had no idea you were in such a jam."

He flicked his other hand at me in a gesture that either meant for me to forget about it or he was batting away an invisible gnat. "You couldn't help. Too far gone," he slurred. "Needed Dev."

Steele straightened up in his chair. When he started to say something, his face broke into a clownish grimace. Picking up his iPad, he typed something with chunky strokes. Usually Steele's typing was as quick and efficient as any good secretary's. That's when I noticed his hands were scraped. Apparently he'd thrown a few punches of his own. When he was done, he handed it to me. I read it silently, then out loud. " 'I've sent you a detailed email of the work I need done this week. Do it and email it to me. I'll review it and get it back to you.' "

I looked up from the iPad. "You mean you're not coming in all week?" I wasn't surprised, given Steele's state, but I was surprised at his willingness to stay home.

He shook his head and gestured for the tablet back. He typed again and returned it to me. " 'I can't, not looking like this,' " I read out loud. " 'Tell people I've got the plague or had a family emergency. Anything but this. Don't even tell Jill. We'll see how this week goes.' "

"In a couple of days it won't be that bad," Greg said to him. "Tell people you were in a car accident. It looks like you went head-to-head with your air bag."

I shook my head. "This isn't about how

he looks, Greg. He can't risk the senior partners of T&T knowing he was arrested."

"I wasn't arrested," Steele mumbled, leaning forward and nearly spraying me with spit in his indignation.

"Okay, calm down." I edited my words. "You don't want the powers that be at T&T knowing you were in a bar fight and almost arrested." I paused, then added, "And you can't let your clients find that out."

Steele put an index finger on the end of his broken nose and pointed his other index finger in my direction. "Ding. Ding. Ding." It came out *dig, dig, dig.*

"I still think you should tell them you were in a car accident," Greg said. "Some of those bruises are going to take time to heal."

"Yeah," I agreed. "It takes time for bruises to go from black and blue to puke green and baby-poop yellow. And the way you drive, everyone would totally believe a car crash. Maybe you could hire someone to crash your Porsche and make it look like an accident." I laughed.

Steele motioned for the tablet. I handed it back to him. He jabbed at the screen keyboard and handed it back to me. " 'Laugh all you want, funny girl, but the car is already totaled. Some goons at the bar destroyed it.' "

"No wonder you were so quick to offer it up in a bet," I fired back.

"That's perfect," declared Greg with enthusiasm, like everything was settled. "Just say you were in a car accident when you finally return to work."

"Is that why you got into a fight?" I asked Steele. "Because some rednecks damaged your car?"

Instead of answering verbally or typing, Steele waved off my question. Whatever was going on, my gut told me it wasn't about the car, not really. Boy, this was frustrating.

He reached out a hand, grabbed the iPad from me, and started typing furiously again. When he was done, he handed it back. " 'OK,' " I read to Greg, " 'tell people I was in a bad car accident. But that's it!!! Tell them I'm working at home for a bit. Have Jill cancel any meetings I have and not reschedule until I tell her. But don't you dare tell anyone the truth!!!' " I even added all the exclamation points in my recitation.

"Okay, okay," I said to Steele. "Consider it done. It's not like I haven't covered your butt for you before. But in return I want to know why you were in Perris. Why in that dive bar? And why did the fight break out?"

"Not happening," Steele slurred in my direction.

# Six

"So what are we going to do about the murder?" The question came out of my mother right after she swallowed a bite of sweet and sour pork.

Across the table, Greg and I stared at each other. He was holding a spring roll just inches from his mouth. I had just shoved a solid forkful of Mongolian beef into mine. I didn't know what part of Mom's comment disturbed me more, the *we* or the part about murder.

Chinese takeout is our fallback dinner when we don't feel like cooking. We both love it and don't mind eating it often. Turns out it's one of my mother's favorite foods, too. So when we got home from San Diego after our stopover at Steele's, it seemed natural to pick some up and have Mom stay for an early dinner. We'd ordered it by phone from the car and picked it up on the way home. Mom had already seen the news about Peter's death the night before. While unpacking the food and setting the table, we told Mom the details of what had happened at the gym, with Greg leaving out the part about our encounter with Peter Tanaka. I'm not exactly sure why he did that, but it did save us a lot of explanation about his personal history with the guy.

"There's nothing to solve, Grace," replied Greg. "Peter Tanaka is dead, and Rocky is being charged with his murder."

"What about the wife?" Mom persisted. "Aren't you going to look for her?"

"The police are looking for her," I answered after swallowing my food. "We've made a few calls, but beyond that we've been told to butt out."

Mom looked at me over the top of her glasses. "And when did that ever stop you before?"

I wiped my mouth with a napkin, when what I really wanted to do was chew on it. "This is one time there is really nothing we can do. Rocky's wife was probably having an affair with the guy. Rocky beat on the guy. The guy died. It's pretty open and shut."

"Odelia's right, Grace," Greg told her. "We discussed it on the way home from Steele's place. There's really nothing for us to get involved with here, no loose ends or investigation. I got in touch with Rocky's brother like Rocky asked, and he's handling everything else, including trying to find Miranda. All we can do is hope Rocky's lawyer can get him a good deal."

"Steele's place?" Mom asked, her brain switching gears quicker than a dog smelling a treat. "So you did get in touch with him?"

"Yes," I told her. "We stopped by his condo on our way back."

Mom seemed concerned. "Is he okay? He sounded funny on the phone."

"He was in a car accident and got a bit banged up," Greg told her, "but he'll be fine." Greg looked over at me, then added, "He just wanted to make sure Odelia knew so she could handle a bunch of things for him this week at the office."

"Yeah," I added. "You know how obsessive Steele is about his work."

Mom still wasn't satisfied. "Maybe I should go over there and take care of him. I could take soup or something. I can ride down with Cruz."

"No!" both Greg and I said at the same time. Mom looked at us with surprised curiosity.

Mom hadn't driven or owned a car since she moved to the retirement home in New

Hampshire. Afraid of the heavy traffic in Southern California, she hadn't even been tempted to drive once she'd moved here. Now I was glad because if she did have wheels, she'd get herself into all kinds of trouble — something she did without driving.

"No, Mom," I said with a calmer voice. "Steele's a bit embarrassed by how he looks right now. He's not only obsessive but very vain." I scooped another helping of veggie fried rice onto my plate. "We got him some groceries, and Cruz will take care of the rest. He was going to see if she would come in a little extra this week."

Cruz was the same Cruz Valenz who also cleans my house. I hired her more than ten years ago to clean my townhouse every other week when I was single. When I married Greg, she moved her duties up the highway to our home in Seal Beach. She's now a weekly fixture in our lives, along with her husband, who takes care of our yard work. Since my mother moved here, Cruz also helps her out once in a while. The two women get along great, and I suspect Cruz, who is in her sixties, keeps Mom company as well as cleans.

Steele's history with housekeepers was about the same as his history with secretaries until I hired Jill — and about the same as his history with girlfriends, but he's on his own there. He went through them all like a whirling dervish, leaving anger and obscenities in his wake. Since I'd done so well in hiring Jill, when his last housekeeper left in a huff several months ago, Steele had asked me to find him a housekeeper, specifically putting mine at the top of his wish list. I'd flat-out told him no. I didn't want Cruz tossing me and Greg aside when Steele pissed her off, as he would definitely do with his fussiness and demands. But when he became obnoxious about it, I caved and approached Cruz. Much to my surprise, she wanted to try it out. She'd lost a couple of clients when the economy tanked and was looking for a good steady gig. She was also thrilled to learn that Steele required her services twice a week, not once every other week like most condo clients. Also, Cruz reminded me, she'd met Steele several times over the years, so it wasn't like she was buying a pig in a poke. Even though she'd said the last part in partial Spanish, I think it meant the same thing. So far, so good. As with Jill, Steele adores Cruz. She cleans and does laundry, mending, grocery shopping, assorted errands, and some cooking for him. She also doesn't take any crap from him. I also think she negotiated top dollar for her time because now she only works for me and Steele, and sometimes for my mother.

"Well, if you're sure." Mom pushed her food around on her plate with her fork.

"You have a good heart, Grace," Greg said to her with a smile. "Why don't you send him a get-well card? I'm sure he'd like that. You can give it to Odelia, and she'll make sure he gets it when she sends him his work."

"Okay, I'll do that. But I still wish we had a murder to work on. It's been kind of dull around here lately. My blog is suffering." Mom resumed eating with gusto. My mother is in her early eighties, taller than me, and a bit slender. The amount of sweet and sour and moo shu she could pack away would put a smile on a truck driver's face. While I had her appetite, I had inherited my father's short, squatty build and penchant for putting on pounds. Mom also writes a blog called An Old Broad's Perspective. It's a homey, chatty monologue about life in general and her adventures as a senior New England transplant in Southern California. It has a surprising amount of regular readers, and Mom even gets fan mail. Who knew?

Shortly after dinner, Greg took Mom

home while I unpacked from our trip and settled in for the night. It had been a busy and emotionally exhausting weekend. As soon as Greg returned, we tucked ourselves in bed with books. Muffin was curled up between us, and Wainwright was on his rug at the foot of our bed. Both seemed very happy to have us home, even though they were sad to see Mom leave. Our little family was in place for the night.

Right before I turned off the lamp on my side to go to sleep, I picked up my cell phone.

"Who are you calling at this hour?" Greg asked.

"No one. I'm texting Zee to let her know we're home. She'd left me one earlier about getting together for lunch tomorrow, and I'd forgotten to respond. Lunch will depend on my workload with Steele out of the office."

Finished, I put the phone back, then grabbed it again.

"Now what did you forget?"

"Nothing — now I'm texting Steele, checking to make sure he's okay."

"Ah," said Greg, not taking his eyes off his book. "You're feeling guilty again."

"Can't I just check up on someone without a reason?"

"Sure, but not in this case. This smacks of guilt." There was a slight snicker in his voice.

Less than thirty seconds later, my phone vibrated a reply. I read it, then put the phone on its charger and turned off the light. "He said he's fine but getting sick of protein shakes. And he sent me three more work-related emails."

Greg laughed.

A few seconds later, Greg's phone vibrated. "It's probably Steele," I said, turning over to face Greg while he checked it out. "He probably wants to ask you again if you think the car accident story will fly."

"No," Greg told me, studying the display. "It's a text from Dev. He said Rocky Henderson has been released."

"Really? That's great news."

"I'll give Rocky a call in the morning and see how he's doing." Greg started to put his phone back on his nightstand when it vibrated again.

"Steele or Dev?" Our phones were getting more late-night action that we were.

"Neither," said Greg with surprise. "It's Rocky. He wants me to call him in the morning."

When Greg finished reading the text, he immediately hit the call button and put the phone on speaker. "Hey, buddy," he said when Rocky answered. "Just got your text, but we're still up. I'm here with Odelia. Your text said you're home and you wanted to talk."

"Yeah," answered Rocky, his voice slow with exhaustion. "Actually, I'm at Lance's right now, but I wanted you guys to know I'm out of the clink. Thanks for everything."

I scooted my face closer to the phone. "Did you make bail?"

"I actually didn't get that far; they let me go. Lucky for me, the beating didn't kill Tanaka. The cops said he was poisoned."

"Poisoned?" My voice squeaked in surprise.

"Yep. They think it's cyanide, but they're not sure yet. Guess it takes a few days for the tests to confirm it."

"Wow!" Greg ran a hand through his hair. "I'm sure glad that's over, at least for you."

"It's not exactly over, which is what I wanted to talk to you about. I need a really big favor."

"Anything," Greg said, meaning it.

"The cops said they found the poison in Tanaka's water bottle and prints on the bottle. They say the prints belong to Miranda."

Greg and I were stunned into silence.

"They still can't find Miranda. I know you

guys have done some detective work in the past. Do you think you could snoop around and see if there might have been anyone else with a reason to kill Tanaka?"

"Seems like it would be a pretty long list," Greg said.

"True," Rocky snorted. "I'm thinking no one would notice you asking a few questions here and there, but they might me. I can't believe Miranda would do something like that, no matter what else she's done."

I finally found my voice. "What exactly did Peter say to you on the court that made you so angry?"

"Let's talk about that tomorrow — if you guys are free, that is."

"What time is good for you?" asked Greg.

"How about after work? I really need to show up at my office tomorrow, and you guys probably do too. Greg, can we meet at your office? It's not far from mine."

"Sure. How about seven o'clock? My staff is mostly gone by then. There's a pizza place almost next door. We'll grab a pizza and some drinks and have dinner at the same time."

"Sounds good," said Rocky with a bit of relief in his voice. "Maybe by then Miranda will show up and be able to prove this is all a lot of nothing."

This time Greg's phone made it to the nightstand without buzzing.

For a long time we lay in bed staring up at the ceiling before either of us spoke. "Do you really think," began Greg, "that Miranda killed Tanaka?" He thought a little more about it. "Maybe Tanaka told her he was going to tell Rocky about their affair so she panicked."

"Hard to say, honey. People have certainly killed for less." I turned toward Greg and snuggled against him. He wrapped an arm around me and drew me close. "One thing is for sure: my mother can't accuse us of having a dull life anymore."

# SEVEN

I really don't know which is worse: having Steele in the office with me within arm's reach or having him work from home and call and email me every fifteen to twenty minutes.

I'd stuck to the agreed-upon script of him having been in a car accident on Sunday. Lying to people in the office and to the T&T mothership in Los Angeles didn't seem to bother me a smidge, and I'm not sure if I should be proud or ashamed. My mother always tells me I'm a lousy liar — a trait she claims I got from my father. She, on the other hand, could win an Oscar for it. Frankly, I was surprised she hadn't called me on the car accident story over dinner the night before. If Greg hadn't been there singing the same tune, she might have fixed her maternal lie detector on me and discovered the truth. The one person I had difficulty looking in the eye and talking about the accident with was Jill, Steele's secretary. She wanted details, and I kept claiming I didn't have any. I knew if I started making up stuff, it would come back to bite me and I'd look like a bigger fool. My plan was to keep any information about Steele simple and to a minimum. Earlier this morning on one of our calls, I'd begged him to let me tell Jill the truth and stressed that she could be trusted, which she could be, but he was adamant that I go to my grave with the bar fight details — or, rather, the few I had — forever locked in my brain. Considering how difficult it was to understand Steele on the phone, I could say that I didn't hear his demand, but I lost that excuse when he texted me the same and underscored it with a dozen exclamation points. That poor punctuation mark was certainly getting a workout.

I'd even begged off lunch with Zee. I gave her a quick call and simply said that Steele had been in a car accident and that I was holding down the fort while he convalesced. She'd pressed for details and I gave her the few I'd given Jill, which was next to nothing. I could have gone to lunch with Zee. I wanted to go to lunch with Zee. I just couldn't risk it. Zee Washington knows me inside and out, and she is even more talented than my mother when it comes to sniffing out lies that dribble from my mouth, full or partial, like spit when I sleep. She can also tell when I'm holding something back just by looking at me.

I really need to work on my duplicity skills. I wonder if there's an app for that?

Near the end of the day, I packed up Steele's mail, along with everything Jill and I had done for him that couldn't be emailed, and headed down to his place. I had planned to send it with a messenger but Steele had insisted that I bring it to him personally. With traffic, time would be tight for getting to our meeting with Rocky Henderson. Laguna Beach is south of where our office is located. Then I'd have to fight traffic north along Pacific Coast Highway to Huntington Beach, where Greg's business, Ocean Breeze Graphics, is located. Hopefully Steele would let me get in and out without too much chitchat or annoyance. If he wasn't going to tell me about Perris, then I saw no reason to stick around and be late for the meeting with Rocky. I'd called Greg before leaving the office to let him know I had to see Steele first, but I only reached his voice mail.

Even though I had a key to Steele's condo — something he'd stashed in the office in case of emergencies — I rang the doorbell and waited. A few seconds later I was let inside by Cruz.

"How's he doing today?" I asked when I entered.

In response, she waved her right hand, palm down, back and forth. "Sometimes good, sometimes not so much. He doesn't like to take the pain pills."

"Is his mouth still swollen?"

She nodded. "I drove him to the dentist today. His teeth are going to be okay. A little loose, but nothing broken."

"That's good news." I stopped her when we were halfway down the entry hall and whispered, "Has he mentioned anything to you about it? The accident, I mean?"

"Not a peep. But," she said, whispering back and shaking an index finger in the air, "those injuries are not from a car crash. I know a beating when I see one."

Without confirming her suspicions, I asked, "Have you asked him about it?"

"Yes, but he threatened to fire me if I asked again."

"Oh, please." I rolled my eyes. "He'd never fire you any more than he'd fire Jill or me. We're his support system — his gals Friday who make his life run smoothly — his Charlie's Angels without the glamour."

She smiled. "I know, but I respect his

privacy, and you should too, Odelia." She patted my arm in a motherly way and winked. "One day we'll know. It just won't be today."

When we got to the dining room, I noticed a couple of beautiful floral arrangements on the table. "Where did these come from?"

"The big one is from the firm," she explained. "The other one is from the Washingtons. It arrived just a few minutes ago."

Leave it to Zee to be speedy on sending get-well wishes, putting the rest of us to shame on good etiquette.

I found Steele sitting on a chaise longue on his terrace, a long balcony that could be entered from either the den or living room. As soon as I stepped outside, I could hear the sound of the waves and call of scavenging gulls from the beach below. Steele was wearing sunglasses and his head was tilted down, making me wonder if he was napping. In spite of the chill in the late afternoon air, he was shirtless. I'd seen Steele without a shirt before when he'd shot hoops with Greg or when we'd gone to cheer him on in some of his races. He was well developed but much more slender than he appeared in his suits, almost to the point of being thin. He had more chest hair than Greg, and I suspected he practiced regular manscaping. What I'd never seen before was the wide pattern of bruising going down the left side of his torso. It looked like a map of the Great Lakes. A gasp escaped my lips before I could stop it.

"You keep staring like that, Grey," Steele said without moving his head, "and you'll have to stuff a couple of dollars into my briefs." His words weren't as slurred as they'd been the day before, but they still weren't as crisp and clear as usual. He pulled up the light throw covering his legs until it reached just under his arms and hid the bruising from my sight.

I put the expanding folder of documents down on the small round glass table next to the chaise. "Should you be out here without a shirt? It's kind of chilly."

"I should go in. I've been out here quite a while already, but the sun felt so good earlier." He moved his head to look at the ocean full on. "I've lived here almost ten years, and I never tire of the view or the sound of the sea." The words came out of his mouth slow and deliberate, like he was testing each one first for pain. "Sometimes I come out here and sit when it's raining. I'll put a chair back by the window, under the overhang so I don't get wet, and sit and listen to the waves and rain together."

In spite of the chill in the air, we were having a warm and fuzzy moment — something rare for us. As much as we care for and about each other, both our working relationship and personal friendship are based on a sort of antagonistic banter. Maybe almost getting beaten to death was making Steele reevaluate his life and relationships.

"So," he said, without turning to look at me, "did you get anything done today or were you and Jill too busy playing in my absence?" He glanced up at me. "I'll bet you took a long lunch with Zee and sat on personal calls all day."

Then again, maybe the beating didn't work magic.

"We got everything done, Steele." I tapped the thick folder on the table next to him. "Here you go." I turned to leave. "Later."

"What's your rush?" Swinging his legs off the chaise in a slow and deliberate movement, he grabbed a nearby sweatshirt and slipped it over his head.

"Greg and I are meeting someone tonight." I consulted my watch. "And you know how traffic can be this time of day."

Steel got to his feet but started to stagger. I dropped my tote bag to the ground and stepped in to help him, but he waved me off. "I'm fine. I just get a little woozy when

I first stand."

"You need to see a doctor, Steele. I'm worried about that huge bruise."

"I have an appointment tomorrow. Besides, it's just a couple of cracked ribs. Doc at urgent care said they'll heal on their own if I take care of them." He gave off a ragged laugh as he hobbled toward the door. "I'll bet you thought if you ever saw me looking like this, it would have been you who'd inflicted the wounds."

"Not that I haven't thought of it from time to time."

He laughed again, then grabbed his left side and went pale. I jumped to his side and helped him move indoors.

"Actually, I always thought it would be one of the women you wined and dumped, or one of their husbands." I paused. "It wasn't, was it?"

"I assure you, Grey, it wasn't." Once inside, I guided Steele to his recliner and helped him ease down into it. He took off his sunglasses and put them on the end table. He looked exhausted from the effort.

Cruz came in from the kitchen and watched him settle in with a look of worry. "Would you like me to stay tonight, Mr. Steele? Because I can."

"No, Cruz, but thanks," he told her. "I

89

really appreciate you coming in extra this week. Tomorrow I have to see my doctor. Can you take me or should I call a car service?"

"It's not a problem," she told him. "I'll take you." She grabbed her purse from the table and slipped into a light jacket. "I made you that albondigas soup you like so much. It's in the refrigerator in plastic containers. Just microwave whatever you want when you're ready to eat. And I cut up some fruit into very small pieces. It's also in the fridge."

"Thanks. I appreciate it." He turned on the TV and flew through the channels until he got to CNN.

"I'll head on out with you, Cruz," I said, then stepped onto the terrace to grab the expanding folder and my purse.

"Grey, can you stay a minute?" Steele requested when I returned. "I promise I won't make you late for your appointment."

I hesitated, really wanting to get on the road, but he looked so pathetic. "Okay, but I can't stay for long."

Cruz waved goodbye to us both and left.

Sitting on the sofa next to his chair, where I'd been the day before, I slipped off my sweater and pulled the documents onto my lap. "I guess you want to go over some of these now." I started pulling a couple of items out of the file.

"No, I'll look at those later." He turned to me, his bruised left eye still looking pretty ugly but not quite as raw as the day before. Considering the injury to his ribs and his eye, I was guessing only Steele's left side was exposed to his attackers, like he was on the ground on his right side when hit or leaning one side against something to protect it.

"Tell me what's going on with your friend Rocky."

"Rocky?" The question surprised me.

"They mentioned something on the local news today about new developments but didn't say much beyond a suspect being released."

"Rocky is who Greg and I are meeting tonight. He was released last night after they discovered Peter Tanaka wasn't killed by the beating."

"What killed him?"

"They told Rocky it was poison — something in his water bottle."

"Really?" Steele sat up straighter in his chair. "Do they know what kind?"

"Maybe cyanide. They're not completely sure yet." I moved the heavy file from my lap onto the sofa beside me and turned to Steele. "Why the interest?"

He shrugged. "Because I'm already bored out of my mind, and I find it interesting." He gave me a lopsided smile, which considering his swollen mouth made him look like a happy gargoyle. "Has his wife shown up yet?"

I shook my head. "No, but now she's the main suspect. Her prints were found on the water bottle. I think Rocky wants me and Greg to poke around and try to figure out what's going on. He's sure his wife didn't kill Peter."

Steele was quiet for a moment, then said, "So what can I do to help?"

"You?" The surprise in my voice was almost a yelp. "Don't you think you have your hands full right now just trying to get well and handle your law practice from home? And what about your car? Shouldn't you be knee deep in insurance crap about that?"

"Relax, Grey. I called the insurance company today, and since it will be a few days before I can drive, there's no sense in my looking for another vehicle. And we're not terribly busy at the office right now. You know that." He swallowed, and I could see talking was hurting his mouth. But did it stop him? No.

Steele took a drink from a water bottle he

picked up from the end table. It was one of those squeeze types runners use. He squirted the water directly into his mouth, without touching his injured lips, and swallowed slowly. "There must be something I can do to help you and Greg. I can make calls, do some research. I need something to keep my mind occupied."

"How about — oh, let's just suggest something silly here — the practice of law?"

"Listen, Grey, before yesterday I worked out in the gym an hour and a half, sometimes two hours a day. It's going to be a while before I can do much of anything like that again, but I can't fill all my time with my job."

"Take up needlepoint," I suggested.

He stared at me. It was his cut-the-bullshit-and-quit-wasting-my-time stare. I saw it often at the office.

"Listen, Steele, I don't know what Rocky is going to want us to do — not really. We might have to help find his wife or look into her relationship with Peter. Or see what Peter was up to behind the scenes."

Instead of responding, Steele pulled out some papers that were under his iPad on the table. He handed them to me. After giving them a quick scan, I looked over at Steele with surprise. "What's this?"

"That, Grey, is a criminal background report on Peter Tanaka. Your brother and the felonious Willie Proctor aren't the only ones with connections."

Willie Proctor is a friend who mostly stays in the shadows. He's on the run from the police because he scammed a lot of people out of their hard-earned cash years ago. He paid the money back eventually, but the charges are still hanging over his head. He also has a lot of underworld connections that Greg and I have found useful, even life-saving, on several occasions. My brother, Clark, a retired cop, works for him in his legal entities, or at least that's the story we're told. We don't want to know more, for obvious reasons.

"Connections, my fat behind," I told Steele. "You got this off of Westlaw. It says so right here."

"Who cares where I got it," snapped Steele. He swallowed hard as a stab of pain radiated across his face. "The point is, I can do research for you while I'm laid up. I can make calls too."

"You're as bad as my mother. She was all hopped up last night about this." I put down the Westlaw printout. "Why is it you all want to be involved in the very things that put my ass in danger?" I took a deep breath.

"All but Zee. I swear, she and Seth are the only sensible people I know."

"Aren't you even going to read that report?" Steele pointed at the papers now sitting on top of the expanding folder. "After all the trouble I went to, and me all banged up." Turning down his swollen lips, he flashed me the most pathetic bruised face I'd ever seen on a grown man, like a GQ model still healing from plastic surgery gone wrong.

"Careful, Steele, or I'll make your eyes a matched set." I got up to leave before my threat became a reality. I'm not given to physical violence as a rule, but Steele was playing the sympathy card until it was a threadbare red flag being flashed at a bull.

"Just read the damn thing," he pushed, obviously not afraid of my physical threat one bit. "That Tanaka's a real piece of work."

I grabbed the printout and stuffed it into my bag, then I pushed the expanding folder closer to him. "I'll read it with Greg tonight, but now I have to go."

While I was putting on my sweater, my cell phone rang. It was Greg. "Hi, honey," I said as soon as I answered. Without waiting for a response, I tacked on, "I'm leaving Steele's right this minute."

"No rush," Greg said from his end. "Rocky cancelled."

"Oh, why?" A part of me was pleased because I was tired and wanted to go home, but in a different part of my body alarms were going off.

"If you're near a TV, quick turn on channel 4."

Without hesitation, I grabbed Steele's remote and aimed it at the TV, turning it to channel 4's local news. Behind the newscaster was a photo of Miranda Henderson. It was a lovely photo showing her bright eyes and smile, and it certainly didn't give the impression that she was a killer. I increased the volume on the TV and put Greg on speaker.

"That's Rocky's wife," I said to Steele.

I expected the news to be that Miranda had been apprehended as a suspect in Peter Tanaka's murder, but that wasn't the case. Rocky's van had been found, and so had Miranda Henderson. Her body had been found inside Rocky's van behind an abandoned warehouse in San Diego.

In shock, I plopped back down on the sofa.

"You watching?" asked Greg from the phone.

"Yes, honey. How awful."

Steele had leaned forward in his chair to pay closer attention to the screen and to hear Greg. "Maybe she committed suicide," he suggested.

"It's a possibility," added Greg.

When the news was over, I told Greg I was going straight home. He said he'd meet me there shortly.

I didn't get up right away from Steele's sofa. My legs felt rubbery and unable to support me.

"You okay, Grey?" Steele asked.

"Yeah, just in shock."

"Take your time. It's a lot to take in." He took the remote from me and muted the sound. "I'm sorry about your friend. Very sorry."

I could tell from Steele's tone, slurred or not, that he meant it.

"In fact, why don't you stay for dinner? I'm sure Greg won't mind. I can heat up some of Cruz's soup for us."

I shook my head. "Thanks, but no thanks." I glanced over at Steele. He was trying hard to be sensitive to the situation even while in his own physical pain. "But I do love her soup."

"It's the best," he agreed, doing his best to normalize the leaden atmosphere created by the news.

We sat there a few more minutes before I finally got to my feet and picked up my bag. "You still interested in helping?"

His good eye lit up like a sparkler on the Fourth of July. "Sure, especially now."

"Find out what you can about cyanide. How easy is it to obtain and from where? How fast does it work? Stuff like that."

"You don't think Rocky's wife killed herself, do you?"

"I don't know about that, but I don't think she killed Peter Tanaka."

I thought about the young woman vomiting in the ladies' room. How her hair had felt like strands of silk in my hands as I held it away from the toilet bowl. How young and vulnerable she'd looked when I'd helped clean up her face and patch her makeup after. How frightened she'd looked at the game on Sunday. Now she was maggot food.

I could tell from Steele's posture that he wasn't so sure. "I've always heard that poison is a woman's weapon."

"Maybe," I admitted. "But it's also a premeditated weapon. I just can't see Miranda Henderson planting poison in a water bottle, then sitting there with a cold heart to watch it do its job."

# EIGHT

I was heading home, my mind only half on my driving. The other half was thinking of Rocky — first accused of murder, then his wife accused of murder, and now losing her. I thought about Miranda and wanted to know more about what had happened to her and why. Where had she gone after leaving Balboa Park? Had she met up with someone? Was she heading to Mexico to disappear? Or was her death just a random, senseless killing? Maybe it was suicide.

Behind me someone blasted their horn. I snapped out of my stupor to find the red light I had been waiting for was now green. I moved forward, quickly going through the intersection before the car in my rearview mirror rammed me through it.

I was halfway home when I got a call from Zee. Using my hands-free feature, I answered it. "Hi."

"When were you going to tell me about

the murder?" Zee launched without even a hello.

"Which one?" I asked calmly, even though I was anything but calm inside.

"Let's start with the murder of the quadriplegic in San Diego. Weren't you and Greg down there this weekend for that tournament?"

"Yes, and we saw the whole thing."

"You saw it? The body or the murder?"

"Both."

"And when were you going to tell me about this?" Before I could answer, Zee continued with her rant. "I was at my mother's all weekend helping her prepare and serve a church luncheon, and I got home late last night. I didn't see the news until tonight."

"I was planning on telling you over lunch today, Zee, but with Steele's accident and all, that didn't happen."

"You could have told me when you called earlier today." From her tone, I knew Zee was standing with one hand on a wide hip, her mouth a thin line of disapproval.

"It didn't seem like a telephone kind of discussion."

"You're not involved with this, are you?"

There it was: the bonus question I knew she'd been dying to ask.

"Like I said, Greg and I saw what happened. We were questioned by the San Diego police, along with the other spectators, then released."

"But aren't the Hendersons friends of yours?" She paused long enough to take a breath. Before I could answer, she added, "That poor woman. Do you think she killed the man at the tournament?"

"I'm not sure, Zee. I'd like to think she didn't, but the police seem to have proof that she did."

"You sound exhausted, Odelia. Are you in your car?"

"Yes. I'm on my way home from dropping off stuff at Steele's, and I am very tired, mentally and physically. Nice flowers, by the way."

"Oh, good. I was hoping they'd get there today. How is Mike?"

"Doing okay. Bored stiff already, but he won't be able to go back to work until probably next week."

"Thank God. He could have been killed."

She didn't know the half of it, and I couldn't tell her. Zee was my best friend. I told her almost everything. This secret business was killing me for sure.

"Yes, he could have," was all I said.

"Odelia, you go straight home, take a long

hot bath in that fancy tub of yours, and go to bed early. That's an order."

I loved it when Zee got all ninja-mom on me. Well, most of the time I loved it. Tonight was one of those times.

"That's the plan, Stan."

She laughed. "I mean it. Shut off your phone and take care of yourself tonight."

"Yes, ma'am."

The next call came from Greg. "You almost home?" he asked.

"Just about. Traffic is horrible tonight."

"You want leftover Chinese? I can fix you a plate and have it hot when you walk through the door."

"That sounds great, honey, but I think I'd rather just have some tomato soup, if you don't mind."

"Want a grilled cheese with that?"

I smiled. Greg not only loved grilled cheese sandwiches but made creative ones. "Sure, but nothing fancy tonight. I think my stomach is a bit on the fritz."

"You got it, sweetheart."

"Zee just called. She saw the news about Rocky and Miranda. She ordered me to take a long hot bath and go to bed early, and I think that's exactly what I'm going to do. How about you?"

"I just got off the phone with Dev. I sent

him a text thanking him for letting us know last night about Rocky, and he called me a few minutes ago."

I stopped at another red light but this time paid attention to the traffic, which I'm sure the car in front of me appreciated. "Did he tell you anything we don't already know?"

"Just that they think she died sometime Sunday afternoon from a gunshot to her temple, and probably not too long after she left the gym. The cops think Miranda probably killed herself because of whatever Peter told Rocky — that she poisoned Tanaka but whatever he disclosed to Rocky would have shined a spotlight on her as a suspect, so she took the easy way out."

*The easy way out.* I hated that phrase. Yes, suicide did seem simpler than staying and facing whatever problems came your way, but there's never anything easy about the permanency of death, especially for those left behind.

When the light turned green, the car in front of me started moving, and I followed it through the intersection. "If it wasn't a suicide, who killed Miranda? And were they involved in Peter's murder too?"

"Dev said the San Diego police will go over every inch of the van, but that it will take time. By the way, I told Dev that

Mike's story is that he was in a car accident, just in case he got asked about it."

"And what did Dev say to that?"

"He laughed, then said okay."

A small giggle escaped my lips, then I said what was on my mind. "Greg, do you really think Miranda killed Peter?"

"Hard to say."

"But when would she have had time to slip something into his water?"

"It was actually a sports drink."

"A what?"

"The poison was mixed with a sports drink — you know, something like Gatorade — probably to mask the taste."

"Have you talked anymore with Rocky?"

"It was actually Lance who called me today," answered Greg. "He said Rocky is absolutely torn up over Miranda."

"No surprise there."

"Rocky is staying with Lance for a few days. Besides, without his van, he can't get around very well. Lance said Rocky's not going into his shop for a few days." Like Greg, Rocky was a small business owner. He operated a machine shop in Santa Ana.

"We should go see him," I suggested. "Just to pay our respects. Any details yet about Miranda's funeral?"

"None, and it probably won't be for a

while. Dev said it might take a bit of time for them to process Miranda's body. Tomorrow I'll check and see if Rocky's up to having company."

I was getting very close to home. With each block, a warm, fuzzy feeling crept through my body like hot chocolate on a cold day. "Honey," I said into the phone as I made a right-hand turn, "I'll be home in about ten minutes. Fire up that soup."

Dinner was relaxing and casual. We ate soup and grilled cheese in front of the TV with Muffin and Wainwright sleeping nearby. Even without verbally agreeing to it, we didn't discuss the two murders, choosing instead to laugh over a silly sitcom.

After dinner, I submerged myself in my whirlpool tub — a gift from Greg two Christmases ago. I'd dumped in some lavender bath stuff, cocooning myself in heavenly scented bubbles. The tub was in our guest bathroom. We'd had to remodel and enlarge the entire bath to get the large tub in, but it had been worth it. Even Greg used it from time to time, especially after a particularly hard game of basketball, but it was mostly a feminine retreat, like now. It was just me, my bubbles, a few scented candles, some soft classical music, and Muffin, who was curled up like a tight little gray bun in the sink, snoozing. I closed my eyes and let the warmth of the gently bubbling water and silkiness of the music relax me into a stupor.

My reverie was interrupted by the sound of our front doorbell, followed by the barking of Wainwright. It was his friendly bark, not his watchdog bark, so it had to be someone we knew. Still, it was after nine — late for someone to be dropping by without a good reason. My mind immediately jumped to Dev. Maybe something important had come up that had to be handled in person.

I was reluctantly hauling my behind out of the warmth and comfort of the tub when Greg opened the door and announced, "Sweetheart, Clark's here."

"Clark?" I grabbed a towel and started drying off. "Is Mom okay?"

"Yes, Grace is fine. Come on out when you can, but don't rush. I think he's going to stay the night."

Wrapped in my favorite thick robe, I padded down the hall and into the living room. Clark immediately stood up from the sofa and wrapped his strong arms around me, hugging me close. He gave me a kiss on my cheek. "You smell great, sis."

"Thanks, but what a surprise."

"A nice one, I hope."

"Of course. It's just that Mom didn't mention anything about you visiting."

"She doesn't know I'm here." He sat back down, and I joined him.

Greg rolled in with a tray across his lap. He handed a mug of coffee to Clark and a mug of hot chocolate to me. "Be right back with my own cocoa. It's brewing right now."

"I hope you didn't go to any trouble," Clark said, taking a big whiff of his coffee. "Smells wonderful."

"Steele gave us one of those Keurig coffee makers last Christmas," I explained to Clark. "Greg still thinks it's a shiny new toy."

"I love the thing," said Greg with enthusiasm as he wheeled back in with his own mug. "I wish we'd gotten one a long time ago." He gave Wainwright a gentle command and the dog stopped slobbering over our guest and went to his bed in the corner.

Clark took a drink of his coffee and smiled appreciatively. "Speaking of Steele, Dev told me he was in a car accident this weekend. How's he doing?"

Greg and I looked at each other with surprise, then I answered, "Steele's pretty banged up, but he'll be fine. When did you talk to Dev?"

"Tonight. We met for dinner." Clark looked over at Greg. "He was just finishing up talking to you when I got to the restaurant."

"I'm surprised," Greg said, "that Dev didn't tell me he was meeting you."

"Yeah," I added. "What's with all the cloak and dagger stuff?"

Clark laughed. "There's no cloak and dagger stuff going on. Sometimes I fly into LA for just a day or two on business, and sometimes Dev and I see each other when I'm in town. Other times I scoot by to see you and Mom. Depends on my time."

"So you're just here for today?" I felt my mouth turn downward. We see Clark off and on, but not nearly as much as we'd like.

"I was going to fly out tonight," he told us, "but decided to stay over and fly out in the morning. I always pack a carry-on just in case. I hope you don't mind me crashing here. I didn't want to bother Mom."

"You're always welcome," Greg told him. "But never worry about disturbing Grace. She's a regular night owl."

I took a drink of my cocoa and eyed my older half brother over the rim. "He's not worried about Mom," I said, flashing a wink at my husband. "He doesn't want Mom to know he's here."

Clark gave off a sigh. He looked good. He used to have a gut but he'd trimmed down considerably since leaving police work for a job in the private sector. His hair was thinner and now totally gray, but his physique was pretty tight for a guy in his mid-sixties.

"Mom has been hounding me to spend more time here, but I've been pretty busy." He took a drink of his coffee. "If I go over there she'll expect me to stay longer, and I have to be on a plane out tomorrow. I have plans tomorrow night that I can't cancel. I'm only staying tonight to talk to you two."

I grew alarmed. Clark may look good, but maybe he had a health problem. "You okay?"

"I'm fine, sis." He slipped an arm around my shoulders and drew me close. "But I sure appreciate the concern."

"If you're worried about Grace, don't be," said Greg. "She seems to be thriving out here. She pals around with my parents and several of the folks at her retirement community, as well as spends time with us."

"No, it's not that, though I do agree moving to Cali has been great for Mom. She even looks younger." He smiled. "By the way, I finally sold the house in Massachusetts. The sale closed last month. I'm now officially a resident of Arizona. I even bought myself a nice place in one of those fancy fifty-five-plus communities with a golf course."

"That's great," I told him, happy that he was happy. "Arizona isn't here, but at least it's closer to us."

"Yeah, but that's not what I want to talk to you about." His voice turned serious on a dime. "Over dinner, Dev told me about the murders of that guy in the wheelchair and the woman suspected of doing it. He said the woman and her husband are good friends of yours."

"That's true," answered Greg. "We've known Rocky and Miranda for several years."

"Here's the thing." Next to me, Clark shifted a bit. "I know I'm talking to two brick walls here when I tell you two to stay out of it."

Clark removed his arm from my shoulders and put his coffee mug on the table in front of the sofa. Then he leaned forward, his arms resting on his legs, hands clasped between his knees, like a father about to have a serious heart-to-heart with a couple of wayward teenagers.

"But whatever *you* do," he continued, "I don't want Mom involved in it. I don't want her going around playing detective like she did last time." Clark looked straight at me when he said the words.

"Hey," I said in protest. "I didn't put that cockamamie idea in her head. She gets those ideas all on her own, believe me."

"And she almost got herself killed, didn't she?" Clark shot back. "As much as I've wanted to shoot her myself a few times, I'm still kind of fond of the old girl."

"She's my mother, too, you know." I twitched my nose in annoyance. "We're on the same page here, Clark, both with wanting to shoot her and keep her safe."

We all paused to take a deep breath and a sip of hot beverages.

I put my mug on the coffee table next to Clark's and turned to face him fully. "Mom has already mentioned getting involved, and we've said no. We're pretending we're not going to do anything."

Clark fixed me with a laser stare. "But you are, aren't you? The two of you are going to look into it?"

"They're friends of ours, Clark," Greg said with conviction. "We're going to do whatever we can to help Rocky."

"Then figure out a way to keep Mom out of it," Clark insisted. "You two are both smart cookies. I'm sure you'll come up with something." He looked at Greg. "How about your parents? Can't they take her someplace for a few days? We can even pay for it."

"Sorry," Greg answered. "My parents are out of town. They're visiting my sister. Besides, last time Grace tried to get *my* mother involved."

"Well, think of something." Clark picked up his mug again and took a drink.

I raised my hand like a kid in school. "I have a great idea," I said with enthusiasm. "You can take Mom back to Arizona with you."

"That would work," agreed Greg. "You can bring her back when you come for Thanksgiving in two weeks."

Clark put his mug back down with a sound thud. "No."

"Why not?" I asked. "I'll bet Mom would be thrilled at the idea of a surprise trip. She just complained to us that she's a bit bored. She's never been to Arizona that I know of. You can show her your new house. She can even help you decorate it. It's a win-win." I was really going for the hard sell.

"I told you I have plans tomorrow night. And don't forget work."

"It's not like Grace needs a sitter," Greg said with a grin. "And if you're seeing a lady friend, you can always go back to her place."

Clark stood up and nearly stepped on Muffin, who'd wandered in from the bathroom. The tiny cat scooted out of the way in the nick of time. "What part of no don't you people understand?"

"Well," I said, sending out my final volley, "if you don't take Mom, then I can't guarantee that I'll be able to keep her nose out of this nasty business."

Clark stretched his arms high above him, reaching for the ceiling, then behind him. He twisted his neck, and it gave off loud crackles and pops. Greg and I eyed each other out of the corners of our eyes and waited it out.

Done with his calisthenics, Clark pulled his phone out of his pocket and jabbed at the screen. "Hey, Mom," he said when the call was answered. "You up for a surprise road trip?"

# NINE

Mom was thrilled to go to Arizona with Clark. Almost as soon as Clark finished his arrangements with her, she put in a call to our home phone. Without letting her know Clark was there, I let her gush on about the trip.

"I'm just worried about a couple of things," she told me.

"Don't worry, Mom. We'll look after your place and water your plants."

"It's not that, but what about the murder investigation? I won't be able to help you."

I rolled my eyes. Clark was right to be concerned, and I felt less guilty about forcing him into taking her to Arizona. "Like Greg and I told you at dinner last night, we're not getting involved. The police are pretty sure Miranda killed Peter, and now that Miranda is dead, it's kind of a closed case." I paused. "You did see the news tonight about Miranda, didn't you?"

"Yes, I did. Very tragic."

"The police are pretty sure she killed herself." I noticed the two men hanging on every word of my side of the conversation, wondering if I could put Mom off the scent enough to ship her off to Arizona. "So there's really nothing we can do." I paused, but not long enough for her to give it much thought. "So we'll see you and Clark back here for Thanksgiving, right?"

"Of course. I promised Renee I'd bake a couple of pies for dinner."

"Love you, Mom," I said, trying to close the conversation.

"Love you, too, but I need to quit jabbering and start packing." She tittered with the excitement of an early bird spotting a worm. "Just think, tomorrow I'll be blogging about Arizona!"

The next morning, after a hearty home-cooked breakfast, we sent Clark off to gather up Mom and her luggage and head to the airport. If she asked, he was going to tell her he had spent the night in Oxnard. He shook hands with Greg and gave me a hug and a kiss. We watched him go down the walk toward his rental car, his overnight bag in his hand. Almost at the curb, he turned and called to us, "Why do I feel like I've been bamboozled?"

"Love you too," I called back with a smile and a wave.

After Clark left, Greg asked me, "You going into the office today, sweetheart?"

"I should, with Steele out."

I usually only work a couple days a week, but I knew Steele would be hot and heavy with emails and projects this week since he'd be out. I picked up my phone and checked my work email. Sure enough, there were several emails from him, sent at various times in the night and this morning. Either he needed to take fewer naps during the day or a sleeping pill at night. I opened the email from him that was not work-related and laughed.

"What is it?" Greg was gathering up his stuff to go to work and stopped.

"Steele. He's as bad as my mother. Yesterday he begged to get involved in the murders with either online research or by making calls."

"Maybe we should have Clark take him to Arizona, too."

I laughed at the thought. Poor Clark. "I ended up giving Steele an assignment," I told Greg. "I asked him to research cyanide poisoning. He did, and it looks like he wrote a term paper on it."

Greg didn't laugh as I expected. He was

listening to a message on his own phone with a dark and concerned face.

"Something wrong at work, honey?"

He shook his head. "It's from Rocky and came in very late last night. We must have slept through it. Listen to this."

He put the phone on speaker and replayed the message. From the phone came a man's voice. He sounded groggy and tired. It also sounded like he was sobbing. "I can't. I can't do this. Sorry."

Panic rose in me. "Is that Rocky?"

Greg showed me the display. It was Rocky's number. Immediately he hit the callback feature. After several rings, voice mail kicked in, and Rocky's usually strong voice told us to leave a message. Greg told him to call us.

Next Greg called Lance, but that call also went to voice mail. Again, Greg left a message to return the call.

"I'm going over to Lance's," Greg announced. He called his office and told Chris Fowler, his right-hand man, that he'd be late but didn't know how late.

"I'm going with you," I told him and placed my own call to T&T, telling Jill I'd be in later.

Lance lived in Costa Mesa, almost on the border of Newport Beach. When I was single I had owned a townhome not more than a mile away, so I knew the neighborhood well. Greg and I took separate vehicles. Once everything checked out, we'd be heading in separate directions. My office was east of Lance's house, and Greg's shop was north. At the last minute Greg left Wainwright, who usually went with him to work, at home.

Lance, a divorced man, lived in a trim ranch-style home painted the color of terra cotta. It was located on a quiet street just a couple of blocks east of Twenty-Second Street in Newport Beach where it borders with Costa Mesa. We pulled up in front of the place but found no cars in the driveway. A closed metal gate extended from one side of the house to the wall bordering the neighboring property. Through the gate we saw no sign of any vehicle.

We made our way up the walk. The front door had several steps leading up to it, so I took those alone and rang the bell.

"There's a ramp in the back," Greg told me. "Lance had it installed for when Rocky visited."

We waited about twenty seconds, then I rang the bell again — this time twice. Still nothing. I pulled out a notepad and pen from my purse. "Greg, I think we should leave a note that we were here."

"Good idea. Leave both our numbers."

I jotted out the note and stuck it on a short nail in the middle of the door, one probably used for hanging a wreath at Christmas time.

Greg and I were heading down the walk, ready to head off to our separate jobs, when a car came down the street and turned into the driveway. It was Lance. He got out of the car and crossed the grass to meet us. He looked like crap. He was a couple of years younger than Rocky and not as buffed in the shoulders. His blond hair was longer and looked greasy and uncombed. Stubble sprouted on his face like tiny weeds.

"We came because we're worried about Rocky," Greg told him. "He called me last night with a really odd message, but I didn't get it until this morning. Is he okay?"

Before answering, Lance rubbed his eyes. They were red. Under them, dark circles clung like leeches. "No, he's not. He's at Hoag Hospital. I've been there all night with him."

"What's happened?" I asked with alarm.

"Rocky tried to kill himself last night," Lance explained in a wet, rough voice. "And he nearly succeeded. I came home last night and found him unconscious."

119

"Oh, no," I gasped. "First Miranda — now him. I'm so very sorry, Lance. Is Rocky going to be okay?"

He shrugged. "He's in a coma. No change at all from last night."

"How can we help?" I offered.

"Thanks," he answered, "but I called our folks this morning from the hospital. They live in Florida and are catching the first plane they can out here. They were going to come for Miranda's funeral, but now they'll come sooner."

"I know Miranda's mother died about two years ago," I said. "But what about her father?"

He shook his head. "He's been out of the picture since Miranda was about ten." He took a deep breath. "You'll have to excuse me, but I have to get to work. I just started a new job, and my boss isn't too keen on family emergencies. I already took Monday off to help Rocky when he was arrested. I can't miss today too, no matter how shitty I feel."

We watched him go into the house, not even stopping to take our note off the front door. As soon as he was inside, Greg's phone rang. It was Dev Frye.

"Hey, Dev," Greg said, answering. "Yeah, we just heard about Rocky from his brother.

We're at Lance's house now." He listened, then said, "Sure, we'd like that. Be right there."

When he finished the call, Greg said to me, "Come on, we're going to the hospital. That was Dev calling to let us know about Rocky. He said if we get there soon, he can get us in to see him. Otherwise we won't be able to because it's restricted to family."

"I'm right behind you," I said, heading for my car.

Hoag Hospital was three miles from Lance's house. Greg and I made it there in just a few minutes and found good parking for both of our vehicles. We rode the elevator up to the floor Dev had indicated to find the detective waiting for us in an area just outside of the ICU.

"Your friend's in pretty bad shape," he announced. "He may not make it."

"Why are you here?" I asked.

"I saw his name on a report this morning and recognized it. We investigate all suicide attempts, Odelia. You know that."

I nodded in response. I did know that. I'd met both Greg and Dev when Sophie London, one of my good friends, had shot herself years ago.

Greg explained to Dev about the call and why we were at Lance's. "According to my phone, the call came in just after eleven thirty." He pulled out his phone and played the voice mail for Dev. "We were already asleep and didn't hear it."

"The brother called the paramedics shortly before twelve thirty," Dev told us.

"How, Dev?" I asked. "Was it pills? On the message he sounds like he's drugged or half in the bag."

"He had a pretty high blood alcohol level, but it was the gunshot to his gut that did the real damage. He almost bled out." Dev turned to Greg. "Isn't your pal a quadriplegic?"

"Yes, he is," Greg answered. "He has pretty good use of his hands, especially his left one, but certainly not a good grip."

Dev wrote the information down on a small pad he always carried with him. "The paramedics recovered the gun, and we're processing it right now. It belonged to his brother."

I grabbed Dev's upper arm. "You don't think Lance tried to murder him, do you?"

Dev didn't remove my hand but covered it with one of his meaty paws in a gesture of comfort. "We won't know that, Odelia, until we check out the gun and everything else. We've already questioned Lance Henderson extensively at the hospital. The gunshot could have been self-inflicted. Your friend could have been aiming for his chest or even his head, but with his impairment caught his stomach instead."

In a nervous gesture, Greg rolled his chair forward and back several times. "Are you working Miranda's case, Dev?"

The big detective shook his head. "Not my jurisdiction, but I'm sure we'll be exchanging information. I've already called Bill Martinez about this. He's working both Tanaka and the Henderson woman since they're probably related."

Dev put away his notepad. "Come on. I knew if you two showed up here they'd turn you away, and I wanted to give you a chance to see him while he's still alive."

Now it was Greg's turn to grab Dev's arm. "Thanks, Dev. We owe you."

"You owe me. Steele owes me." Dev snorted. "I've got IOUs coming out my backside these days."

When we entered the ICU, Dev flashed his badge at a nurse manning the central station.

"Just ten minutes, Detective, not a minute more."

Dev grunted and kept walking, entering one of the glass-walled rooms. We followed.

In the bed was a pale, shrunken man

hooked up to tubes and machines. It didn't look like Rocky Henderson, but a poor facsimile of him — a copy of a copy of a copy — a grainy, faded image of the man who just days before was commanding his troop of wheelchair athletes down a hard-wood floor in search of a victory. That was just three short days ago.

I covered my face with my hands and sobbed. Greg slipped an arm around my waist and buried his face into my side.

# TEN

It was difficult for us to drag ourselves away from Rocky, not knowing if we'd ever see him alive again, but the nurse was adamant about the ten minutes. Once we were back in the waiting room, Dev gave us his standard lecture, which was really just a rerun of Clark's comments the night before.

*Don't get involved, but I know I'm talking to myself here. Blah. Blah. Blah.*

It's not that we don't appreciate how people are worried for us and care so much about us; we do. But we also care about our friends, and Rocky and Miranda are friends, and friends don't let friend's deaths go unresolved.

It had also been difficult to say goodbye to Greg at the hospital and head to work. He was my rock, and I wanted to cling to him like suffocating moss lest anything befall him. Seeing Rocky in that hospital bed and knowing Miranda was dead made me paranoid about my own better half. If Rocky had tried to kill himself, had it been over grief in losing Miranda or had it been about what Tanaka had said and how he and Miranda had last parted? You hear stories all the time about the guilt people feel when a loved one dies and their last words to each other were harsh and in anger. Sensing my fears, Greg had wiped the tears from my eyes and kissed me gently before saying goodbye.

"We're going to get to the bottom of this," he promised.

Words failed me. I could only nod and climb into my car with my husband's comforting touch and words of confidence as security. I clung to them like a child clutches a teddy bear.

When I got to the office, Jill rolled her eyes — not at me but in general — as she announced, "Steele's been going nuts trying to reach you."

"I know, I know," I said as I passed her desk and headed to my office. "My cell phone was going ballistic, so I turned it off. I was at Hoag and couldn't talk to him."

At the mention of the local hospital, Jill got up from her desk and followed me into my office. "Everything okay? It's not your mother, is it?"

"No. Mom's good. In fact, she's on her way to Arizona with Clark as we speak." I sat down in my chair and put my purse in my lower desk drawer. "Remember our friend who was found dead in the van?"

She nodded, her mouth pursed with concern. "The woman suspected of killing that quad rugby player?"

"Yes. Well, her husband is in a coma at Hoag. They don't know if he tried to shoot himself or if someone else did it and tried to make it look like he did it to himself."

Jill gasped and dropped into my visitor's chair with a solid thud. "Oh my God!" She ran a hand through her short-cropped brown hair, forming shallow furrows like freshly plowed rows with her fingers.

"They also don't know if he's going to make it or not. Greg and I dropped by Rocky's brother's house this morning to check on him and ran into his brother, who was returning from the hospital. He found Rocky last night when he got home."

Jill put a hand to her mouth a moment, then said, "Odelia, I'm so very sorry. What can I do to help?"

I leaned back in my chair. "Thanks, Jill; nothing right now. Greg and I are going to check with some of our other friends in the rugby league and see what's going on. He's going to call several of them today while I try not to lose my mind and kill Steele."

"If you want me to lie to Steele and say you never came in, I'll do it."

I studied Jill. Lying was not something she did lightly or well. She hated it when Steele wanted her to lie about his whereabouts and usually managed to get around it with evasiveness. I'm sure it was one of the reasons Steele didn't want her to know the truth about his injuries.

"Thanks, Jill, but for now, Greg and I just have to think everything through and piece it together." I paused before tacking on as an afterthought, "And stay out of the way of the police."

"Is Detective Frye on this case?"

"Yeah, at least on the part concerning Rocky, and he knows the detective working Miranda's death and Peter Tanaka's."

"He's a good man, that Dev Frye."

"The best," I agreed. "He's already told us to keep out of it."

In spite of the gravity of the situation, Jill let out a short snort. "Sorry. I couldn't help myself." She got up and headed back to her desk. "You know if you need Sally and me to do anything for you, you just need to ask."

Sally Kipman was Jill's partner. She and I had gone to high school together when the

Grand Canyon was just a wheel rut in a dirt road. Sally had also chummed along with me several times when I'd stuck my nose where it didn't belong. Unlike Jill, she didn't have scruples about lying and subterfuge when it was called upon.

"Thanks, Jill. That's much appreciated, but for now I'll deal with Steele myself and see what Greg comes up with." That had been the decision between Greg and me. He would call his buddies in the wheelchair athlete community and I would find whatever I could on Peter Tanaka. We had also agreed to let Steele do some of our research, knowing if we didn't, he'd never leave us alone.

"I'm going to call Steele right now," I announced. "Anything you want me to tell him?"

Jill got up to leave. "Nah. Just do me a favor and mention my name as little as possible."

Before I could make the call, Jolene McHugh showed up at my office door. Jolene was an attorney who had migrated over to T&T with Steele from Woobie, officially known as Wallace, Boer, Brown, and Yates, our last law firm. Jolene had started with Woobie fresh out of law school. Now she was a seasoned veteran and a senior associate on partner track with T&T.

"Got a minute, Odelia?" she asked.

"Sure, Jolene, but do you?"

We both laughed, knowing I was referencing her advanced state of pregnancy. It was her first child, and she planned on working right up until the moment the baby, a boy, popped into the world. After the birth, Jolene would be on maternity leave for two months. With some difficulty, she lowered her swollen body into the chair Jill had just vacated and blew out a breath of relief that fluttered her copper bangs.

She started to speak, then laid a hand on her belly. Her pale face blanched to an even brighter white, making her freckles look like an advanced case of measles. "Wow," she said once she caught her breath, "that was a good kick."

My forehead bunched, worried that Jolene was going to drop the kid in my office. Like Prissy in *Gone with the Wind,* I don't know nuthin' 'bout birthin' babies. My right hand instinctively went to my cell phone, ready to hit the preprogrammed 9-1-1 should the need present itself.

Jolene took a deep breath. "I have a lot of stuff for you to take to Steele when you go over there today. He isn't due until next week, but I don't think Bubba is going to last that long."

Bubba was the nickname Jolene and her husband had given the fetus as soon as they'd learned it was a boy. They were keeping mum on the real name they had chosen for the baby. I tightened my grip on my phone. Jolene noticed.

"Relax, Odelia," she said with a short laugh. "Bubba may come soon, but I don't think it will be today, and certainly not this minute."

"Looks to me like Bubba's not going to last until lunch."

Jolene shifted in the chair, her discomfort obvious. "The sooner the better at this point."

I smiled at her. I really enjoyed working with Jolene and watching her grow from a raw, fresh-faced law school graduate into the brilliant attorney she was today. She and Steele didn't always get along, but she'd learned to hold her own with him, and he respected her for it and found her work and support nearly flawless. Whenever he was out for any extended time, like vacation or now, Jolene was in charge of the office. When she'd announced her pregnancy, Steele had smiled and given her hearty public congratulations. Alone with me behind closed doors, he'd nearly started banging his head against the wall, worried in advance about the effect her maternity leave would have on the firm and, more importantly, on him. If Bubba came now, with Steele laid up, Steele just might overdose on pain pills.

"I hadn't planned on seeing Steele today," I told Jolene. "I was there last night."

"Oh." She adjusted her bulk in the chair again, trying to find some degree of comfort. She was losing the battle. "I spoke to him about thirty minutes ago and he said you were dropping by tonight with a pouch of office stuff."

"Not that I know of," I told her, "but I was about to call him myself." I hesitated, studying Jolene. Her belly looked like it was rippling and expanding before my very eyes. I half expected Bubba to pop out doing a Fred Astaire impersonation, including top hat and tails. Or maybe he'd enter the world like The Rock, with bulging muscles and a fierce attitude. Either way, he was an active little sucker. "Um, does Steele know that you might not make it until your due date?"

"I didn't tell him," Jolene admitted. "He has enough to worry about without this. Besides, he'll be back next week, won't he?"

"I believe that's the plan."

"Even if Bubba comes today, it will only

be a few days without one of us here. I'm sure any of the other attorneys would be able to take the reins for that short time." She grabbed the arms of the chair and slowly hoisted herself to her feet.

"Are you sure you should be here?" I asked.

"Except for feeling like a hippo with swollen ankles, I'm fine." She shot me a smile that morphed into a grimace as her belly took another kick. "But I promise, if things change, I'll head for Hoag."

The mention of the local hospital brought me back to my morning visit with Rocky, changing my own smile.

"You okay, Odelia? Your face just dropped."

"I'm fine," I assured her. "It's just that Greg and I were at Hoag this morning, visiting a friend who is in a coma."

"I'm so very sorry." She waddled to the door and paused. "Steele didn't say much about his injuries, but I could tell something was wrong with his mouth." She fixed me with narrowed eyes. "Gossip around the firm is that he really had plastic surgery and is only saying he was in a car accident."

Forgetting Rocky for a moment, I let out a loud guffaw, which really did sound like *guffaw.* "I can assure you, Jolene, Steele did not have cosmetic surgery, although if his injuries had been any worse, he might have needed it."

"Is that handsome face of his messed up?"

"He looks like he took a good beating." I love it when I can tell the truth and people think it means something else.

"A friend of mine went face-first into an air bag last summer," she said with a nod of understanding. "It saved her life, but it wasn't pretty."

As soon as Jolene left, I got up, closed my door, and called Steele. "Hey," I said as soon as he answered.

" 'Hey'? That's all you have to say?" His voice was still slurred, but it wasn't as bad as yesterday. "I've been calling you all morning."

"I was at Hoag."

"Is Grace okay?"

I love how instantly everyone was concerned about my aged mother. It made me feel warm and fuzzy that people were interested in my family, even though the old bird would probably outlive us all.

"No, it's not Mom. It's Rocky Henderson." I filled Steele in on what had happened and our plans.

When I finished, he asked, "Did you read the information I sent you about cyanide?"

134

"Sorry, I haven't had a chance. Clark dropped by last night, and this morning we were dealing with the Rocky situation."

"Then let me give you the Cliff's Notes — it's quite interesting. Cyanide kills in minutes on an empty stomach but can take several hours on a full one."

I thought about the time frame of Peter Tanaka's death. He'd seemed fine one minute but went downhill fast after the time-out. "I'd say there's a good chance he hadn't eaten anything or much of anything before he died. It happened so quickly — almost in the blink of an eye."

"The taste of the sports drink probably masked the poison. Or he might not have noticed anything off in the excitement of the game." Steele paused, and I thought I heard him gulp some liquid. "The question, Grey, is who put it in his water bottle? Whoever did this had to have access to it without raising any suspicion. Would Miranda have had access to it?"

"That's a good question. And would she have had access to the poison? How easy is it to get?"

"It's obtainable, but not as easy as you might think. The government really clamped down on it after the Tylenol poisonings in the '80s. Do you remember that?"

I dug through my brain. "Didn't someone lace capsules of Tylenol with cyanide, causing the deaths of several people?"

"Yes. It was in the Chicago area, and they never found the killer. That event caused most drug companies to stop using capsules for over-the-counter drugs and to develop better tamper-proof packaging."

"Okay," I said, filing the information away in my brain. "So where would someone get cyanide today?"

"Well, it's not like it's on sale at Target, priced at two for five dollars. Forms of cyanide are used in pest control, especially in the wild or in industry, as well as in mining and even electroplating jewelry. If someone has connections to one of these industries, it could be fairly easy to get. It would be a little more difficult for other people, but not impossible." He laughed. "You can order a do-it-yourself electroplating kit online that comes with a form of cyanide, but the kits aren't cheap, although most home kits now come with a non-cyanide solution."

I shook my head. "You really got into this, didn't you?"

"You know how I love research."

I paused, then said slowly, "Should I worry about drinking anything at your place in the future?"

"Not if you stay in line, Grey."

I smiled to myself. "Speaking of which, what is this BS about my stopping by your place tonight? Jolene just told me she has stuff for me to drop off."

Steele sighed. It was the sigh that signaled I'd forgotten something important, or at least something important to him. I waited, knowing that after the dramatic pause he would enlighten me as to my alleged goof.

"I think that went without saying, Grey. Every night this week, you'll need to bring by any work that can't be scanned and emailed and take back to the office the work I've finished."

"I don't recall agreeing to be your errand girl, Steele, and I don't have time for it, not with everything else going on. I'll send a messenger." When he paused, I added, "Or I could send someone from the office."

I knew Steele wasn't so much of an ass he wouldn't understand about my personal time crunch, and I knew he would not want someone from T&T showing up at his door looking the way he did. Cruz might not be the only one who immediately pegged his injuries for what they really were.

"Use a service," he finally answered, "but tell them to leave it by the front door, no signature required."

"Okay, will do, but what about work you have coming back to the office?"

"There's not much, just some letters. I'll email them to Jill, and she can print and sign them for me."

"Now, if you will excuse me," I told Steele, "I need to get the work you emailed to me last night done before I call the messenger."

"What about Tanaka's criminal report?" Steele asked. "Anything you want me to follow up on with regard to that?"

"What report?" I asked, truly puzzled.

Another big sigh. This one was deeper and longer and relayed that I must be slipping into senility. "The report I gave you last night that you were going to show to Greg," Steele reminded me.

"Oh, *that* report." I started digging through my bag.

"You never showed it to Greg, did you? I'll bet it's still in that overnight bag you call a purse. It's probably wedged between your makeup bag and a Snickers bar."

A lot he knew. It was under the toasted cranberry bagel I'd picked up on my way in and forgot about. I pulled the report out and used a fingertip to wipe away a small gob of melted cream cheese that had oozed onto it from the hastily wrapped bagel.

"You're right, at least about not showing it to Greg. With everything that was going on last night and this morning, I forgot. Cut me some slack, would ya?"

He paused. "You're right. You do have a lot going on. Sorry."

I froze. Had Steele actually apologized to me? I pulled the phone away from my ear and stared at it, then tapped it like it was on the fritz. "I'm sorry, Steele, what did you just say?"

Another deep sigh. "I said I was sorry, Grey. Make me say it again and I'll set the dogs on you the next time you drop by."

"You don't have a dog, singular or plural."

"I'll rent a whole pack just for the occasion."

I grinned at the phone. It was nice to see that even though Steele had had the crap beaten out of him, his assailants hadn't bludgeoned his spirit.

"I'll scan this to Greg when I get off the phone," I told my boss. "That way he'll see it sooner." I scanned the report, running my eyes over it to see if there was anything of note. "Are there Cliff's Notes to this, too?"

Another deep sigh from his end.

"Do you have a slow leak, Steele?"

"Basically, Tanaka was a real jerk," Steele said after letting go with another longer, deeper, and very exaggerated sigh just to annoy me, "but it sounds like you already knew that. He's had a few scrapes with the law for public brawling. He even served sixty days for one assault. He was also arrested on a few domestic violence charges, but those were eventually dropped. Seems the guy liked to get physical with most anyone, male and female, but mostly women."

"Anger issues? Maybe over his injuries?"

"Could be, or it could be he was an ass before whatever happened to put him in a chair."

I made a mental note to ask Greg if he knew how Peter Tanaka became a quad. My eye snagged on something in the report. "Is this a drug charge?"

"That, Grey, *is* the big news. Seems Tanaka was also a drug dealer."

"Dealer, user, or both?"

"Not sure about the using, but considering his athletic abilities, if he was using it would have been steroids or some other performance-enhancement drugs, not the hard stuff."

I read the information with a more focused eye. "It doesn't say that here."

140

"No, it doesn't. I placed a few calls early this morning. Those charges were for selling heroin and cocaine."

"Were you impersonating an attorney again, Steele?"

He laughed. With the swelling of his mouth, it came out almost like he was clearing his throat. "According to my source, Tanaka was suspected for a long time of being a small-time dealer in Canada, but due to some bad handling of the evidence, they had to drop the charges. They were hoping to leverage those charges to find out the names of the higher-ups."

I looked once again at the list of Tanaka's criminal history, wishing the whole story was there. Maybe it was scratched in the margins or between the lines with invisible ink, like the stuff we made in elementary school with lemon juice that could only be seen when held over a light bulb. Or maybe we needed to make a few more calls. "This drug arrest happened earlier this year," I said to Steele. "I wonder if that's why he left Canada and returned to California."

"Could be. Maybe things got too hot for him. My source said Tanaka was under constant surveillance after he was released."

"Did you tell your source that he was murdered?"

"Sure did, and he was only surprised that it hadn't happened sooner."

I waited for more information, but Steele was quiet on the other end. "Did your source offer up any suggestions as to who might have done it?"

"He said it could have been most anyone — an angry husband or boyfriend, a battered woman, or even his drug supplier. Or maybe Peter Tanaka made a whole new set of disreputable friends when he returned to Southern California."

# ELEVEN

After I scanned the report and sent it to Greg, I took a careful look at it. Steele had provided more than just a criminal report, which was on top. He'd also discovered a lot of personal information about Peter Tanaka. He had grown up in Altadena, California, and would have turned thirty-two in just three months. He had graduated from Pasadena High School and from Pasadena City College, transferring to Cal State LA to complete a bachelor's degree. According to the report in my hand, Tanaka never received his degree, dropping out in his last year. His current address was listed in Altadena. None of this came from West-law. It was on another page without the legal search engine's footer.

It seemed my boss did have sources out-side of his usual legal research packages. Did he hire a private eye to get this informa-tion? Not that he'd ever tell me, but I definitely planned on asking Steele the next time I was eyeball to eyeball with him.

I looked again at the report and wondered if Tanaka had dropped out of college before or after the event that had landed him full-time in a wheelchair. I didn't have to wonder long. The information on the next page informed me that he had been injured in a bad car accident his senior year in college. He and a few friends had been drinking and joy riding along the winding Angeles Crest Highway when their vehicle went over an embankment. There had been three people in the vehicle. The driver and one passenger, a woman, had been killed. Tanaka had been thrown away from the vehicle, breaking his back in several places and leaving him a quadriplegic.

I closed my eyes against the horror. The words of the report stretched across the page in a clinical formation of black against white, like industrious ants marching across a clean kitchen counter. Still, the tragedy and senselessness wasn't dampened. Peter Tanaka had not only been crippled for life, he'd lost two friends, all because they didn't believe they were too drunk to drive. I read more of the report. It seemed that the accident had only involved their car. It was a small glimmer of light. At least they hadn't plowed into someone else, inflicting carnage upon innocent people.

Putting down the report, I went back to thinking about where Steele might have gotten the information. The way the report was written and formatted on the page reminded me of something, or at least of someone. With a few taps on my keyboard, I found the name in our firm's online contact list and placed a call to the number indicated. The call was answered on the fourth ring by a woman who sounded out of breath.

"Barbara?" I asked.

"Yes." The voice was cautious — not "danger" cautious but the kind of care reserved for when you're not sure if you've just answered a call from a solicitor.

"Barbara, this is Odelia Grey. I work for Mike Steele."

"Odelia, of course." The voice changed from cautious to friendly. "How are you?"

Barbara Marracino's late husband, Larry, had worked as a freelance corporate investigator. Like a police dog sniffing out drugs, Larry could follow the money or dubious transactions or track down owners or partners who wanted to remain silent. If something smelled of rotten fish in the business world, he'd find out why — for a price. Over the years Steele had used his services, mostly when he wanted to make sure the people opposite a client on a big deal were aboveboard. I'd heard that after Larry passed away a few years ago, Barbara had taken over his business — not the actual field work but the computer end of it. We hadn't needed such services in quite some time, and I wondered if Barbara was still in the business.

"I'm fine, thanks. And yourself?"

"Not bad for an old broad with creaky joints. I'm mostly housebound these days with my bad knees and back, but my son and his wife visit often with the grandkids. And I keep busy with my research business."

"So I see from the report I'm holding." I had no concrete evidence that Barbara had prepared the report on Tanaka, but I plunged forward on my hunch. If it wasn't Barbara feeding Steele this information, no harm. I'd just cross her off the list, which was short since it contained only her name and Clark's. I wouldn't put it past Steele to call my brother about something like this. He'd figured out that Clark now worked for Willie, and I wouldn't put it past Clark to keep silent about work he might be doing for Steele.

"Do you have any more to give Steele on this Tanaka guy?" I asked Barbara, hoping it was her. I really didn't want to ask Clark about it.

"Yes," she answered. "As a matter of fact, just this morning I confirmed the information on his family. Should I send it to Mr. Steele or to you?"

I let loose the breath I was holding and smiled with self-satisfaction. "How about to both of us." Not wanting this run through the T&T system, I gave her my personal email address.

"Will do." She cackled softly. "This must be off the books, because Mr. Steele used his personal email account too."

"Yes, way off the books. In fact, it's something personal for me and my husband, and Steele is helping us with it."

"Do you want the information I pulled on Miranda and Richard Henderson, too?"

"Steele had you look into them?" I tried my best to keep the surprise out of my voice. Greg and I had discussed our need to question some of their other friends, especially Miranda's, but it never occurred to me that it would occur to Steele. I'd only asked him to research cyanide.

"Yes. He emailed me yesterday about it."

"Do you have employment information on the Hendersons?"

"Sure do."

"Then copy me on that, too," I told her, silently thanking Steele for saving me time in ferreting out Miranda's work information. I knew she was a dental hygienist but had no idea where. "Did Steele also ask you to run a check on cyanide poisoning?"

"No," Barbara answered, "but I can if you like. Most of my assignments are for writers, especially crime writers. You'd be amazed at what they ask me to research. It's a really good setup, especially for someone with my limited physical capacity, and it doesn't involve all the running around that Larry did." She paused. "It was so nice to hear from you and Mr. Steele. It has been a while. Do you think you'll be needing my services beyond this?"

"We just might, Barbara. We'll let you know." I had never thought of using Barbara Marracino before for my nosiness and was kicking myself. She could have saved me a lot of time in the past on the things that weren't deep and dark. I usually went to Clark and Willie for that information, but the general stuff I did on my own with what resources I could muster. I was sure Barbara had many more streams of information than I knew of, and she had more time. And using her would help keep my activities off of Clark and Willie's radar, more or less.

Leave it to Steele to think of her.

Before I said goodbye to Barbara, I glanced at the report and thought of something else. "Barbara, do you also have information on the two people who were killed in that car accident involving Peter Tanaka?"

"No, just their names, which is in the information I sent. Do you want me to locate their people?"

"Yes, that would be very helpful. Thanks."

"Glad for the work."

For a moment I considered asking Barbara to go way, way off the books and investigate what had happened to Steele in Perris, but I quickly changed my mind. Cruz was right. One day we would know, and if Steele ever got wind that I was having him investigated, he'd never forgive me. And I wouldn't blame him. No matter how snarky we were with each other, when push came to shove, we were also dead loyal to each other. Steele had had my back on numerous occasions, especially when it came time for me to leave Woobie, and I'd had his just as many times. For the time being, I'd just have to sit on my hands when it came to Steele and focus on the issues and people at hand — and the work I needed to get done for the firm. Surprisingly, there wasn't much. Steele had sent email instructions on some things he needed done, and I had a couple of minor things for other attorneys that I had dispatched quickly before digging into Steele's work.

Coming in so late, I'd lost track of time and was surprised when I checked the time to see it was well past my usual lunch hour. My squashed bagel still sat in its loose wrapper on my desk, looking forlorn and unappetizing, but I gnawed on it anyway, downing the bites with slurps of cold morning coffee from my mug. I had more important things on my mind at the moment than digging up a better lunch. I wanted to use the time to set out my plan of attack on the information Barbara had provided, which now included the names and last known addresses of the families of two people killed in Tanaka's car accident. The woman's name had been Heather Stuart; the driver's, Wayne Mercer.

My divide-and-conquer plotting was interrupted by my cell phone. It was Greg. "Hi, honey," I said upon answering. "Did you get the emails I sent you? I sent two."

"Yep, looking at them now," he answered. "It's the first chance I've had all day. That drug stuff is interesting. Considering the way Miranda died, if it isn't suicide, my money is on a drug dealer connection."

"On the surface it looks that way," I told him, "but do you really think Miranda was involved in drugs?"

"Maybe not, but if she was involved with Tanaka, the drug dealers might have taken her out, thinking she knew too much."

"But why hurt Rocky? I don't think he knew anything about an affair with Tanaka until right before Peter died, so he wouldn't know anything about the drugs unless he was also a loose end they wanted tied up."

"Could be," Greg replied, "but we still don't know if Rocky's injury was self-inflicted or a murder attempt. That might be totally unrelated to Tanaka and Miranda's murders. Could be that Rocky had just reached the end of his rope with the murder and Miranda's death crashing down on him." He paused. "Interesting information on Tanaka's accident. In all the time I'd spent around him years ago, I'd never heard about this. I only knew it was a vehicle accident, not that other people were killed."

"I know it's a long shot, but I wanted to rule out a long-held grudge."

"Good idea," said Greg. "But since Tanaka wasn't the driver, he wasn't directly responsible for what happened. I doubt it has any

151

bearing on what's happening now."

"That's what I thought after reading the report. Still, if we run out of leads, we can try this. Meanwhile, I think I should start with questioning some of Miranda's friends and coworkers. I'd like to see if they knew anything about Miranda and Peter Tanaka. I'll try to get in touch with someone this afternoon."

"Great," said Greg. "Things are quieting down here at the shop, so maybe I'll check in with some of the other players and see what they know. I also want to contact the coach of the Vipers. Even though the team is based in Ventura, I understand the coach lives down here."

"Really?" I was surprised, still picturing the small, wiry man pointing at Rocky while he shouted *asesino* over and over. Ventura was about eighty or so miles from here.

"That's not unusual. Players have to live within one hundred and fifty miles of the teams they play on. It might be the same for the coaches. The Vipers are sponsored by a health care company based in Ventura."

"So why don't we reach out to our prospective leads and circle back later?" I suggested. "Once we know which direction we're heading, we can decide if we're going together or separately."

"Sounds like a plan," Greg agreed. "Are you going to Steele's tonight?"

"No. He wanted me to, but I got him to agree to my sending the work to him by messenger."

Greg laughed, then gave me a kiss good-bye with a promise to call me back in a few hours.

# Twelve

After talking to Greg, I ran to the ladies' room. On my way back to my office I heard someone call my name. I stopped in the hallway, not sure where it was coming from. I stood still and held my breath, listening for it again like it was an elusive bird call or a comment from God.

"Odelia," I heard again, followed by "in here."

I turned toward the voice. It was coming from an empty office, one furnished with the bare-bones necessities of a desk, desk chair, visitor's chair, and a computer. It was the office we reserved for visiting attorneys from the head office. I peeked inside to find Simon Tobin, one of the founding partners of Templin and Tobin, sitting at the desk, staring in my direction. He waved me inside.

In a way, it *was* God.

"Do you have a bit of time for me, Odelia?" he asked.

"You pay me to have time for you, Mr. Tobin."

My remark caused him to grant me a wry half smile. "Good answer, and please call me Simon."

I stepped inside. With the grand gesture of a gentleman from a Jane Austen novel, he stood up and indicated the chair opposite him. When I sat down, he walked to the door and gently closed it before returning to his seat. Steele would have kept working and snapped at me to catch the door on my way in.

I'd met Simon Tobin in person only once before, and that was during my orientation to the firm, which took place at the large home office in Los Angeles the first week I started working for T&T. The staff in LA seemed to like and respect him a great deal. Since then, I'd seen him numerous times during business department meetings, which were conducted by video between the two offices, but had had no direct contact since he had a paralegal at his disposal in LA.

"I didn't know you were coming to Newport Beach, Simon," I said as I willed myself not to fidget in my seat. "Since Mike Steele's out, maybe you'd be more comfortable in his office."

Simon waved off the idea with the flip of an elegant hand. "No need," he told me. "I'm only here for today and tomorrow, and I have appointments outside the office most of tomorrow."

Simon Tobin reminded me — and everyone else who met him — of Tim Gunn of *Project Runway* fame, right down to being impeccably tailored, silver haired, and gay.

"But speaking of Mike," Simon continued, "how is he doing? Have you seen him?"

"Yes, I have. My husband and I visited him on Monday, and I was there last night going over some work with him." I left out the part that during his convalescence Steele was working for me researching poison and murder, leaving Simon to assume anything he wanted from my words.

"Do you think he'll be back in the office next week?"

"Why don't you call and ask him that yourself?" Then, lest Simon think I was being cheeky, I tacked on, "I think Steele would be a more accurate gauge of his own recovery."

Another half smile as Simon's steely blue eyes studied me from behind expensive, trendy frames. "I called him last night and he told me he'd be back on Monday, but frankly he didn't sound all that well."

I nodded, understanding what he meant. "Steele got hit in the face pretty hard and his mouth is swollen, but each day he sounds a little bit better — at least he did when I spoke to him a couple of hours ago. And when I saw him yesterday he was moving around a lot more than when we saw him on Monday."

Simon still didn't look convinced. "I don't want him to rush back if he's seriously injured, but at the same time Jolene looks . . . well, she looks about to take her leave. If they are both going to be out at the same time, I need to make sure the business department is properly covered in this office."

"I understand, but we're not terribly busy right now, and so far Steele has been able to handle everything from home. He's told me he plans on being back Monday, and I have no reason to think otherwise." I paused, then added, "Why don't you drop by and see for yourself? He lives just down in Laguna Beach, and I'm sure he'd welcome the visit."

*Liar, liar, pants on fire!* rang in my head in a chorus of schoolyard chants. It wasn't just a lie, it was a whopper of a lie. The last thing Steele wanted was a name partner of T&T on his doorstep. I'm sure if he'd heard me utter those words to Simon Tobin, he would have strangled me on the spot. But there it was — a bluff, played in the hope it would put Simon off from any more concerns about Steele.

"No," Simon answered after a few seconds of consideration, "but I think I will give him another call later."

"Okay." Inside, I was huffing and puffing with relief. "We have a messenger taking things to him at the end of the day, so if you have anything you want to get to Steele, just leave it with Jill, his secretary. She sits just outside his office."

"Thank you, Odelia."

I got up to leave, but Simon motioned for me to remain. I settled back in the chair and waited. Whatever else was on Simon's mind, he was having trouble spitting it out. Maybe his fancy silk tie was choking him? I didn't look directly at him but studied the said tie, trying to place the designer and failing, only recognizing that it was very expensive. Steele preferred to dress in Armani, and my husband was a Gap guy. For a fleeting moment, I worried that I was being fired, but the idea came and went as fast as a silverfish slithering along a bathroom baseboard. Maybe Simon wanted to ask more about Steele but was concerned about saying too much, knowing Steele and I were close.

Finally, Simon cleared his throat. "I understand, Odelia, that sometimes you get involved in some rather . . . well . . . unorthodox events."

*Uh-oh. Maybe I* was *getting fired.*

I leaned forward a couple of inches. "Um, can you be more specific, Simon?"

"Investigations, Odelia. From time to time, don't you and your husband get embroiled in some dangerous undertakings?"

I leaned back. "Not willingly, I can assure you." After pausing no longer than half a heartbeat, I went on the defense. "Mike Steele told me the partners of T&T knew that before you hired me."

Simon gave me another crooked half smile. "That we did, though not all of us were pleased with your extracurricular activities. To be honest with you, I was one of those with concerns."

The silverfish was back, this time pausing long enough to take a good look around. Big boss or not, I fixed Simon with my best laser stare. "Are you taking advantage of Steele being out of the office to fire me?"

Surprised by my direct question, Simon held up both of his hands, palms outward, as if I might hit him. "Oh no, Odelia. On the contrary, we're quite pleased with your work and how smoothly you keep Mike on track." A meaningful pause; a lowering of the hands. "As you know, he can be a bit of a loose cannon from time to time."

"Yes, but a lucrative cannon for the firm, correct?" I grew so bold as to give him a nod and a wink.

"A very lucrative one," he agreed, nodding back. "But this isn't about Mike or about your position." He glanced at the door to make sure it was shut tight before beginning. "This is personal."

"Personal?" I leaned forward again, my big boobs almost resting on the desk. "Me personal? Or you personal?"

"Personal with regards to me." Simon straightened his already ramrod posture. "Specifically with regards to my mother."

Considering that most of my misguided adventures start with a dead body, I became alarmed. "I hope your mother is all right?"

"She's fine, at least physically. She's in her early eighties, and, until recently, I would have said mentally she's sharp as a tack." Simon stood up, went to the window, and stared out of it. I remained silent, getting the vibe that he was sorting out his thoughts. "Lately, though, I've begun to worry about her mental faculties." He turned to face me. "She seems all there. She's not leaving the milk in the pantry or putting the mail down the garbage disposal. Nothing like that."

"Isn't this something you should be discussing with her doctor?"

He shook his head. "No, I believe you're the right person for this." He took a step back toward the desk, but instead of sitting, he placed his hands on the chair's back, as if needing it to hold himself erect. His face was lined with worry. "Lately my mother has been talking about investing in a business with a new acquaintance of hers, and nothing I say or do will dissuade her. She's quite determined. I think this other woman, another elderly lady, has her quite persuaded, if not brainwashed."

"Why don't you hire a private investigator to look into this acquaintance and the business proposal?"

"Do you know who my mother is?" The question wasn't thrown at me in an arrogant manner but as a casual query.

I dug through my limited cache of office information, then shook my head. "Mrs. Tobin?" I ventured.

He chuckled but swallowed it halfway through. "My mother is Frances Albright, better known as Fanny Albright."

The name sounded familiar. I dug deeper. Of their own accord, my eyebrows shot north in surprise. "The heiress who was kidnapped in the 1940s and found five years later?"

"Yes. It happened before she married my father."

"Wasn't she supposedly taken by some big shot in the Middle East — some sheik or something?"

"I'm surprised you would know that, seeing you weren't even born at the time."

I took a deep breath. "What I remember is a story from several years ago. Fanny — I mean, Mrs. Tobin — was in the news for . . . um . . . something, and the story about her kidnapping was dredged up." The something was allegedly shoplifting in Beverly Hills, then slapping the security guard silly when he tried to intervene, but I wasn't about to admit to a boss that I remembered that tidbit about his mother. My late father had remembered the kidnapping with clarity, and when the story about the shoplifting came out he told me that most of the nation believed Fanny Albright to be a spoiled rich kid who staged the kidnapping just to embarrass her society mother and father. I also didn't tell the second T in T&T about that.

"That is my mother, although it was determined that the shoplifting incident was a misunderstanding."

*Uh-huh. Fanny Albright must be gal pals with Winona Ryder and Lindsay Lohan.*

As if reading my thoughts, Simon quickly tacked on in a clipped tone, "Mother was under the influence of a new prescription at the time. Her doctor provided an affidavit to that fact, and she was never charged."

"I still don't understand why you need me for this, Simon. A professional PI could do a much better job of it."

"Because PIs have also been known to sell information to the tabloids or have leaks among their staff, that's why." He took his seat again. "I was very impressed when I learned how you conducted yourself at your last firm, especially at the end of its existence. You know how to keep quiet and you obviously know how to snoop around. Your loyalty to your employer is legendary, especially your loyalty to Mike Steele."

"Legendary? That's a bit overblown, isn't it?" I scoffed, thinking he was watching too much TV. "I simply have the backs of those who have mine, Simon. And I believe in professional confidentiality."

"And that's why I want you to handle this, Odelia. Steele's out for a few more days.

163

You said yourself your workload is light. Take the next few days out of the office and look into it for me. Please. I'll tell people I've given you a special project in Mike's absence. I am also aware that you usually only work part-time, so don't worry, you'll be paid for any time you work on this, as well as for any expenses you incur."

Yes, my workload at the office was light, even with covering for Steele, but my workload outside the office was anything but breezy and carefree. And it wouldn't be the first time a law firm had assigned me to a secret project. Woobie had assigned me the task of looking for Steele when he went missing years ago and was accused of sabotaging a case. I didn't believe for an instant he'd done anything wrong and had been worried about his safety and proving his innocence. As for the rest, I wondered if I should tell Simon I was already looking into a murder involving friends.

I looked away, giving it thought. No. I needed to keep my mouth shut about Rocky and Miranda, but if no one expected me to be at the office for the next few days, then I could easily look into that mess without people wondering where I was. Of course, I'd also have to look into the problem with Simon's mother, but how difficult could that be? Simon said Fanny's new BFF was another old lady. I may be in my fifties, but I was pretty sure I could handle an old lady — unless, of course, that old lady was my own mother, in which case all bets were off.

I turned back toward him, reading his face, looking for clues to another worry. I sat up straight and plowed forward with what was on my mind. "What would happen if I didn't take the assignment?"

He seemed surprised by the question, but I couldn't tell if the surprise was from my boldness or from the idea that I might say no to a bigwig partner. After a few seconds, he said, "Nothing, Odelia. I promise you that. If you decide not to help me, I will be disappointed, but in no way will it affect your position or future at Templin and Tobin."

We locked eyes. I'd been set up by powerful partners before, specifically at Woobie. Steele might be an ass, but he would never set me up or hang me out to dry. He wielded loyalty I could count on, no matter what else he did that was annoying. *Legendary loyalty.* I smiled at the thought.

"Does that smile mean you'll do it?"

I started, then realized Simon had misread my facial expression. I took a deep breath and made up my mind. "Give me any information you have and I'll look into it. I can't promise the results you want, but I can probably dig up something about this person."

"I really appreciate this, Odelia." From his jacket pocket he retrieved a Mont Blanc pen and started jotting on a nearby legal pad. "Here is the name of the woman who befriended my mother and the name of her company. I know that tomorrow they are having lunch at Bouchon in Beverly Hills. I tried to get Mother to come to Newport Beach with me just to get her away from this person for a day or two, but she wouldn't budge. She's very headstrong."

"I know the type. My mother's the same way and the same age."

He ripped the sheet of paper off the pad and handed it to me. The woman in question was named Eudora Fox. Her company's name was Little Foxes.

"I don't know if the company is a corporation or an LLC," Simon told me. "I checked Westlaw, but it doesn't appear to be set up anywhere yet."

"Did you check the Delaware website?" I asked. "Entities formed in Delaware don't always show up on Westlaw."

"No, I didn't. I only checked Westlaw."

"Don't worry, I'll check." I folded the

piece of paper. "Do you have a photo of your mother?" I asked. "Or better yet, a photo of her with this person?"

He gave my request some thought before his face broke with satisfaction. "You know, I do. Just last weekend Mother invited my partner and me to brunch. Eudora was there." He pulled out his smartphone and started going through the photos. "Here's one. It was taken on the patio after we'd eaten."

He handed me his phone. Displayed was a photo of Simon in immaculate but casual clothing. Behind him was a sparkling swimming pool. He was seated between two older women. He had his arm snug around the one to his right, and I guessed her to be Fanny Albright Tobin. She must have been quite stunning in her youth because even in her eighties she was beautiful. To Simon's left was a woman who looked to be younger than Fanny, maybe in her late sixties or early seventies; it was difficult to tell. She was just as beautifully groomed as Fanny and decked out in pearls even with her resort wear, but she was not quite as attractive. With a flick of my fingers, I enlarged the photo for a closer look. Something about Eudora Fox nagged at me, but I couldn't get a handle on it. I had been spending so

167

much time at my mother's retirement community, maybe all old ladies were beginning to look alike.

I handed the phone back to Simon. "Could you email that photo to me, along with your mother's address?" Knowing better than to touch a man's Mont Blanc, I plucked a stray cheap pen from a nearby pencil cup and jotted my personal email on the legal pad. "Send it here, not to my office account."

He nodded, agreeing to the request. "You'll be getting it from my personal account as well. In fact, I'd prefer all communication on this be through that avenue or my private cell phone, which I'll also provide."

I stood up and so did he. Simon extended his hand to me. I took it and he pumped it gently. Instead of his half smile, his face was wreathed with relief. "Thank you, Odelia. I really appreciate this."

# THIRTEEN

As soon as I got back to my office, I closed the door and placed a call. "Hi, Barbara, it's Odelia again."

"Do you need more information?" she asked in an upbeat and hopeful tone.

"Yes, I do, but this is just for me. It has nothing to do with Mike Steele, so don't copy him. I'll pay you directly."

"I can always use the work."

"I want you to find out everything you can on a Eudora Fox." I spelled the name out for her. "I believe she's located in the Los Angeles area or at least in Southern California. Older lady, pushing seventy or thereabouts."

"Aren't we all." I heard a hearty laugh.

"And check out a company called Little Foxes."

"Got it. When do you need it?"

"Right away. Again, send it to my personal email. Also, text me if you find anything really interesting." I gave her my cell number.

"I'm on it."

Next, I made sure all the work Steele had given me was done, and what couldn't be emailed I took out to Jill's desk and handed off to her. "Steele agreed to let a messenger drop off the package today. Just have him leave it by Steele's door."

"How did you manage that?" she asked with suspicion.

"Sometimes Steele can be reasonable."

"Ha! What did you blackmail him with?"

"What can I say?" I answered with a shrug. "I have photos of him with barnyard animals."

"It wouldn't surprise me." She took the documents and placed them on a pile. "Jolene's are also ready to go. I'll pack them up shortly."

"You might also want to check with Simon Tobin before you do. He's set up camp in the visitor's office and might have something for Steele."

"Is that where you've been?"

I nodded. "He's nervous about Jolene going out on maternity leave before Steele comes back."

She snorted. "As if you and I couldn't run things for a few days without them."

"About that," I said to Jill. "Simon gave me a big research project that includes footwork. I might be out of the office for the next few days, so it looks like you're on your own. You okay with that?"

"Oh, please!" She rolled her eyes, but there was a twinkle behind them. "Just make sure you answer your phone when Steele calls so he doesn't bother me."

I gave her a crisp salute and returned to my office.

With Barbara doing my footwork on Simon's problem, I turned my attention to my real concern. After studying the information Barbara had given me on Miranda, I looked up Coastal Dental Spa online. It was one of those fancy dental offices that offered patients a full line of cosmetic dental work in addition to the usual services, along with massages and designer water while they waited. I knew that because in addition to what I was reading on the Internet, it was also where Zee and Seth had started getting their dental work done a few years back. Zee raved about the place and had been trying to get me to try it, but I'd been going to my dentist, who was now older than dirt, a very long time. Maybe when he retired I'd try Coastal. Then again, why not now?

Picking up the phone, I called Coastal.

The office was here in Newport Beach, over by the Fashion Island mall. I had no idea if my plan would work, but it might flush out someone who knew Miranda well.

"Hi," I said to the woman who answered. "I'd like to schedule a cleaning." My boobs had once been pressed into service to ferret out a killer. Why not my teeth?

"Are you an existing patient?" the receptionist asked in a clear, professional voice.

"No, but your office came highly recommended by a friend."

"May I ask who referred you to our office?"

"Zenobia Washington."

"Excellent. When would you like to come in for your checkup?"

"I don't need a checkup right now, just a cleaning." I paused. "Is it possible to request a hygienist? My friend said she really liked the work of someone named Mandy or Miranda. She said she was very good but gentle."

There was a long pause on the other end, then, "I'm sorry, but Miranda doesn't work here any longer. I'm sure you'll be quite happy with Seema."

"I don't know," I said, not to sound too eager. "Is she experienced? I'm very sensitive."

"Seema has been with us several years, and our patients seem quite pleased with her work."

"Can I get in to see her around five thirty tonight?"

"I'm sorry, but she takes her last patient at three, and today she is totally booked."

"How early does she come in?"

"Her first cleaning is at eight. I can put you down for eight o'clock next Tuesday morning."

I drew out my answer as if contemplating the appointment time, then said, "Okay. That sounds fine." I gave the woman my name and contact number, then jotted down a note reminding myself to cancel the appoint by Friday if I found Seema in the meantime. If I couldn't connect with her, then a cleaning next Tuesday might be in order, even though I'd had one just three months ago.

It was almost three o'clock. I needed to get moving. If Seema's last appointment was at three, there was a good possibility that she worked until four or a little after. I needed to get my butt down there and stake out a spot to watch and wait, the plan being to ambush the woman as she left the office. It would help if I knew what she looked like, but I didn't even have a last name. On a thread of hope, I checked out Coastal's website. Sometimes businesses posted photos of happy employees. Unfortunately, Coastal wasn't one of them. I placed another call.

"Zee," I said as soon as she answered, "what is the name of the dental hygienist you go to at Coastal Dental Spa?"

"Seema. Why? Are you finally going to give them a try?"

"Maybe. Did you ever go to any of their other hygienists?"

"Once when Seema was on vacation. It was a woman named Carlene, I think, but she's not there any longer."

"Did you never meet any other hygienists?"

"What's this about, Odelia?"

"It turns out that Miranda Henderson worked for Coastal Dental Spa as a hygienist. I want to question Seema. What does she look like?"

"When are you going to meet her?"

"In about an hour. I have to get a move on if I'm going to make it."

Zee paused. I could almost hear her brain crunching and whirling, cutting through my bullshit like a wood chipper. "Pick me up on your way there," she ordered. "I'm going with you."

"No, you're not."

"Are you at the office?"

"Yes," I admitted.

"My house is practically on the way to Coastal from there. By the time you get here, I'll be ready."

I knew better than to argue with Zee. I also knew that Seema might be more willing to talk to me with a friendly face by my side.

We pulled up in front of the office building housing the dental practice just after three thirty. True to her word, Zee was ready when I got to her house and was even waiting on the curb to save time. Along the way, I gave her a quick rundown on Rocky and what we'd found out so far on Peter Tanaka.

Coastal Dental Spa was in an office building that housed mostly medical services. Long and only four stories high, it was built wide instead of tall, like me.

"Is this the only entrance?" I asked Zee as we pulled into a parking place near the large glass entryway. Through the doors we could see a gleaming lobby with elevator banks in the center. To the far left was a pharmacy.

"Yes," she answered as she unbuckled her seat belt and opened her door. "Although I'm sure there's a delivery entrance in the back somewhere." When I didn't move to get out of the car, Zee froze, her door opened several inches. "Do you really have an appointment with Seema?" She narrowed her knowing eyes at me.

"Yes, I do," I said with a twitch of my nose. I paused. Zee continued staring at me, her dark brown eyes boring into my brain like a termite looking for wood, but in her case she was searching for the truth. "Okay," I admitted. "It's for next Tuesday at eight."

"Odelia Grey," Zee snapped. "You're here to ambush this poor girl, aren't you?"

"Ambush is such an ugly word, Zee. Let's just say I'm here to ask her a few questions, and I didn't want her to bolt before I got the chance."

Zee looked alarmed. "You don't think Seema is involved, do you?"

"Not at this time, but her coworker was just murdered, and I'm sure the police have or will question her. I wanted to catch her off-guard with questions of my own."

"It's called an ambush, Odelia, no matter how you spin it, and I'm now an accomplice. This is a woman who puts her hands in my mouth at least twice a year."

"Hey," I protested. "I never invited you along — that was your idea. I just wanted to know what Seema looked like so I could recognize her. You can sit in the car if you like. In fact, it might be better if you do. You know how I hate to get you involved in this stuff."

Zee took a deep breath and turned to look at the office building. "Come on," she finally said. "Let's wait for her in the lobby."

We had barely sat down on a bench in the lobby when Zee nudged me and pointed at a young woman emerging from one of the elevators. She was dressed in a sage green uniform similar to medical scrubs but nicer, over which was a thick sweater. Zee approached her first.

"Seema," she said to the woman.

Seema had been digging in her purse when we approached. She looked up upon hearing her name and smiled when she recognized Zee. "Mrs. Washington. What a nice surprise." She pulled car keys from the purse. "Do you have an appointment in the building?"

"No, I — we," Zee indicated me, "we came to see you."

From her olive skin, black hair, and dark, luminous eyes, I guessed Seema's ethnicity to be something Middle Eastern, maybe Persian or Armenian. The eyes, enhanced by perfectly applied liner and mascara, widened at Zee's confession. "But the office is closing soon, and the doctor is with someone. Is this a dental emergency?"

"No, it's not. My friend here . . ."

When Zee stumbled to come up with an explanation, I jumped in. "My name is Odelia Grey. My husband and I were good friends with Miranda and Rocky Henderson."

At the mention of Miranda's name, Seema bit her lip. After a short moment, she said, "I am so sorry. She was a nice person. I will miss her."

"Did you know that her husband is in a coma at Hoag?"

At my question, Seema's eyes widened even more. "But wasn't he the one who killed that guy in San Diego?"

I shook my head. "No, the police released him. They got in a fight, but that isn't what caused Peter Tanaka's death. We think Rocky tried to kill himself over losing Miranda."

The slender shoulders in the uniform sagged. "The police came by yesterday and questioned some of us about Miranda, but they didn't say anything about Rocky."

"It happened late last night," Zee added.

I stepped closer to Seema. "May I ask you some questions of my own?"

At the request, Seema took a step back. "I have to pick up my kids."

"Please," I implored. "My husband and I were there when Rocky and that guy fought and the guy died. We saw it happen. My husband, who is also in a wheelchair, knew them both."

While she considered my plea, Seema played with her hair, which was long and fastened into a ponytail. "I don't know how much help I can be. Miranda and I worked together for a few years, but we didn't hang out."

"Please, Seema," added Zee. "Just a few questions and we'll be on our way."

As if punctuating her decision, Seema swept the ponytail over her shoulder to her back. "Okay, but it will have to be fast because of my kids."

I steered her over to the bench. Zee followed.

"Seema," I started after sitting down next to her. "The man who died said something to Rocky about Miranda right before the fight. It's what triggered Rocky's temper. Was Miranda having an affair with Peter Tanaka?"

Seema shifted with discomfort. "How would I know that?"

"I work in an office," I told her. "I know a lot of girl talk happens in the lunch room and the ladies' room. It's difficult to keep

179

secrets when you work closely with someone." My thoughts immediately shot to
Steele. He was obviously keeping a big
secret about his injuries or why they had
happened. I brushed those thoughts aside
to focus on the issue at hand. There would
be time later to figure out what was going
on with Steele.

Zee reached a hand out and lightly
touched Seema's arm. "This might help
Rocky. The police believe Miranda killed
that man, but Odelia here doesn't. Doesn't
poor Rocky deserve to know the truth?"

Seema took a deep breath, leaning back
until her shoulders touched the marble wall
behind the bench. "Yes, I think Miranda
was seeing someone on the side."

"Was it Peter Tanaka?" I asked.

"I never got his name," Seema said, looking from me to Zee, "but several times I
heard Miranda lying to her husband on the
phone. You know, telling him she had to
work late when she didn't or was meeting
friends for a drink, then telling me she
couldn't wait to go straight home. Something was definitely up with her."

"Any idea how long this had been going
on?" I asked.

Seema closed her eyes and gave it some
thought. "Off and on for a while, but about

four months ago it became more apparent that something was off with that marriage. A few times Rocky called the office looking for her. She only worked three days a week, but I got the feeling her husband thought she worked more or at least different days than she did. Each time the receptionist buzzed me and asked what she should tell him. She didn't want to lie to Rocky, but she didn't want to get Miranda in trouble with either Rocky or the doctor, who wouldn't like it if he found out. I told the receptionist to tell him that Miranda had stepped out but that she'd give her the message to call him. The next day I told Miranda that whatever she was doing, to keep us out of her lies to her husband."

It certainly did sound like Miranda had something going on the side with Tanaka. "What did Miranda say to that?" I asked.

"She apologized, and it seemed genuine. I asked her if she and Rocky were having problems and told her if she needed to talk, I was here for her." Seema shook her head slowly. "Husbands. We've all been down that rough road, you know?"

Both Zee and I nodded, fully understanding Seema's comment. Even the best of marriages travel some broken track once in a while.

"Did Miranda ever take you up on that offer?" asked Zee.

"Not really. She just promised not to put us in the middle anymore."

I scratched my nose. Something certainly smelled off.

Seema stood up and consulted her watch. "I really have to get going. I have to get the kids home and start dinner."

Zee and I stood up with her. "Thank you, Seema," I said. "But one last question. Did the police ask you about this?"

"Yes. They seemed to think Miranda was cheating on Rocky too, and with this Tanaka guy."

A cool November night was in progress when we stepped from the building into the parking lot. Salty dampness from the nearby ocean penetrated the early evening air and my suit jacket.

"I really appreciate you taking time to talk to us," I told Seema as I pulled my jacket around me tighter.

"No problem. I'm very sorry about Miranda."

Seema took a couple of steps away, and we headed for my car. We weren't quite inside when Seema jogged over to where we were parked. "There's something else," she said. "It's probably nothing, but I just

182

thought of it. Something I didn't tell the police."

Zee and I reversed our progress and came to stand by Seema next to my car. "What is it?" I asked.

"Around the time that I noticed things were kind of off with Miranda, she started showing up with a few new things. First it was a pair of diamond earrings, then a necklace. And just a few weeks ago she had a new purse. I never said anything about the jewelry, but the purse was awesome. It was a Kate Spade satchel in a killer peacock color. She said Rocky had bought it for her with a bonus he received from work. I thought maybe it was a sign that they were getting past the rough spot." Seema leaned against my car and looked out toward the road beyond the parking area as she tried to remember details. "Then, about two weeks ago, I stayed a little late to finish up a patient and saw her come out of the ladies' room in the building's lobby and leave. She wasn't in her uniform. She was dressed to kill in a very expensive-looking dress and shoes."

"Maybe she was meeting Rocky for dinner?" suggested Zee.

"Maybe," said Seema, "but why didn't she change upstairs in our ladies' room? That's what most of us do when we have plans right after work. It's much nicer and roomier than the ladies' room off the lobby."

"Seema," I said, "do you remember what day that was? Can you narrow it down a bit?"

She played with her ponytail, then nodded. "I'm pretty sure it was a Wednesday, because I never book late patients except on Wednesdays when my husband can pick up the kids." She paused, obviously thinking about something else. "This is just my opinion, but in the time I worked with Miranda I never knew Rocky to buy her expensive things. In fact, I got the feeling they couldn't afford stuff like that, but I know she had a taste for them. The only thing she ever said to me about her marriage was that she and Rocky wanted different things out of life. Maybe she found someone to give her those things."

We thanked her again and parted.

Once in the car, I pulled my smartphone out of my tote bag, which I'd stashed behind my seat. Opening the calendar app, I started looking at dates for the past two weeks. From the passenger's side, Zee craned her neck to look at the screen with me. "Miranda was not meeting Rocky that night," I told her, still looking at my calendar. "Two Wednesdays ago, Rocky was with Greg and some of their buddies at a guys-only birthday bash for another friend." I showed her the entry on the calendar: *Greg @ Matt's bday party.* I remember Greg telling me Rocky was there because he said Rocky got stinking drunk and had to be taken home.

"So she and that Tanaka guy were having an affair." Zee settled in her seat and shook her head.

"Sure sounds like it." Something was nagging at me. I started arranging the information Seema had just given us, and it wasn't adding up, like my checkbook most months. If not for Greg, it would never balance. Forget my checkbook — we're talking about my life.

"What's wrong?" asked Zee. "I know that look. Something isn't sitting well with you."

"You're right, something is off." I turned in my seat to look at Zee. "Seema said Miranda had been sporting some new stuff — nice stuff. I didn't know Tanaka except for that one time we met, but he didn't strike me as the type who would give a woman expensive gifts. He has a record of abusing women, not indulging them."

"Seema said Rocky bought Miranda that purse."

"Maybe, but if Seth gave you such a lovely purse, wouldn't you use it all the time? Especially at first?"

"He does, and I do." As an example, Zee held up her bag. It was a Coach satchel given to her by Seth on her last birthday.

"At the tournament, Miranda wasn't carrying a Kate Spade bag of any kind. She was carrying a cheap black microfiber bag. I remember it because I picked it up and handed it to her when she got down off the bleachers to go to the ladies' room during one of the games." I paused and squinted, trying to squeeze the information into place. "No, if she owned a peacock-blue Kate Spade bag, it was not from Rocky. It would be easy to slip a small piece of jewelry or some earrings past someone, but not a large leather bag."

"Are you thinking she might have been seeing someone besides that Peter guy?"

"Maybe, or I'm wrong and Tanaka was the type to give nice gifts, maybe as apologies after smacking them around. I don't know what he did for work, but dollars to donuts Miranda was hiding that bag from Rocky."

"Didn't you say he was in the drug business in Canada? Maybe he's still pushing drugs. That would bring in a lot of cash."

"True."

My cell phone was still in my hand, and it startled me when it buzzed, announcing a text message. It was from Barbara.

*NOTHING ON EUDORA FOX ANYWHERE — EXCEPT A DEATH CERTIFICATE.*

"Hang on, Zee. I have to deal with this."

"Work?" she asked.

"Sort of." I called Barbara. "Nothing?" I asked as soon as she answered.

"Nothing except that someone by the same name died last year in Wyoming. She was about the right age though, and nothing on Little Foxes either. Do you have any other clues?"

"Not at the moment. Thanks. I'll be back in touch." I ended the call. "Crap," I said out loud.

"What's wrong?" asked Zee, whom I had almost forgotten about while my mind swirled with information, or lack thereof, about Eudora Fox.

"It looks like I'm driving to Beverly Hills tomorrow. I hate going into LA during the week."

"I'll go with you," Zee offered. "I can keep you company on the drive and go shopping while you have your meeting."

"It's not a meeting exactly. More like surveillance. Something for one of the LA partners." I plugged my phone into the car's system and buckled my seat belt. "Looks like I'm lunching tomorrow at Bouchon."

Zee squealed with delight. "I love that place and haven't been in a long time."

An idea picked at my brain. *Why not?* I asked myself. Two ladies lunching would not seem out of order to two other ladies who were lunching, while one woman dining alone at such a nice place might receive a few glances. And it was just surveillance. It wasn't like I was going to tackle a criminal to the floor. If the fake Eudora was up to something, it was probably a con, not anything that would cause bullets to fly at the famous French eatery. But having Zee along would also mean it would take more time. I had hoped to check out Peter Tanaka's family tomorrow. Included in Barbara's report was a current address for Tanaka's widowed mother. It was the same as the address listed for Peter. Altadena was nowhere near Beverly Hills, nor was it anywhere near where I lived. I had figured on driving a lot tomorrow, just not to Beverly Hills. It wasn't Zee who was putting a wrench in my plans, it was the need to check out the situation with Fanny Tobin and her gal pal that was mucking up my schedule.

"Pick you up at nine thirty?" I asked Zee. "That way we'll miss most of rush hour and can get in a little shopping before."

"Sounds like a plan," Zee said with delight. "But how about I pick *you* up and around nine instead of nine thirty."

"I'll be ready," I told her. I hate driving in LA traffic, so her offer sounded like heaven to me.

"Have you made the reservation?"

"Reservation?" I asked.

"You should have reservations for Bouchon, silly."

"No." Before I could say anything more, Zee whipped out her own smartphone and located the restaurant's number on the Internet.

"What time?" she asked.

Simon hadn't told me what time his mother and Eudora Fox were having lunch. "I'm not sure," I told Zee, "so make it for twelve thirty. That way I'll see them either halfway through their lunch or as they come in, unless they are lunching later in the day."

"How old are these women?" she asked.

"Seventyish, eightyish."

"Then they will be having lunch earlier." She checked her phone again. "They open for lunch at eleven thirty. I think we should shoot for noon instead of twelve thirty."

I glanced over and nodded in agreement. When it came to social calendars and procedures, Zee was the guru. Quick as a bunny drooling over newly sprouted carrots, she placed the call and made a reservation for lunch the next day.

On the way back to Zee's, my cell phone rang. I ignored it.

"Aren't you going to get that?" asked Zee.

"No. It's just Steele."

Zee cocked her head to listen to the ring. A second later, she turned to me, open-mouthed. "You have the theme from *Jaws* as Michael Steele's ringtone?" The question came out in a half laugh, half scold. "Does he know that?"

"Of course not. Why would he call me if he's within earshot?"

The phone stopped ringing. A few seconds later it started up again.

"Odelia," Zee admonished. "I know he can be annoying, but he might need something."

*What he needs is a good swift kick in someplace not already battered.*

With a sigh, I hit the button on my steering wheel that activated the phone. "Hey, Steele."

"What did you say to Tobin?" he barked, slurring half the words.

190

Before he could go further, I cut him off at the path. "Steele, I'm in the car, and Zee is with me. Be polite and say hello."

The knowledge that I wasn't alone put a stop to the rant I was sure was coming.

"Hi, Zee," Steele said. He spoke slowly in an effort to speak clearly. "Thank you so much for the lovely flowers. Thank Seth for me, too."

"You're welcome, Mike," answered Zee. "How are you feeling?"

"Better, thanks. I'll be back to normal in no time."

"Normal for you, maybe," I quipped. "Normal like other people might take a lot longer and require a couple of surgeries."

Zee shot me a glare befitting an old maid schoolteacher and looked ready to rap my knuckles.

"If there's anything I can do for you," Zee said toward the phone, "just give me a call. I can be in Laguna Beach in a jiffy."

"Thanks, Zee," he answered. "I appreciate that. Other people seem to think this is a joke."

I rolled my eyes. "Steele, I'll call you back about that work thing after I drop Zee off at home." I cut off the call.

"Really, Odelia," Zee said. "Mike isn't just your boss but your friend. You really should be nicer to him, especially since he was almost killed in a car accident."

*Car accident, my ass.* That man was going to owe me after this. In fact, I intended to jump the payback line in front of Dev.

"If I was nice to Steele," I told Zee, keeping my eyes on the road, "he'd freak out, sure that he was dying and only I knew about it."

# FOURTEEN

I had just dropped Zee off at her home when my phone rang. It was Greg.

"Hi, honey," I said with a smile. "I was just about to call you. I'm heading home now. What would you like for dinner? Your choice is chicken or chicken."

"That's what I'm calling you about," he replied. "I called a few of Rocky's teammates, including their coach. I told them about Rocky, and they're pretty torn up about it. They are spreading the word among the team."

"I can imagine. Were you able to broach the subject of Miranda with any of them or wasn't it a good time?"

"I did manage to bring it up. Mostly I asked if they knew of anything wrong between Miranda and Rocky."

"And?"

"Kevin and Jeremy didn't seem to know of anything out of whack, but they also said that they only saw them at practices and games."

"Well, I found out that Miranda was probably having an affair with someone. I just spoke to one of her coworkers, and Rocky may or may not have had a clue. It depends on how observant he was or how much denial he was swallowing."

"Interesting, especially since I got a similar vibe when I spoke to Mona Seidman today," said Greg.

"I remember Cory saying something about it right after Peter died."

"They might know something more," Greg said, "so I invited Mona and Cory over for dinner tonight. That's why I'm calling. You don't mind, do you?"

"Not at all, but I don't have enough chicken thawed."

"Don't worry about that. I already called Leoni's and ordered a pan of their lasagna and garlic bread. I'll pick it up on the way home. If you slap together a salad, we're done."

"Sounds good to me," I agreed. "I'll stop by the bakery and pick up something for dessert."

"I told them to come by around seven thirty. Is that enough time for you?"

I checked the time on the car's dashboard

clock. It was nearly five thirty. "Plenty of time. See you soon, honey."

"Love you," my darling husband said instead of goodbye.

"Love you back."

I'd just hung up when I remembered my deal with Simon Tobin. I called Greg back.

"What's up, sweetheart?" he answered. "You want me to also order a salad?"

"No, we have the stuff at home to whip one up. It's just that I forgot to tell you about my day at work. It was . . . well, unusual."

"Steele unusual or unusual in general?"

Most of my odd days at the office usually involved Steele. "Weird unusual." I told him about my meeting with Simon, including the fact that Barbara couldn't find anyone by the name of Eudora Fox above ground.

"Huh," he answered when I'd finished. "As if you don't have enough to do with Steele and Rocky."

"Yeah, but Simon doesn't know about the Rocky and Miranda stuff, and Steele's been pretty low-key today. This might give me a chance to be absent from the office without much notice."

"So tomorrow you're going to Beverly Hills for the day?"

"Looks that way, but I should be back

mid-afternoon, so if you line up any other people to talk to, I'll be around then. I had hoped to talk to Peter Tanaka's mother tomorrow. Her information is on that report."

"I'd like to do that one with you, if I can. If she's hesitant at all, my being in a wheelchair might soften her up a bit. Maybe we can see her tomorrow night. Let me see what I can set up."

With a replay of vows of love, we hung up.

I was heading up the 405 toward home when my cell phone warned me of a shark in the water. Crap, I'd forgotten to call Steele back after I dropped off Zee. "Hi, Steele," I said, infusing my voice with as much false perkiness as possible.

"You alone now?" he asked.

"Yes. I'm on the 405 going north. It's slow going."

"Good. Then we'll have time for a little chat." The sarcasm in his voice was enhanced by the slur, which was worse than it had been this morning. Either he was tired, on his meds, or both.

"Chat away. I'm going nowhere fast."

"What in the hell were you thinking telling Simon Tobin he could drop by my place?"

My heart nearly stopped, the perkiness draining out of me like old motor oil. "He didn't, did he?"

"No, he didn't, but he said you suggested that I'd welcome the company. Really, Grey? Are you trying to tank my career with T&T?"

"Of course not! It was a bluff."

"A bluff!" It came out *buff,* with the L having gone totally AWOL.

"Yes," I confirmed, "a *buff.*"

The car to my right was trying to merge into my lane in the almost-stopped traffic. I waved at him to go ahead and held back while the vehicle inched ahead and slowly drifted into my lane in front of me. The driver waved his thanks to me through his rearview mirror. I waved back. I firmly believe in traffic karma. If you cut people off and won't let someone merge, somewhere down the line you're going to be treated the same on the highway. If you're nice to others on the road, you might actually be rewarded with a decent parking spot at the mall.

"I didn't think for a minute he'd go visit you," I continued saying to Steele, "or else I wouldn't have done it." That wasn't entirely true. I had hoped Tobin wouldn't head to Laguna Beach. "What's the big woo anyway? If he had, he would have seen a guy who looks like he went one-on-one with an air bag at high speed, just like he was told." I paused. "Look, Steele, Tobin was asking a lot of questions about how you're doing and if you'll be back on Monday. He was antsy about the management of our office with Jolene about to pop. If I had hemmed and hawed about anything, he would have smelled something funny. By inviting him to see for himself, he bought into the story."

From the other end I heard a muffled sound. It could have been a swear word or a cough; I wasn't sure which. "He also informed me," Steele said, "that he's putting you on a special project in my absence."

"Yep. I start tomorrow."

"What is it?"

I paused, preparing myself to walk through a minefield. "I don't think I'm at liberty to discuss it, Steele."

"You can't discuss it with me? I'm your boss."

"I can't discuss it with anyone, but rest assured it has nothing to do with you."

There was a long silence from the other end. It gave me time to concentrate on my driving and move my car into the right lane. My exit would be coming up soon.

"I have to go, Steele. I'm almost at my

exit and have some errands to run before I go home. Greg and I are having company for dinner."

"Wait a damn minute," Steele snapped. "Is Tobin having you snoop around on something personal for him?"

"Speaking of snooping," I said, ignoring his question, "nice job bringing in Barbara Marracino for the research."

"Nice try at deflection, Grey, but it's not going to work."

"Wish I'd thought of using Barbara."

"That's why I get the big bucks," he quipped. "Now back to this secret project."

"I'll be out of the office tomorrow and Friday for sure," I told Steele, moving the conversation forward at a good clip before he could grill me further. "I'll be in LA tomorrow. Jill can handle anything that comes up, and I'm just a phone call away."

"What about the investigation into Rocky and Miranda?"

"Greg and I are still on it," I assured him. "And as soon as I have something more for you to do, I'll let you know. Or should I just contact Barbara directly?"

"Smart ass. Just let me know if you need anything else."

The lasagna from Leoni's was to die for. We

often ordered it when we needed extra food for a party or even to take to a potluck. I had put together a large salad of fresh greens and assorted vegetables. For dessert I'd picked up a small cake. A little wine, cold beer, a few candles, and some linen napkins, and we had an impromptu dinner party. Too bad the subject would be murder and the activities of a dead woman.

Greg got right down to business as I served up the lasagna. "So you think Miranda was fooling around on Rocky with Peter Tanaka?" he asked Mona just as I placed a plate of food in front of her.

"I think there's a good possibility of that," she answered.

"There were a few times at recent scrimmages when I saw them talking alone together," added Cory. "One time I overheard them when they thought no one could see them. It definitely sounded like they had something going."

From a bag hanging on her wheelchair, Mona removed a looped grip of some sort. Using her semi-functioning hands, she wiggled a fork into one end of the grip. I started to help but a glance and a smile from Cory held me back, letting me know that Mona would want to do it on her own. It was the same with Greg. He preferred doing things for himself but didn't hesitate to ask when he knew he needed some assistance. But Greg had full use of his hands and arms. Then I remembered how hard Mona played quad rugby. Anyone who could play that brutal team sport could certainly feed herself. Once the fork was in place, she slipped the grip over her hand and dug into her lasagna. Cory pulled a bendable straw from her bag and placed it in her wine, which I'd served to her in a sturdy tumbler instead of an easily tipped wine glass. Mona shot Cory a smile of thanks and affection.

I've learned a lot since meeting and marrying Greg Stevens. I've learned to share and play better with others. I've learned to be more of a team player, which was difficult for me since I'd pretty much been on my own most of my life. I've learned to be less pig-headed and that compromise isn't necessarily a dirty word. But some of the most valuable things I've learned are not to take everyday things for granted and that most any obstacle can be overcome.

Mona stopped eating and turned to her husband. "Cory, tell them what you told the police."

Cory wiped his mouth with a napkin before speaking. "It's just that I saw them together right before Tanaka died." He picked up his wine glass and took a sip. "It was during the break before the playoff game. I'd slipped out for a smoke."

"I didn't know you smoked," Greg said.

Cory laughed a little. "I don't as a rule, only when I get really nervous."

"He tends to smoke at the games," added Mona.

"Yeah," Cory said. "Especially when it's tense. That's what I was doing when I saw Tanaka and Miranda before at the scrimmage. At the tournament I slipped out before the playoff game began, to chain smoke." He laughed.

"I was outside then, too," I said, "but didn't see you."

"At first I didn't stay near the building with the other smokers. I walked around the parking lot to wear off some of the tension. Later, right before the game started, I lit up a second one while in the smoking area." Another short laugh. "I think I get more worked up over these games than Mona does."

"It's true," Mona agreed, shaking her head. "He takes them quite personally. You'd think it was him being battered on the court. He seldom smokes in the off-season."

My thoughts flashed back to Mona getting rammed hard by Tanaka and how Cory had nearly leapt onto the court after him. I could see how it would be difficult to stand by and watch a loved one being treated that way, even in a rough sport.

"Anyway, I was walking through the parking lot, having my first smoke, when I saw Miranda coming out of Tanaka's van. It wasn't parked with the others close to the building, but on the far edge. Tanaka was with her and they seemed to be having an argument, but I couldn't tell what it was about. I even ducked behind a couple of cars and tried to get closer, but I was afraid they'd see me."

He looked at Mona, and she nodded for him to continue. Cory took a deep breath, then added, "I saw her handing him a couple of sports bottles from inside his van."

Again my mind flashed back to that day. Tanaka was parked on the far side of the lot. I remember noticing him coming from that direction even before I'd met him. And he did have a couple of bottles in his lap when I collided with him. I'd forgotten that.

"That would account for her fingerprints being on the water bottles," noted Greg.

"Is that why the police said she was a suspect?" asked Mona.

"Yes," Greg answered. "There was cyanide in the sports drink in at least one of those bottles, possibly all of them. That's what killed Tanaka. Miranda's prints were on them. A friend who's a cop told us that. He didn't say if there were any other prints besides hers."

"He's not investigating Tanaka's murder," I clarified. "He lives up here but is a friend of Bill Martinez, the detective on the case. But our friend is investigating what happened to Rocky."

After a short pause during which Mona looked down at her plate, no doubt thinking of Rocky — her friend and team captain — she raised her head and asked, "So Miranda poisoned Tanaka?"

"Well," I answered, "her prints were on the water bottles with the poison, but that doesn't mean she put the poison in the bottle."

"Still, it seems pretty incriminating," said Cory.

"Something has been bothering me," I told them. "Wouldn't the water or sports drink have been provided by the team and put in the drinking bottles in the gym? Greg's basketball team supplies it when they have tournaments."

The other three looked around the table

at each other as they thought about it. Mona spoke first. "It depends. The tournament does provide water and drinks, but many of us bring our favorites, and most of us bring our own sports bottles since they are easier for us to hold than a commercial bottle."

"So maybe Miranda didn't put the cyanide into Tanaka's drink," I ventured. "It could have been someone else. Someone who might have filled his bottle at the game."

"You mean like his coach?" asked Cory.

I shrugged. "I'm just saying someone else might have had an opportunity to slip the poison into his bottle."

Mona took a sip of her wine through the straw, her fine brows meeting in the middle as she gave it serious thought. "It doesn't explain who killed Miranda," she finally said. "It sounds to me like someone poisoned Peter Tanaka, then took out Miranda."

Greg speared a tomato from his salad bowl with his fork. "The police think she committed suicide but are still investigating. But if it was murder, any idea why?" He popped the tomato into his mouth and chewed while he waited for an answer.

Cory and Mona exchanged glances, but it

was Mona who spoke. "It was rumored Tanaka left Canada because of a drug charge."

"Even here," Cory added, "it was starting to get around that Tanaka could get his hands on most anything anyone wanted, especially coke or weed."

"Did he have a regular job?" I asked, toying with my garlic bread.

"Not that we ever heard," answered Cory, "but we hardly knew him. Maybe selling drugs was how he supported himself."

"I know when he was living in the area before," Greg said, "he was living off of a substantial insurance settlement he'd gotten from the accident that put him in the chair, along with some money his father had left him. As I recall, his family is quite well off."

"Tanaka wanted to play for the Lunatics again," Mona explained, "but Coach and Rocky were dead set against it. Coach had heard about the drug stuff from a friend of his in Canada. He told the team about it in a meeting. Between that and Tanaka's reputation for being a dirty player, most of us didn't want him on the team."

I swallowed the lasagna in my mouth before speaking. "What about the Vipers — didn't they care about Tanaka's reputation?"

Mona took another sip from her straw

before answering. "The Vipers were struggling. They'd just lost a couple of key players. Rocky tried to warn their coach, but he needed to fill his roster."

Greg glanced at me, then at Cory and Mona. "Did Tanaka know that Rocky tried to get him banned from the Vipers, too?"

Mona shook her head. "I don't know, but probably. I mean, we all knew it, so I'm sure Tanaka got wind of it through someone."

"Was Tanaka close to any of the players on the Lunatics?" I asked.

She shrugged. "When I started playing, Tanaka was already gone."

"I've seen him horsing around with Kevin Spelling," Cory said, "but nothing that I'd call tight. When Tanaka came to the scrimmages, people were friendly enough but generally kept their distance."

Greg nodded and took a drink of wine. "I remember Tanaka and Kevin Spelling being close once upon a time."

"That makes sense," Mona commented. "Kevin was one of the few players who wanted Tanaka back on the Lunatics."

"But he went after Kevin during the game just as viciously as he did Rocky," I pointed out.

"That's part of the game," Mona explained. "You don't hold back on the court just because you're friends off of it. We often play against some of our closest friends."

Seeing Cory's clean plate, I asked if he wanted more lasagna. In response, he smiled and lifted his plate toward me. Greg also took another serving. I scooped out the second helpings while Greg refilled wine glasses.

"Do you think," I began as I settled back down in my seat, "that Tanaka went after Miranda out of revenge for not getting on the Lunatics?"

"It's likely," admitted Cory. "At least from what we've heard about him and seen for ourselves."

Over dessert and coffee we moved the conversation to more pleasant topics. Mona, who worked in customer service at a large company, had just been promoted. Cory, who was in sales, was having a big year in spite of the economy. They had recently bought a house and were remodeling it to accommodate Mona's needs. After dinner we gave them a tour of our home, which had been featured in a magazine for the physically challenged.

"Well," I said to Greg as I came out of the bathroom later that evening, "everything the Seidmans said seems to collaborate Miranda dating Tanaka."

I was putting lotion on my arms and hands before bed. Greg, as always, was reading, with one eye on the TV that was tuned to the late news.

"Sure does," he said, without looking at me. "And the possible drug connection." He glanced my way. "Makes you wonder if Miranda knew about the drug dealing or was even involved with it."

"We don't know for sure that Tanaka was dealing down here, and maybe I was wrong about the purse." I stepped over Wainwright, who was already snoozing on the rug at the foot of our bed, and made my way to my side of the bed. "Maybe Tanaka did buy it for her." I'd told Greg about the handbag and my theory about it while we were setting the table for dinner.

Greg put his book facedown on his chest. "If she was involved with Tanaka's drug business, maybe she bought it herself."

I climbed into bed, pushing aside Muffin with my leg to make room. For a tiny cat, she could be a real bed hog. "Could be, honey. Whether it was a gift or she bought it herself, it would be hard to explain to Rocky where it or the money for it came from. Unless I'm totally off-base and Rocky bought it for her and she just didn't want to bring it to San Diego."

Greg picked his book back up. "You know more about women and their handbags than I do, sweetheart, so I'm going to back your gut feeling on this."

Something still wasn't sitting right. I turned to Greg, remembering something I'd forgotten to tell him. "Honey, do you remember that party you went to a few weeks ago? The birthday party for Matt?"

Greg stopped reading and looked at me. "Sure. What about it?"

"Rocky was there, right?"

"Yes, he was. He and Matt are tight."

"What about Peter Tanaka? Was he there?"

Greg closed his eyes and concentrated. "Yeah, come to think of it, he was. He came in near the end of the party, and I spent the rest of the night avoiding him. Fortunately, it was a big place and there were lots of guys there. Why?"

I told him what Seema had told us about Miranda getting dressed to kill that night in the lobby bathroom. "There's a good possibility," I said when I was finished, "that Miranda was seeing someone other than Tanaka."

"Or," Greg pointed out, "they had an early night because she wasn't sure what time Rocky would be home and Tanaka came to the party after." He paused. "Or she was dressing for one of those wild girls' nights out. After all, that birthday party was a guys' night out."

I made sure my cell phone was on its charger, then said, "But if it was something like that, I don't think Miranda would have dressed in secret. She obviously did not want anyone from her office knowing about her change of clothing."

Greg turned off his light. "By the way, I called Lance on my way home tonight. There's no change in Rocky's condition."

"Do you think Lance might know something about Miranda and Tanaka's relationship?"

Greg shut off the TV and his light and settled the covers over his chest. "Rocky didn't seem to know, so why should Lance? Seems like if he knew, he might have told his brother."

"If your sister-in-law was cheating on your brother, would you tell him?" I asked Greg.

Greg was silent for a moment. "It would be difficult, but yes, I probably would say something to my brother if I found out his wife was cheating."

I couldn't for a minute imagine Greg's brother and his wife having problems. They seemed as goofy for each other as Greg and I were. But it could happen.

"Whatever Tanaka told Rocky at the game," Greg said, "it seemed to come as a complete surprise."

"I agree. Whatever it was, it hit Rocky hard."

"And," Greg said, after kissing me goodnight, "even if Miranda did kill Tanaka, who killed her? That definitely smacks of at least another party, if not more, or suicide. If Tanaka was involved in drugs and Miranda knew, maybe it was the drug people who killed them both. Miranda's death certainly seemed like something that type of criminal would do — bump someone off and make it look like they did it themselves. Maybe this other party took out both Rocky and Miranda?"

Question marks were flying around the room like gnats, but nothing stood out as the winner.

"Like Mona said," I told him, "it does seem like Miranda might have killed Tanaka and then someone killed her. Maybe it was just a matter of cleaning up loose ends."

I shivered and pulled the quilt up under my chin as I thought about why Miranda would get involved with Tanaka in the first place. She and Rocky always seemed happy enough — not blissful but okay. But I've known many couples who looked happy on the outside but were miserable behind closed doors. With that thought I snuggled closer to my husband, who instinctively lifted an arm so I could get closer. Once I was in place, he wrapped both of his arms around me and almost instantly fell asleep. I sighed with contentment. Greg and I were happy in the public eye and even happier behind closed doors.

Sleep did not come to me as easily as it did to Greg. Something was off — something I was overlooking. With the house quiet except for the snores of my husband and the occasional snuffling from Wainwright, my brain went into overdrive going over and over everything that had been shoved into it over the past few days.

Slipping out of bed, I went into the kitchen and made myself a cup of hot chocolate. I was halfway through the creamy beverage when what was nagging at me presented itself front and center. After finishing my drink, I went back to bed.

Greg stirred. "Everything okay?" he asked. He opened his eyes to slits and drew me close, snuggling his lips against my forehead.

"I don't think Miranda was seeing Peter Tanaka," I told him.

"Why not?" His eyes opened all the way and turned to look at me.

"Miranda hated quad rugby."

Greg came more awake. "What?"

"She told me so. She despised it and the time Rocky devoted to it. I'm pretty sure she'd never date another player."

# FIFTEEN

I hate driving to LA during the week, even when I'm not physically doing the driving and even when traffic is not snarled. Zee and I were on our way to Beverly Hills, the city of the rich and famous, sitting like a bejeweled island among the hustle and bustle of greater Los Angeles. One of the ways to spot when the city of Los Angeles stops and the city limits of Beverly Hills begins are the telltale white scrolled street signs throughout the expensive enclave. LA street signs are a dark color and plain.

Before leaving home I had placed a call to Dev Frye but had only reached voice mail. I had wanted to run some of my ideas past him. Maybe they would help the police find the killer or killers. He returned the call while Zee and I were on our way to Beverly Hills.

"Do you mind?" I asked Zee when my phone rang. "It's Dev."

"Go right ahead," she replied.

"Hi, Dev," I said into my phone. "Thanks for calling back."

"Your message said you have something on the Henderson case," Dev said.

"Just a hunch or two, but I think it's worth looking into or at least passing along to the detective in San Diego."

"I'm all ears."

Pleased that Dev wasn't going to start by chewing me out for snooping, I told him what I had learned from Seema and my theory that Miranda was not seeing Peter Tanaka but someone else. "I don't know what Miranda was hiding from her husband," I told Dev when I was done giving him all the info, "but I'd almost bet it was not an affair with Tanaka, though it was something Tanaka knew about."

"Funny you should mention the secret fancy duds," Dev replied. "We went through Miranda Henderson's car. The trunk was filled with expensive clothing, shoes, and jewelry all packed in suitcases, ready to go. There was even a very large stash of cash. It looked like she was living a secret life separate from her husband. And it looked like she was getting ready to bolt."

"You mean leave him?" I asked. Zee glanced over at me, her brows clearly raised over the top of her sunglasses.

"Sure looks that way."

"Any indication of another person involved?"

"None that we could see, but we're pulling her phone records." Dev paused. "Are you sure there were no problems between the Hendersons?"

"The only crack I ever saw was her dislike for quad rugby. I know Rocky spent a lot of time on the sport, and they always seemed happy enough, but you never know. Did you talk to Lance Henderson?"

"Yeah, I did. The guy's all torn up over this, but he did say his brother had been moody lately — something about his job. Seems Rocky Henderson was about to lose his business. He also said the couple had been on and off for some time due to stress over finances."

"I had no idea they were having financial problems," I said with surprise. "And I don't think Greg did either. Rocky did tell Greg he wanted to talk to him about something while we were in San Diego, but of course that never happened. Maybe it was about his business. Maybe he needed some advice."

"His brother also said he'd been drinking a lot more lately."

"Rocky and Greg were at a party together about two weeks ago, and Greg said Rocky got totally bombed at it." Quickly I digested the pieces of information. "Okay, so Rocky's business was failing, but his wife was squirreling away expensive stuff and cash."

"Yeah," said Dev. "Doesn't look like she was much of a team player in that relationship." Dev cleared his throat. "One more thing, Odelia. It has been determined that Rocky's gunshot was self-inflicted, which is making more sense with everything that's coming to light. The guy was losing his business, in debt up to his eyeballs, drinking too much, and then finds out his wife is messing around behind his back."

"Not to mention she's a murder suspect, then is murdered herself."

"Yeah," Dev said, "whether she was killed or put the bullet in her own brain, it was a recipe for disaster for sure."

"Has there been any progress on the murders?"

"None, but Martinez is hard at work, I can assure you. I'll keep you updated as much as possible." He paused. "And don't take this as encouragement, but thanks for the information. I'll pass it along to Martinez."

"And I'll bring Greg up to date on what

you told me. I appreciate you keeping us in the loop as much as you can."

"How's Steele doing?"

"Much better. He's still a pain in the ass, but everything considered, he's on the mend."

"Good. And what about you? You sound like you're in a car."

"Yes, Zee and I are heading to Beverly Hills today for some lunch and shopping."

"Good again," Dev said, this time with a slightly upbeat tone. "That should keep you both out of trouble for a bit."

After ending the call, my eyes filled with tears. I reached into my tote and pulled out a tissue, dabbing my eyes carefully so I wouldn't disturb my eye makeup.

"You okay?" asked Zee.

I nodded, then filled her in on Dev's side of the conversation. "Greg and I had no idea about Rocky's business," I told her. "Our friend had been suffering, and we didn't know it. Did we miss the signs?"

"Don't beat yourself up, Odelia. Maybe that was what he wanted to talk to Greg about."

"Maybe, but why hadn't he said something sooner?"

"Pride maybe. No one likes to admit they need help, especially like that. He might have been trying to fix the problem on his own first."

I blew my nose. "Had the incident in San Diego not occurred, Greg and I might have been able to help in some way. Greg's a whiz in business, and we might have been able to help out financially as well. That still would not have changed Rocky's marriage, but maybe it was Rocky's failing business that had triggered Miranda's unhappiness and plans to leave."

"It's not your fault, sweetie." Zee glanced over and gave me an encouraging smile. "Why don't you give Greg a call and let him know, unless you'd rather wait until you can tell him tonight."

I wiped my nose again. "No, he should know this sooner than later." Picking up my cell again, I called Greg and gave him the sad update.

# SIXTEEN

Zee maneuvered her car through the streets from the freeway to the iconic shopping district of Beverly Hills as deftly as an alien flying its spaceship home. With a sagging spirit I watched out the window as the storefronts became more glitzy with each passing block. We have many of the same stores in Orange County, but shopping Beverly Hills and the famed Rodeo Drive had an energy all its own, even if you're only window shopping. And window shopping was pretty much all that was going to happen today. None of these stores carried plus sizes, and some of the ultra-luxurious stores were locked and you were admitted only by appointment. But even if I had started out with the goal of conspicuous consumption, it was dampened now. I silently told myself to shape up. I was here to do a job for Simon Tobin and hoped putting that forward in my mind might keep me from whipping myself into a depressed frenzy over the Hendersons.

One thing I will say about Beverly Hills is that it has plenty of parking. You can pay large amounts of money for valet parking at some of the private garages or use city parking, which was free for three hours. Zee pulled into a city garage just off of Rodeo. As she took the ticket from the automatic machine at the gate, she said, "I need to pick something up for Hannah at Juicy, but we'll move the car closer to the restaurant when we're done walking around."

I nodded, half listening, my mind occupied now with what I was going to do when I spotted the bogus Eudora Fox. Should I say something to her, letting her know I knew she was a fake? I could wait and hope she'd go to the ladies' room, then follow her and pounce. Or should I even approach her and Mrs. Tobin at all? I had no plan going in outside of simply observing. I guess I had hoped that seeing this person might jar some ideas loose on how best to handle the situation. I hadn't told Tobin yet about my findings — or, rather, Barbara's findings. After I got a good look at this Eudora knockoff, I'd give him a buzz.

"Oh, look," said Zee with hushed excitement as we walked up Rodeo Drive. "Isn't that Heidi Klum?"

I shook off the fog inside my head and turned to look at the tall, leggy blond she was referring to a few feet up ahead to our left. It sure looked like the German bombshell. "I think so," I answered without much excitement.

Zee turned to me once we passed the woman and confirmed our suspicions. "Are you worried about lunch? Or are you still feeling guilty about Rocky and Miranda?"

"Both," I admitted. "But mostly I'm concerned about lunch right now. I'm wondering if coming here today was a mistake."

"Why?"

"Because I have no idea what I'm going to do besides have a nice meal at someone else's expense and watch the two of them, hoping they don't think I'm a stalker."

That was the truth, but only part of it. The other part was concern about Zee. When I'd told Greg about Zee coming with me today, he'd been less than enthusiastic.

"I like the idea of you not going alone, sweetheart," he'd told me over breakfast this morning, "but if something about this turns out to be more than you bargained for, Zee could get caught in the middle. And it wouldn't be the first time."

"Through no fault of mine," I'd quickly added in protest.

"Maybe not, but it tends to happen."

I looked over at my dearest friend, who had stopped in her tracks to *ooh* and *ahh* over shoes in a store window. Even though Zee had been subjected to dead bodies and even violence over the years through association with me, she still insisted on tagging along once in a while. But this was just surveillance and lunch — nothing else. I shook the worry off and joined her to drool over the spectacular footwear in the window, all of which were too high for me to wear and too expensive for me to buy, and which reminded me of the cache of high-end items found in Miranda's car.

After shopping, we moved the car several blocks away to the public parking closest to Bouchon, which was on Canon Drive near Wilshire Boulevard. The parking was underground and automated like all the others. I'd never eaten at this restaurant, but Zee had and led the way up the elevators to the restaurant's lobby, which was on the second floor of the building. By the time the doors to the elevator opened, I'd managed to shove the Hendersons aside and aim my focus on the task at hand.

"Remind me," Zee said as we approached the maître d', "to go to their bakery before we leave. It's on the first floor. Seth loves their bacon cheddar scones and chocolate croissants and would kill me if I didn't bring something home. I just hope they're not sold out."

As we were led to our table, I scanned the dining room. It was decorated simply but with elegance and was a good size but not huge. Every table and booth appeared to be visible except those on the balcony, but it was too chilly today for most people to be seated outside, especially two elderly ladies. People were already seated, and I tried not to gawk as I surveyed the diners. Most of the people seated were in pairs, but most were business people. Then I spotted them. They were in a booth against the far wall with food already in front of them. When the waiter tried to steer us in another direction, I gently asked for a different table — an empty one I spotted closer to my targets, thinking it didn't matter how close we got since neither of them knew us.

*Wrong!*

As soon as Zee and I took our seats and were handed our menus, I glanced over at Fanny Albright Tobin and her companion. A gasp, thick and heavy, rose in my throat, threatening to spill onto the table. I squelched it as best I could in an attempt to not garner attention.

"You okay?" Zee asked.

I nodded and took a big drink from the water glass the waiter had just put in front of me, nearly drinking it down in one long gulp. "Just something caught in my throat," I squeaked when I was finished with the water.

I looked over at Fanny Tobin's table again. I had to be mistaken. The cold hand clutching my gut and squeezing the life from me told me I wasn't. The hair was different — longer; a softer, lighter color; and better styled — and she was wearing makeup, but it was *her. It couldn't be,* I told myself, trying to convince my eyes they were mistaken. But it was. And if I had any doubt, it was dispelled when she turned her head my way and saw me, giving a short double-take. Her face morphed from surprise to curiosity to amusement as her smallish eyes settled on me, clinging to my face and suffocating me like plastic wrap. She smiled, showing even, gleaming white teeth. Dollars to donuts she'd had an expensive whitening job and possibly some cap work done on them since the last time we'd met.

My first instinct was to grab Zee and run

from the restaurant, bypassing the toothy maître d', the trip to the bakery — hell, even the elevator. Maybe we could pull off a Butch and Sundance move and jump from the balcony to save time. My second instinct told my first one to hold the phone; it wanted to know what in the hell was going on and wasn't about to leave without an answer. The two instincts went to war in my brain, with the second calling the first a chicken — and the first one clucking in response.

"Would you like to hear today's specials?"

Startled, I looked up to find our waiter standing next to the table. "Could you give us a few more minutes?" I asked him, my voice wavering in its indecision.

Before he left, Zee said to him, "Would you please bring us both iced tea to start." He gave her a professional smile and went off to get our drinks.

"Odelia, are you sure you're okay?" Zee asked me, looking concerned. Her back was to the Tobin table, which was about two to three yards away. I looked at Zee, keeping one eye focused just beyond her shoulder.

"Maybe we should go," I suggested.

"We just got here." Before the words were out of her mouth, she remembered I was on a mission. Leaning toward me, she whis-

227

pered, "Is she not here?"

"Oh," I whispered back, "she's here, and so is her friend." I closed my eyes, wishing I could click my heels and take both of us back to Orange County like we'd never left — or at least send Zee back. Maybe I didn't need ruby slippers; maybe I needed a transporter. I could shove Zee into it and beam her back to her cozy home in Newport Beach, leaving me to deal with this situation on my own. But I didn't have either. What I had was the mother of one of my bosses, who was in more danger than first thought, and my best friend, who may end up in the line of fire. Again.

*Do something,* I told myself. *Anything but pee your pants will do.*

My left eye joined my right eye in staring back at Eudora Fox, better known to law enforcement as Elaine Powers, and better known to me as Mother — the head of a women-only group of professional assassins. The woman hanging out with Simon's mother had made whacking people for money a cottage industry. Like my pal Willie, Mother was adept at slipping through the fingers of the law, and she popped up in the oddest places. My lips formed a weak smile, but my eyelids blinked like a faulty neon sign in disbelief.

The waiter returned bearing goblets of iced tea. He placed them in front of us, breaking my shock and jarring my brain out of a frozen stupor. I looked over at Zee and said in my best forced casual voice, "You ready to order?"

After the waiter described the specials and we made our selections, Zee whispered, "You know the person Fanny Tobin is with, don't you?"

In response, I nodded but said nothing. I took a sip from my iced tea and did a quick computation of possibilities. Was Mother here because Fanny Tobin was in need of her unconventional services, or was she here because Fanny was the target and Mother needed to get close before doing the deed? Either was a good possibility, but Simon had said Eudora Fox wanted Fanny to invest in her business. That could be a cover. Or perhaps Mother was looking for venture capital. Maybe she was expanding her hit-woman services by opening chain locations; I'd love to see that prospectus.

"Yes, Zee, I do," I answered, saying no more. The last thing I needed was for Zee to know that the woman sitting a few yards behind her was Mother. With Mother having shown up a few times in my life in the past few years, Zee knew who she was, even if she'd never had the displeasure of a face-to-face meeting, as I had, and Mother knew way too much about Zee by her association with me.

The waiter appeared again, this time with a small, slender loaf of fresh baked bread, which he placed directly on the table with a small crock of butter. The warm, comforting scent of the bread washed over me like a hug but wasn't enough to soothe my agitated mind.

"You must try this bread," Zee gushed. "It's heavenly." As she tore off a chunk, my focus returned to Mother, who was now communicating to me with her eyes. She wanted to make contact — that much was obvious. It was even more obvious when she excused herself from her table and with a slight nod of her head indicated for me to follow.

I took a long pull from my iced tea. After about ten seconds I said to Zee, "I'm going to the ladies' room. I'll be right back."

Something in her eyes told me she wasn't believing me. She turned in her seat to glance back at Fanny's table. Seeing the older woman alone, she put two and two together. "Should I go with you?"

I shook my head and gave her a fake smile. "Nah, I've got this. Piece o' cake."

What I really wanted to do was to tell Zee who I was following, instruct her to wait ten minutes, and, if I didn't return, to call the police — oh, and to tell Greg my last thoughts were of him.

# SEVENTEEN

When arriving at the restaurant, the elevators spill open onto a narrow marble hallway. A short distance to the right are the restrooms, which I'd noticed when we'd arrived. From there you enter an elaborate but small waiting area with a reservation desk. Beyond that is the hostess desk and the main dining room. I found Mother waiting for me past the reservation desk area just inside the narrow hallway leading to the elevator. Seeing me, she waved for me to follow her and disappeared into the women's restroom. I swallowed and headed in that direction.

"Odelia Grey," Mother said, turning my name into a statement of mixed amusement and disbelief. "Is your showing up here a coincidence?"

I bent to look under the stall doors.

"Don't worry," Mother said. "I already checked."

I straightened, half wishing I had spotted a pair of pumps under one of the doors, but since there wasn't any I had no choice but to move forward with my mission.

"You look good, Mother," I said. "Or should I say Elaine? Or would you prefer Eudora?" Letting her know I knew her current alias was a bold move on my part, but it quickly established that this wasn't a coincidence.

Usually quick of mind and mouth, she didn't answer but instead studied me up and down while her mind chewed on the situation.

"Is that suit a St. John knit?" I asked to fill the silence. "Quite a step up since the first time I saw you. On that memorable occasion, I believe you were wearing an old sweatshirt with something about bingo on the front. This is a good look for you. Your hair is nice too."

"And the last time you saw me we were both in our birthday suits." She gave me a small smile. "Since we're becoming such good friends, Odelia, why don't you call me Elaine."

"Well." I paused to take a short breath. "Well, *Elaine*. I'm not here for you specifically, but to look after Mrs. Tobin. I had no idea you were Eudora Fox or pretending to be Eudora Fox until I saw you when we came in." I paused again, then quickly added, "Did you know the real Eudora Fox? Seems she died last year in Wyoming. Was she one of your targets or a client?"

"Neither," Elaine answered. "She was a distant cousin. A crazy old bag with thirteen cats." After checking to make sure it was dry, she leaned against the vanity and crossed her arms. "So what's your connection to Fanny?"

"I work for her son, Simon Tobin."

"You don't work with that pain-in-the-ass Mike Steele any longer?"

"Oh, I still work for him," I assured her, "but both of us are now employed by Templin and Tobin. Simon asked me to check out his mother's new companion. He had concerns."

Elaine gave a tight-mouthed chuckle. "He should be concerned. She's a self-absorbed nut job with loads of money — easy pickings for someone like me."

"So she's not a client or a target of your hit business?" I ventured.

"Neither. She's a mark."

"So you're into fraud and larceny now?"

Again Elaine chuckled. She turned toward the mirror and started fussing with her hair. "A good business is a diverse business." She opened her purse and my heart stopped, but instead of the gun I feared she was toting, Elaine pulled out a tube of lipstick and started touching up her lips. "I'd think," she said, touching a smear at the corner of her mouth with a fingertip, "considering your friendship with William Proctor, that you'd be a bit more tolerant of financial crimes."

"I've never condoned Willie's embezzlement of that money," I told her. "He knows that."

She popped the lipstick back into her designer bag and looked at me with expectation. "So where do we go from here, Odelia?"

I squared my shoulders. "Leave Fanny Tobin alone."

Elaine raised one nicely shaped eyebrow at me.

"Please," I tacked on.

"And if I don't?" She crossed her arms in front of her again, reminding me of the principal of my elementary school when she was waiting for an answer you knew would earn you a detention.

I shrugged, as I always did in school when sent before the principal. "There's really no way I can make you stop screwing with Mrs. Tobin, Elaine. I'm simply asking that you don't."

"You could always blow the whistle on me," she suggested.

"And put me, my friends, and my family in mortal danger? No, thanks."

"I've always said you were smart." She uncrossed her arms.

"I'm sure there are other old people you could prey on without messing with this lady." I thought about my own mother, then I quickly added, "Not that I'm suggesting you continue with this despicable crime wave, but if you do, can you do it elsewhere?"

"What makes you think I haven't already?"

I was growing weary. I wanted this conversation over so I could return to my table before Zee began to worry.

"I need to get back," I told Elaine. "Please don't mess with Fanny Tobin," I said, stating my request again, "or hurt her. I would consider it a huge personal favor."

"I thought I did you a huge personal favor the last time we met."

I hung my head. "Yes, you did. A monumental one."

She studied me as she gave it some thought. "Oh, okay, Odelia, I'll leave Fanny alone." She said it with a juvenile roll of her eyes, as if I'd just asked her to turn her music down. "What can I say, I have a soft spot for you."

"Thank you," I said with relief.

Elaine picked up her purse and started for one of the stalls. "Why don't you rejoin your friend Mrs. Washington and enjoy your lunch. The food here is quite good."

"What will you tell Fanny?"

"Probably something like I don't feel well and need to leave. Then I'll disappear, and she'll never hear from me again." She cocked her head to one side. "And what will you tell your boss?"

"Why do I need to say anything? I'll let him think you took off before I could find out anything about you."

She smiled. "Don't be so modest, Odelia. Tell him the truth, or at least part of it. Tell him you found Eudora to be a fraud and confronted her, ordering her to leave his mother alone or you'd go to the police. Take the credit and let him think you're a hero — nothing wrong with that. Might get you a nice year-end bonus."

She must have seen the hesitation on my face because she followed it up with, "Just don't tell him the *entire* truth."

"I wouldn't dream of it." I held my right hand out to her. She looked at it a moment like it might be some sort of a trap, then took it. We shook. "Thank you, Elaine."

"One more thing, Odelia," she said, not letting go my hand. Elaine had a surprisingly strong grip for a woman of her age. "Every time we cross paths, you cost me money. The next time, I might not be so generous."

I left the ladies' room, but just outside the door I had another thought and returned. Elaine was in one of the stalls doing her business. "Pssst, Elaine — it's me, Odelia."

"Now what? Did you come back to make sure I wiped my ass?"

"Did you see the news about the woman who was found dead in a van in San Diego this past weekend?"

Silence. Then, "You mean the one they think killed that guy in the wheelchair?"

"Yes." I took a deep breath then surged forward. "Did you have anything to do with that?"

More silence. I waited, shifting from foot to foot. A moment later I heard her flush. Seconds later she emerged from the stall smoothing down the skirt of her knit suit. "If it was a hit, it wasn't us."

"Do you know anything about Peter Tanaka's death? He was the wheelchair athlete who died."

"Again, not us." She washed her hands, then considered me while she dried them.

"You don't think that woman killed him?"

"I don't know if she did or not." I looked at Elaine's reflection in the mirror. "That woman was Miranda Henderson. She and her husband are friends with me and Greg."

Elaine stared at my reflection. "How do you do it, Odelia? How do you always manage to get so close to murder and mayhem? For me, it's a business; for you, it's . . . ," her voice trailed off as she tried to find the appropriate word.

I lifted one shoulder in response and helped her out. "It's a gift."

Elaine chuckled.

"Seriously, Elaine." I turned away from the mirror to look at her directly. "My husband and I are looking into Miranda's death as a favor to her husband." I cast my eyes down at the thought of Rocky. "He's currently in the hospital in a coma. They think he tried to kill himself after Miranda died."

"Maybe the husband killed them both," she suggested, "then offed himself."

"Unlikely. He's in a wheelchair too. And he was in jail, charged with beating Peter, when she died."

Elaine stared at me like I had two heads. "You do remember who you're talking to, don't you? Who's to say he didn't hire out

239

the hit on both of them, got in the fight to cover it up, then tried to kill himself? Were they screwing around behind his back?"

My eyes widened at the thought, which hadn't entered my mind and probably not Greg's either. In spite of my theory about Miranda not getting involved with another quad player, I said, "Possibly."

Elaine picked up her purse by its handle. "Well, there you go. A motive if ever there was one. But I can assure you, if either or both were professional jobs, it wasn't my crew. I choose the jobs personally."

True to her word, shortly after we returned to our respective tables, Elaine made some excuse to Fanny and left the restaurant. Fanny stayed behind and finished her meal, and Zee and I enjoyed ours.

"Okay," Zee said once we were back in the car and heading home. "Now that we're alone, are you going to tell me what happened with that woman?" We'd stopped by the Bouchon bakery on our way out, and both of us had picked up baked goods to take home. The car's interior smelled decadent with buttery goodness.

"I confronted her and told her to back off of Mrs. Tobin. She agreed."

"Just like that?"

"She was running a scam on her, and I

told her if she didn't cease, I'd go to the police."

Zee glanced over at me. "So who is she?"

"No one."

"Odelia Grey, don't you dare lie to me. You nearly had a heart attack when you recognized her."

It was a long drive back to Orange County, and I knew Zee would not let the matter rest. "You know that hit woman I've come across on occasion?"

I watched Zee as she dug through her memory. When her eyes popped open, resembling two fried eggs with a chocolate yolk, I knew she'd hit pay dirt. "That was Mother, the contract killer?"

"Yep."

"And just like that she agreed to leave Fanny Tobin alone?"

"She said she has a soft spot for me. And she wasn't going to kill Fanny," I clarified, "just steal her money."

A horn blared at us when we ran a stop sign. Zee pulled her Mercedes over to the curb and parked. She was visibly shaken.

Reaching over, I patted the hand closest to me. It was still curled around the steering wheel, clutching it with a white-knuckled death grip.

"Why don't you let me drive," I suggested.

# EIGHTEEN

After a quick and early supper of leftover lasagna, Greg and I hit the road for Altadena to visit June Tanaka, Peter's mother. Since we caught the tail end of rush hour, traffic was bad. There was no easy way to get from our place to the Tanaka home, located forty-five miles away in the foothills above Pasadena, without navigating one freeway after another, moving slowly forward like modern covered wagons ambling across an asphalt prairie. Greg maneuvered the freeway system deftly and with patience, but even with him at the wheel, between the trip to Beverly Hills and the drive to Altadena, I was road weary.

"You're sure she's okay about us coming?" I asked. Over our rushed dinner we'd discussed my day and what Dev had disclosed, but we hadn't had time to talk about Greg's findings. It wasn't that I hogged the conversation but that my darling husband got caught in a rut when I mentioned that Eudora Fox was really Elaine Powers.

*"Mother?"* he'd asked, nearly dropping the small salad and bottle of dressing he was shuttling to the kitchen table. "Mother the contract killer?"

"The very same," I'd assured him as I took our reheated dinner out of the microwave. "So did you have a chance to call any of the other players?"

"Not so fast." Greg slid the salad and dressing onto the table and rolled over to me, nearly trapping me in the kitchen. It was clear he wasn't going to budge until he got answers.

I put the container of hot food on the counter and looked at him, hands on my hips. It had been a trying day, and I was not in the best mood. "Yes," I confirmed again. "It was Mother, and she agreed to leave Fanny Tobin alone."

"Just because she likes you?" Greg didn't sound convinced.

"That's what she said." I picked the food up again. "Why don't you feed the animals before we get started," I suggested. Both Wainwright and Muffin were sitting by their respective food bowls with large, pleading eyes, patiently waiting for their dinner, but I'd made the comment more to get Greg out of my way. He backed up his wheelchair and headed for the low cabinet where we kept the dog and cat food, but I knew he was not backing up his brain. When something was on his mind, he stuck to the topic like Krazy Glue. I put the food on the table and sat down.

Finished with feeding the animals, Greg rolled up to his place at the table. "Do you really believe Elaine Powers is just going to drop Fanny Tobin like a bad habit after investing time and effort into buttering up the old lady?"

"Greg, I don't really have a choice but to trust what she said. If I tell anyone who she is, she could retaliate. She's like a poisonous snake you see sleeping on the edge of a hiking path. If you leave it alone, you'll be okay. If you poke it, be ready to be bitten. Besides," I said, "no matter who or what she is, she saved my bacon not too long ago, didn't she?"

Greg blew out a long deep breath. "Yeah, she did. But I still don't like the idea of her being in our lives again. She just keeps popping up like a bad rash."

"Funny," I said with no humor while scooping lasagna onto Greg's plate. "She sort of said the same thing about me."

I put the plate down in front of my husband and dished out a helping for myself from the serving dish. Using salad tongs, Greg added salad to his plate, then to mine. I started eating, but Greg did not. Instead, he studied the mushrooms and tomatoes nestled among the micro greens as if they might say something brilliant or break into song. In the background, our dog and cat chomped their respective kibble with gusto.

I put down my fork and put a hand on Greg's forearm. "It's going to be okay, honey. I really do think Elaine will be true to her word and leave Mrs. Tobin alone. And I don't think she'll be bothering me either."

"That's good news," he said, giving me an unsure smile. "Even though I've never met her, she strikes me as some kind of scary."

"She is, Greg, but she's had plenty of opportunities to harm me and never has, and I don't think it has anything to do with our relationship with Willie. At least not anymore." I speared a tomato wedge. "By the way, I asked Elaine if she had anything to do with the deaths of Miranda or Peter Tanaka."

Greg stared at me, his fork stopped halfway to his mouth. "And?"

"And Elaine said she had heard about Miranda, but she assured me neither her or her people had anything to do with it."

He put down his fork, the metal hitting the plate with an off-key *ding*. "Odelia, do you really think she'd admit it if she was involved? That would be an admission of murder."

"Well, I believe her." I stuck a bite of food into my mouth with a hard chomp and chewed.

I thought about Mother/Elaine. I'd met her three times, and each time she'd exuded a confidence that didn't strike me as fake, nor did it appear cocky. She was good at what she did and knew it. Did she feel empowered by the fact that she could and did have people killed without them ever seeing it coming?

I was confident in my work as a paralegal. I knew my stuff and served our clients to the best of my ability. I was also confident in my undying love for Greg and in his love for me. And I was confident in my relationships with Zee and Seth, Clark and Mom, and all the other people who were part of my personal solar system, even Mike Steele. Did Elaine have that kind of emotional confidence or was her foundation wrapped up totally in her nefarious pursuits? Willie was confident like that, too. A small, nerdy-looking guy, he walked the earth like he owned it and was untouchable, which he pretty much had been so far. But it wasn't until he married Sybil that Greg and I noticed true peace on his face.

Criminal confidence — was there such a thing? Neither appeared crazy, as most criminals on the news did; rather, they appeared confident that they were above the normal behavior, moral expectations, and consequences of the rest of us, like they were playing a game and excelling at it. Then again, if they didn't go into their questionable activities with such assurance, they would fail before they even started.

After the discussion about Elaine, Greg and I had eaten dinner and cleaned up the kitchen in near silence. I was still wrestling with the issue of morality and confidence. Who knew what was going on in my darling husband's head. Now that we were in the van and heading for Altadena, I asked Greg the question that had gotten lost during dinner. "Were you able to talk to any of the other players today?"

He nodded. "Yeah. I found out the Lunatics are having a practice on Sunday down in Oceanside." He glanced at me. "You want to go?"

"I think we should go, but isn't it kind of weird that they're having a practice just a week after what happened?"

"Originally it was called off," he explained, "but a lot of the team is in a funk, and Coach Warren thought it might help to burn off some of their anxiety to hold it anyway."

"What about the coach of the Vipers? Did you reach him yet?"

"I got his number from Coach Warren and called, but I only reached voice mail. He hasn't returned the call yet. His name is Rob Rios and he lives in Long Beach. He's a PE and math teacher at a high school. I'm hoping we can contact him this weekend."

"Speaking of voice mail," I said. "I received an odd one myself today."

Greg shot me a grin. "More odd than running into the Queen Mother of murder?"

"No, that topped the cake. But the message was still odd. It was left on my voice mail at work by someone named Michelle Jeselnick. I asked Jill if she knew who she was, but she didn't."

"Maybe Steele knows."

"That's the weird thing," I answered. "In her voice mail, this Michelle begged me not to say anything to Steele about her call."

Greg's head shot my way, then turned back to watch the road. "That is odd. So you don't think it's a client?"

I shook my head. "I asked Jill to do a

search of our firm's data base to see if this woman's name popped up anywhere in any documents or in our contacts, and it didn't."

"What did she want?"

"She didn't say. Just that she'd call back and that she'd appreciate my keeping the call a secret from Steele."

"Maybe she's one of Steele's jilted girl-friends."

"Could be," I agreed, "but usually Jill and I know the names of the women he dates. Steele puts everything on his calendar, including the names and phone numbers of his romantic victims." I laughed. "Jill's theory is that he does that so if he ever goes missing again, it will give us a jumpstart on where the body is buried."

"She didn't leave a number?" Greg looked over at me again. It was dark out now, and the lights of the dash reflected off his strong chin.

"Nope."

"Maybe it has something to do with what happened in Perris."

"But why call me? And how would anyone out there know to call me about Steele? It must have something to do with work for her to know my name and where to call."

"Good point, sweetheart. I guess you'll just have to wait until she calls again." He changed lanes.

"You know what's really odd," I said. "Steele didn't call me today. Not a peep. He called Jill and arranged to have some documents scanned and sent to him, but not so much as a slurred sniffle my way. I told him I had something to do for Simon. Maybe Steele's miffed at me."

"That's because I called him." Greg grinned at me like he'd just arranged a birthday surprise.

I stared at him. "What did you do, bribe him to leave me alone today?"

"It was much easier than that. I simply called to see how he was doing."

I narrowed my eyes at him. "That's it?"

"Yep. I checked on him and let him know he wasn't forgotten. I asked him if he needed anything." When I looked away, Greg added, "Seems you did a well-check on our broken boy, too." He laughed. "Steele told me you called."

"Yes, I'll admit it, I caved and called him. I got worried when I didn't hear anything. And I was right, he was miffed over Simon."

"And you also know a couple of his golf and tennis buddies had been in and out today to visit, so he'd been otherwise occupied."

I nodded. "And he said another's coming

over tonight to watch a game on TV." I turned to Greg. "He went ballistic when he thought I was sending Simon Tobin to his place, but his pals are in and out of there today like it's a hot new brewery."

"Ah, but Simon is the head of the firm," Greg explained. "These guys are his friends. That's a big difference. Besides, it's been five days since he was in his accident, and I'm sure by now he's looking more like the story you and I are peddling on his behalf."

Greg was right. Simon was not one of Steele's inner circle, which was comprised of a handful of other professional men — many of which he'd gone to college and law school with. I knew many of them, and most would keep his secret if he decided to tell them, but I doubted he would.

"While you were making calls, did you also check on Rocky?"

"I talked to Lance this afternoon," Greg told me, "but I didn't mention anything about what Dev told you. I figure the poor guy has already been questioned to hell and back about that. Rocky is about the same. Their parents got into town this morning and are staying at Rocky and Miranda's place, although Lance said they will probably spend most of their time at the hospital."

I took a deep breath. I didn't want to switch topics, but I wanted to move the discussion from the heavy sense of loss to theory, to remove the closeness of it until we were just looking at the facts. Maybe then we'd see something we'd been missing. Like when you're looking for a needle dropped on a carpet, sometimes it's best to get off your hands and knees, stand up, and look at it from a distance.

"Let's review what we know," I suggested. It was a perfect time, as we were still stuck in traffic with quite a few miles to go. "Miranda's fingerprints were on the water bottles, and Cory saw Miranda hand Peter the bottles from his van."

"That doesn't mean she put the poison in the drink, though," Greg pointed out.

"True," I agreed. "Peter says something to Rocky about Miranda that makes Rocky go ballistic and beat the crap out of Peter, all while the poison is doing its thing in his body. Miranda takes off and winds up in Rocky's van, shot in the head. Then Rocky tries to off himself."

I took a deep breath and held it for a count of five. "The thing is, we don't know what Peter Tanaka said to Rocky to set him off. That might be the key we're missing. We're assuming it's about Miranda fooling around on Rocky with Peter, but what if it was something else?"

"Cory said it sounded like Tanaka and Miranda were hooking up, and he saw and heard them fighting. A breakup gone bad, maybe?"

"Yes, but I still think if Miranda was cheating on Rocky, it wouldn't be with another quad rugby player. She'd be wanting to get away from it. Maybe Peter knew what she was doing — and with whom — and was simply the messenger bringing the news to Rocky. Maybe it was his leverage to get the upper hand when he needed it in the game."

"Now there's a thought," Greg agreed. "And certainly something he'd do."

"And then there's the drug angle," I said. "Maybe Peter was selling drugs and double-crossed someone. Maybe Miranda knew that or was even involved in his drug business. She had to have gotten all that new stuff and cash found in her car from somewhere."

"Miranda could have been pressed by the drug guys into killing Tanaka," Greg suggested, "then they killed her to cover it up."

I suddenly remembered something Elaine Powers had said. "Mother threw out another theory. She said maybe Rocky already knew about a possible affair between Peter and Miranda and hired a hit out on both of them while he played the outraged husband."

Greg shook his head back and forth with vigor. "I can't believe that of Rocky Henderson. He's no saint, but he's not a murderer."

I shook a finger in Greg's direction. "Jealousy and betrayal have sent decent people over the edge before, and Rocky came darn close to beating Tanaka to death."

Greg shot me a look. "If you ever betray me, I'd be destroyed, but I'd like to think I would never kill others or myself." In the shadows I couldn't tell if he was smiling or serious.

"Trust me," I told my husband with a slight snort, "the only men I'd ever leave you for are Ben and Jerry."

"That's a comfort." Now I could clearly see him smiling.

With all the information laid out like cards in a game of solitaire, we rode along with our own thoughts as we tried to see which card went where.

"At least I have that favor for Simon Tobin off my plate," I finally said, breaking the silence as we got nearer to Altadena.

"Did you call Tobin and tell him about your lunch?"

"No," I answered. "I'll do it tomorrow. I don't want him to think it was that easy."

Again, Greg shot a look my way that was hard to read. "It was too easy, if you ask me."

I kept my mouth shut because, frankly, I was thinking the same thing, but until Mother showed me the price tag for her favor, I was keeping my wallet in my purse.

When we reached Altadena, we had a little trouble locating the Tanaka home. It was located at the top of a quiet street nestled against the hills. There were very few streetlights in the neighborhood, and most of the homes were behind hedges or walls. We crawled along, reading each number in the semi dark, until we spotted the one we were searching for on the side of an open stone gate. Greg turned through the gate. The drive was circular, with a short appendage dead-ending next to a three-car garage for additional parking. The house was a sprawling ranch in slate gray with white trim and shutters. All around the perimeter were mature trees and shrubs, with well-tended flower beds edging the driveway and in front of the main entrance. The place had a feeling of peace, serenity, and harmony with nature — not exactly where I expected Peter Tanaka to hang his hat, considering the chaos he seemed to thrive on.

Not surprisingly, the drive, walkway, and entrance to the house were wheelchair friendly. A woman whom I placed around thirty opened the door shortly after we rang the doorbell, as if she'd been waiting on the other side for a finger to press the buzzer.

We introduced ourselves. She was dressed in gray leggings and a turquoise sweater that hugged her slight frame. "I'm Ann Tanaka, Peter's sister," she told us, flipping her waterfall of inky black hair off her shoulder. Her face was pretty, round, and grim, her mouth a tight slash without color. "My mother is expecting you."

Ann showed us down a short entryway that opened into a very large great room and dining area. The interior of the house gleamed with polished hardwood floors, furniture with clean lines and low profiles, and minimal clutter. One wall was a bank of large windows that afforded a spectacular view down the hill and across the valley. Just beyond the windows was a swimming pool and patio. On the patio a small firepit glowed amber and orange against the night. Walls held impressive modern art; shelves held sculpture. In one corner a baby grand piano stood sentry. On it was a carefully arranged grouping of framed photos. It was a cultured and sophisticated home.

Standing at the windows, looking out, was a woman with ramrod posture dressed in black wool slacks and a black sweater. Her hair was also jet black and bobbed short. She turned when we approached.

"Mrs. Tanaka," Greg said when we got close. "I'm Greg Stevens, and this is my wife, Odelia Grey. Thank you for agreeing to see us tonight."

I gave her a sad smile and held out the potted orchid we'd picked up before getting on the freeway. "With our condolences."

The woman gave Ann a nod. Ann stepped forward and took the plant. "Thank you," she said.

Mrs. Tanaka had a round little face like her daughter's and sharp dark eyes ringed with exhaustion. She looked to be near sixty years in age and in very good physical condition — an older version of her daughter. Without a word, she walked toward a sofa and several chairs and held out a slender, delicate hand indicating for us to take a seat. I sat on the sofa. Greg positioned his chair near me. Mrs. Tanaka took a seat on the edge of an upholstered chair. Again she nodded to Ann, who disappeared with

257

the plant.

"You were friends of Peter's?" she asked, her voice soft but in no way timid.

"I've known him a long time," said Greg. "My wife just met him at the tournament. We're very sorry for your loss, Mrs. Tanaka."

"But were you friends?" Mrs. Tanaka asked pointedly, her small cherry mouth barely moving.

I looked at Greg. He looked directly at Mrs. Tanaka and said, "No. We were not friends."

"Honesty is always the best policy, is it not?" she said, not taking her eyes from Greg.

"Yes, it is." Greg cleared his throat. "Peter and I had our issues over the years, but I am still sorry for what happened."

"My daughter recognized your name and informed me that you once dated Linda, the girl Peter took to Canada several years back. Was that the problem between you?"

"Mostly, but obviously that's in the past." Greg reached over, took my hand, and squeezed it. "To be perfectly honest with you, Odelia and I were at the tournament when Peter died. We're close friends of the Hendersons, and we're trying to find out what really happened."

"You don't believe that that Miranda

person killed my son?" Mrs. Tanaka took her eyes from Greg and looked at me. Not a smidgen of emotion showed on her face.

"We're not sure, Mrs. Tanaka," I told her. "But it doesn't seem like something she'd do."

"Her husband is in the hospital in a coma," Greg said. "He may have tried to kill himself after his wife died."

Mrs. Tanaka moved her eyes to Greg. "And that would be the man who tried to beat my son to death before the poison did its job, correct?"

Greg hesitated, then said, "Yes."

"Frankly, Mr. Stevens, I don't care if your friend lives or dies." Still no emotion from her, like an alabaster sculpture that could talk. "His wife killed Peter, and he beat him. I know my son was far from perfect, but he did not deserve to die."

"We agree, Mrs. Tanaka," I said. "But we also don't think Miranda Henderson killed him."

"The police believe she did."

"She's a suspect," I clarified. "It hasn't been determined yet if she actually killed him."

"And if she didn't kill him," Greg added, looking directly at her, "wouldn't you want to know who did and bring that person to justice? And Miranda was killed not too long after Peter's death. It could have been the same person who murdered them both."

"I don't care who killed that woman or that her husband tried to kill himself. All that matters is that my only son is dead. Will anything I say or do, or anything you ask me, bring him back to me?"

"No, ma'am," answered Greg with a slow, sad shake of his head.

Ann appeared toting a tray with a lovely Japanese teapot and matching cups. She placed it on the coffee table. Her mother nodded to her and she began to pour three cups of tea, after which she handed a delicate porcelain cup to each of us and stepped back. Ann didn't take tea or a seat but remained standing, face blank, head slightly bowed, like an obedient servant awaiting her next command.

"If you feel that way," I asked, returning my attention to Mrs. Tanaka, "why did you agree to see us?"

"Because I wanted to see what you had to say," Mrs. Tanaka answered. "None of the quad rugby players from any of the teams have so much as called. Only his coach has taken the time to pay his respects. But you're not one of the players, are you?" she asked Greg. "You're not a quadriplegic."

"No, I'm not," he answered. "I met Peter playing basketball."

Her head started to droop, but she corrected it, holding it up and straight ahead. She pursed her lips. "Peter was everything to me. After my husband died, even more so. I have nothing now."

I shot a glance at Ann in time to see her jaw stiffen at her mother's words. "You have Ann," I said, returning my attention to Mrs. Tanaka. "The two of you can be each other's strength in this tragic time."

Mrs. Tanaka didn't look at her daughter but straight at us when she answered. "Yes, I still have Ann."

"Mrs. Tanaka," Greg said, "did Peter have any girlfriends that you knew of?" He took a sip of the hot tea while he waited for the answer.

"He was very popular with women," Mrs. Tanaka answered, a very slight smile appearing momentarily on her lips. "More so before his accident, but still after."

"There's speculation," Greg continued, "that he was dating Miranda Henderson."

"A married woman? I doubt that. Not when he had so many other women around him." She took a delicate drink of her tea.

"But," I added, "we have reason to believe they knew each other beyond just the quad rugby connection."

At that point, Mrs. Tanaka did glance at Ann. "Tell them," she said to her daughter. "Tell them what you told the police."

Ann hesitated, looking ready to bolt instead of answering.

"Tell them," her mother ordered. "They need to know about their friend — what kind of person she was."

Ann took a deep breath and looked at us. "They did know each other, but not in the way you think. Miranda Henderson was a . . . a call girl."

"What?" came out of Greg with a loud snap, like a tree branch breaking in two. He put his teacup down on the table and leaned forward.

"So Peter was paying Miranda to sleep with him?" I asked, startled myself. I wasn't naïve; I knew a lot of men in wheelchairs paid escorts. Greg had even confessed to me that he had done it a couple of times when he was younger.

Ann shook her head. "No. But he found out and . . ." Her words drifted off.

"Tell them everything," her mother urged with sharpness. She put her tea down and I followed suit, worrying that if the news gave me another shock, I might slosh it.

After a hard swallow, Ann said, without

looking at us, "Peter found out about it and was blackmailing her. I heard him talking to her on the phone a few times and asked him about it. He told me he saw her working as a prostitute at a party he attended a few months ago."

"He admitted to you he was blackmailing Miranda Henderson?" I asked.

Ann said nothing but nodded in response.

Mrs. Tanaka squared her shoulders. "Like I said, my son was no angel, but you can see that the Henderson woman did have a very strong motive to murder him."

I kept my eyes on Ann. "You told this to the police?"

She nodded again.

Considering the timing of my conversation with Dev, I wondered if Dev had known about Ann Tanaka's allegations when he and I had spoken.

"Did the police tell you," I said to Ann, moving the conversation along, "that right before Rocky went after your brother, Peter said something to him to enrage him?"

"Yes," June Tanaka answered for her daughter. "They told us that, but they also said no one heard what Peter said to the man."

"I'm wondering," I continued, keeping to my train of thought, "if that's what Peter

263

told Rocky that made him go nuts. When Rocky confronted his wife, she took off."

"And," added Greg, "a friend of ours overheard Peter and Miranda fighting right before that game."

Ann's eyes met Greg's. "Someone heard them?"

"Yes, he was near Peter's van, but he couldn't tell what they were fighting about. He'd also seen them together before, talking at scrimmages."

"It still doesn't mean they were involved," snapped Mrs. Tanaka, finally showing some emotion, even if it was anger. "Or give that horrible woman the right to kill my son."

"We're still not saying Miranda killed Peter," I said with defiance. "We heard that he was selling drugs in Canada — maybe his criminal connections took him out. Miranda might have known something about it and ended up as collateral damage."

"This is not as open and shut as you might think, ladies," Greg said to the Tanaka women.

"My son did have some issues in Canada, but he left them there, I can assure you," Mrs. Tanaka said, her voice clipped and cold.

"That's not what we heard," said Greg. "We were told it was well known among the rugby players that he was the man with the drug connection."

Mrs. Tanaka stood up and signaled to her daughter with her eyes. Ann quickly gathered up the tea things and started to leave with them. Obviously, our cozy little chat was done.

I got to my feet. "May I use your powder room before we leave?"

"Follow Ann," Mrs. Tanaka said curtly. "She'll show you where it is." She turned to Greg. "You can wait for your wife here, then please leave." Mrs. Tanaka turned and, with head held erect, disappeared through an arched door in the opposite direction. A moment later, we heard a door shut.

"I'll be right back, honey," I said to Greg, then followed Ann.

She went through a formal dining room and into a large, well-lit kitchen with gleaming high-end fixtures and appliances. After placing the tea things on a counter, she gestured to a small corridor. "It's through that door to your right."

When I came out of the bathroom, I found Greg in the kitchen with Ann, clearly in defiance of his orders from Mrs. Tanaka. I gave them both a smile as I approached. Ann was at the sink, washing out the delicate teapot and cups. Greg had positioned his wheelchair near her but not so close as to appear intimidating. When he saw me, he said, "I just asked Ann what Peter did for work."

I looked at the young woman, waiting for her answer along with Greg.

"Nothing," she said quietly, her head bent over the sink. She put the last cup on a rack next to several sports bottles upended to dry.

"Those Peter's?" I asked, indicating the sports bottles.

"Some of them," Ann answered. "Some are mine. We liked the same type. I run long distance, marathons mostly."

"Did you fill them for him before games?" I asked. "Or did he fill them at the games?"

She stared at me with wide-eyed shock. "Are you asking if I poisoned my own brother?"

"No," I clarified. "I'm asking when did the bottles get filled with his sports drink last weekend, here or at the game?"

Her face relaxed. "Of course. I'm sorry I snapped at you. Everything has been so overwhelming." She took a deep breath. "As I told the police, generally we filled several bottles here before he left. We'd also fill up a two-and-a-half gallon cooler with water and add a large powder packet to it. He'd keep that jug in his van to refill his individual bottles as he needed it."

"Was he blackmailing anyone else that you know of?" Greg asked.

"Who knows," she said, her voice filled with exhaustion. She leaned against the sink. "As to how he supported himself, my father left him — the both of us — a lot of money when he died, but it's held in trust with my mother in charge of it until we turn thirty-two, which will be soon. Then all the money comes to us equally."

"The two of you get it at the same time?" I asked. "Are you twins?"

She nodded. "Yes, we are. He was the eldest by four minutes." She started to tear up. Grabbing the dish towel, she dabbed at her eyes before continuing. "Mother paid most of Peter's expenses and gave him an allowance, but she was very tightfisted with the funds. No matter how often Peter asked her for more, she refused."

"Is she just as stringent with your money?" I asked.

She gave me a wry smile, then said, keeping her voice low, "My expenses for college and grad school were paid for as long as I went to a school close by. Like Peter, I'm given a small monthly allowance stipulated by the trust, but not a dime more. I have a job now, but it's not enough to buy a place of my own."

"So you're still living here?" Greg asked.

She nodded. "Yes, until I get the trust money. After that, I'm leaving home and not looking back."

"Did Peter return to California when things got too hot for him with the drug charges?" I asked.

Ann hesitated, then sighed. "I might as well tell you since I told all this to the police." She swallowed, then continued. "Yes. That was part of the deal. Mother paid for his legal fees and got the charges dropped, but he had to return home. Otherwise he would have been on his own." She turned to look back out the window at the lights shimmering around the pool. "He should never have returned. I told him if he came back she'd mess with his head, but he didn't listen. If he had, he'd still be alive. But he was the crown prince — the center of the Tanaka universe. No matter what he did, Mother would protect him, and no matter where he went, she would always have a hold on him."

"Why are you telling us this, Ann?" Greg asked. "Just because you told the police, it doesn't mean you have to tell us."

"Because I want you to know who Peter

was or at least part of why he was who he was." She turned back around. "I loved my brother, but I know he's done bad things, even to me. He was arrogant enough before his accident, but after it his sense of entitlement became unbearable as Mother doted on him even more. I think in her heart she actually thinks Peter becoming a quad was a good thing. It made him more dependent on her. One of the reasons he went to Canada was to get away from her, or at least to cause her pain. The two of them had a sick codependence thing going on."

"And what about you?" I asked. "Where did you fit in?"

Another wry smile. "I was in the background, handmaiden for the two of them. I often got caught in the middle of their fights and pettiness."

She stopped and held her breath, listening. "You should leave. Mother will be angry if she hears us speaking."

We started to go, then I turned around. "One more question, Ann. Who gets Peter's half of the trust now that he's dead?"

She looked me straight in the eye when she answered, her head held high, and I saw her mother in her clear as day. "I do, and I think I've earned every single penny."

# NINETEEN

"I am beginning to see why Peter Tanaka battered women," I said once we were heading home.

"Ya think?" Greg shot at me as he turned the van onto the freeway's on-ramp. "That mother is a piece of work. If Ann doesn't leave that house soon, she might end up just like her — controlling and bitter."

"I think she's already there, honey. At least the bitter part."

Greg glanced at me. "Bitter enough to have poisoned Peter?"

I shrugged. "It certainly crossed my mind."

I plucked my cell phone out of my bag and hit speed dial.

"Who are you calling?" Greg asked.

"Dev." I put the phone on speaker. The sound of it ringing on the other end echoed in the van.

"Hi, Odelia," answered Dev after the

second ring.

"Hi back at ya," I replied. "Greg and I are in the van, but we have a few questions for you and didn't want to wait until tomorrow. Are you free to talk now?"

"Shoot," came the gravelly voice. "I'm home with my feet up and a beer in my hand. I have all the time in the world for you."

Greg and I exchanged smiles, both glad to hear our friend was getting some well-deserved down time.

"It seems that Miranda might have been a call girl," I told him. "Do you know anything about that?"

There was a long pause on the other end, then a deep sigh. "Yeah, I heard the same, and some of the items found in the car back up the possibility."

"Did you know this when we spoke this morning?"

"I did," Dev answered.

"Then why didn't you tell me?"

"We have no concrete proof, just some-one's say so and a few items that might or might not be used for professional reasons. If she was a pro, she might have been an independent, but Martinez is going to ask around to see if she worked with any known agencies. The amount of money hidden in the car suggests that whatever she was doing, it was at a high level."

Again Greg and I exchanged glances. "That's a delicate way of putting it," commented Greg.

"Hey," Dev said, "that's the facts. There was no sign of an agency or pimp, but that doesn't mean there wasn't one." Dev paused. "You must have been speaking with the Tanakas."

No sense denying it. "Yes," I told him. "We just left Peter's mother and sister. The sister said Peter was blackmailing Miranda about her activities."

"Looks that way from what Martinez has told me, although it's difficult to tell. It wouldn't have been for huge sums of money, and all transactions, like with drugs, would have been carried out in cash so there would be little to no paper trail. Martinez found a small gun vault in Tanaka's van with a lot of cash inside, including one envelope containing a thousand dollars. Miranda's fingerprints were on the envelope."

I looked out the windshield as an idea came to me. "That could be why she was in the van with Tanaka," I said into the phone. "Cory Seidman saw them together. She could have been giving Tanaka a payment. And while there, she might have handed him the water bottles that were already filled. That could be how her prints got on them."

I remembered what Ann said about the jug of sports drink. "Dev, was there also a large jug in the van containing the sports drink?"

"Yes, there was. It was the kind you take on picnics, with a spigot. According to Martinez, it also had poison in it, and Miranda's prints were on it too. She could have put the poison in, then made sure he refilled his single bottles with it."

"Or," I suggested, "maybe his sister put the poison in the jug and sent it off with him, and he only got to the poison when he refilled the next day."

There was silence while the three of us chewed on the information. I thought I heard Dev stifle a belch, but I wasn't sure.

Greg shook his head, not on board with my theory. "Tanaka would have used part of the contents of that jug on Saturday. If the poison was in it, he would have gotten it then. Most players stay overnight on Saturday in San Diego," he explained. "If that jug needed to be refilled on Sunday with a fresh batch, it would have been done at the hotel before Tanaka left for the game."

"So that leaves Ann off the hook," I noted.

"Was Tanaka able to fill it himself?" asked Dev.

"I'm not so sure about the jug because it would be heavy," Greg answered. "But once it was filled with water and placed in his van, he'd be able to mix in the drink powder and refill his single bottles himself. He was like Rocky — he had limited use of his hands but still decent function. But honestly, two-and-a-half gallons should have lasted him most of the weekend, especially if he supplemented his sports drink with drinking regular water."

"The timeline for Tanaka's hydration is the key here," Dev noted. "If he used any part of that jug before the final game, he would have died if the poison was in it already. That poison wasn't added until later, closer to the playoff game."

"Dev's right," Greg said, glancing my way. "The poison in the jug could only have been put in later in the day on Sunday."

"It still could have been Miranda," Dev noted. "She could have slipped the poison into the jug somewhere along the line. Besides Tanaka's, her prints were the only ones on the jug and the bottles."

"Not his sister's or his mother's?" Greg asked with surprise.

"Nope," Dev answered.

"Then who filled it and put it in the van for Tanaka?" asked Greg. "If it was done at home, it would have been one of the Tanaka women, and their prints would be on it. I'm thinking that whoever put the poison in there wiped the jug down good after, indicating that it was done before Tanaka and Miranda touched it — another reason I'm leaning toward Miranda not being the killer."

"By the way, how is Rocky? Do you know?" I asked.

"Still in a coma," Dev told us. "Doc still doesn't think he'll come out of it anytime soon, if at all. I went to the hospital today and met with Rocky's folks to tell them the outcome of the investigation. Nice people. I hate that part of my job. I'll never get used to it."

There was more silence, more this time out of respect for Rocky and his family.

"So who killed Miranda?" Greg finally asked, breaking the silence and not giving up on his train of thought.

"No one killed Miranda," Dev announced. "It was determined this afternoon that she committed suicide."

"How's that?" I held my breath, waiting for the next slap of news.

"The gun that fired the bullet that killed

her was found in the van on the floor by her body," Dev told us. "The gun was registered to Peter Tanaka. Martinez thinks Miranda took it from the van after giving him the poison."

"So her death is being considered a suicide too, like Rocky's shooting?" asked Greg.

"Looks that way."

"But how would she have been able to get into the lock box to get the gun?" Greg asked. "I doubt Tanaka gave her the key."

"Martinez said the box was found unlocked when they searched the van after Tanaka's death. Martinez and his people think that somehow Miranda got ahold of the gun when she gave Tanaka the payoff or went back for it."

"But even if Miranda went back to grab the gun after Rocky confronted her, and somehow got into the vault," I said, working through the theory as I talked, "wouldn't she have also grabbed the money, at least her own?"

"Were her fingerprints on the vault?" asked Greg, bombarding Dev with a question on the heels of mine.

"No mention of her prints being on the vault," Dev told us. "But they were on the gun. As for the money, if she intended to kill herself, she wouldn't be worrying about money."

Greg and I were speechless to the point we almost forgot about Dev being on the phone.

"You folks still there?" asked a voice from the phone in my hand.

"Yeah, Dev. We are," I told him. "We're just having a difficult time processing all of it. There's just too many pieces and loose ends to connect them cleanly."

"And no witnesses outside of Cory Seidman saying he heard Miranda and Tanaka arguing shortly before Tanaka died." We could hear Dev take a drink of something.

"The general consensus," Dev said, continuing, "is that Miranda Henderson was a working girl, and Peter Tanaka found out and was blackmailing her. She gave him a payoff and took the opportunity to slip something into his drink. She might have taken the gun while the vault was open and he was otherwise occupied or went back later and somehow got it open. Who knows, maybe Tanaka left her alone for a minute to take a whiz, giving her an opportunity. Or maybe he left his van open for her to leave the money and slip away, but instead she poisoned him and took the gun. Could be Tanaka didn't make sure the vault was locked tight before he went into the gym. The key to the vault was found among his stuff at the game."

"There seems to be a lot of loose ends, Dev," Greg said.

"I agree, but it's not my case, and the bulk of it is fitting together enough to consider it a murder-suicide. As for Ann Tanaka, her prints weren't found on the sport bottles or the jug or the vault. Believe me, after interviewing that family, Martinez had them on the short list of suspects, especially the sister."

"Because of the trust money she's due to inherit?" I asked.

Dev gave a soft chuckle. "I don't know why you're asking me questions you already know the answers to."

"Confirmation, Dev," I said.

"Well, you have it. The sister was looked into because of the money and because it came to light that Peter knocked her around from time to time, but she had an alibi for the timeframe and nothing to do with those water bottles."

"What?" This time the surprise came from Greg. "What about the mother — didn't she stop the battering?"

"More like covered it up for years. Started even before the accident that put him in the chair, though it does seem like it lessened as they got older. Martinez isn't sure if it continued after they were adults or not, but if it did, there isn't any evidence of it."

"Peter Tanaka was arrested for battering women in Canada," I told Dev. "So it is something he continued, maybe just not with his sister."

"Now how in the hell do you know that?" Dev asked. "No, never mind — I don't want to know. I know you have your special ways."

"It doesn't take a rocket scientist to pull up criminal records on Westlaw," I answered, not wanting him to know that Steele was helping with the research, although I'm sure he was thinking either Clark or Willie was helping. "I do work in a law firm, you know."

"Well," continued Dev, "according to Martinez, neither the mother nor the sister would discuss it beyond saying Peter had anger management issues and was getting help."

"Ann's comment about the trust is making sense now," Greg said.

"What comment?" asked Dev.

I held the phone closer to me. "When we asked Ann who would get Peter's share of the trust now that he's dead, she said she would and that she had earned it."

"That's really a screwed-up family," Greg shot in the direction of the phone. "More than most."

"Yeah, that's the sense I got from Martinez. I haven't had the pleasure myself."

"We're almost home," I told Dev. "We appreciate the update, even if it isn't good news."

"No problem. If I hear anything else I'll let you know, but really you two can back off. It looks like this is all on Miranda, and there's nothing you can do to change the facts."

When we got home it felt like the air had been let out of our tires, meaning mine and Greg's, not the van's. We were mentally and physically exhausted. We washed up and crawled into bed. Greg didn't even read or watch the news. I forgot to brush my teeth. When I realized I hadn't brushed them, I decided they wouldn't fall out overnight and turned off the light.

"Where do we go from here?" Greg asked in the darkness of our bedroom.

"Is there anywhere else to go?"

I felt him shrug under the covers. "How about we take tomorrow off from looking into this. Maybe some distance will help. We can go to the practice on Sunday. It might just be what Dev said — Miranda killed Peter and then herself. Just because we thought we knew her doesn't mean we did."

"Yes, you're probably right." I turned to face him. "Maybe I won't go into the office tomorrow. I'll just spend the day here getting caught up on some stuff."

"I thought Simon told you to take the rest of the week off."

"Not take it off, but take it to work on his project. Since I finished it so quickly, I really should look into my other work."

"Nah," Greg told me after giving me a goodnight kiss. "I say give Simon a call tomorrow with your update and call it a day. Maybe check in with Steele, but that's it."

# TWENTY

I followed my hubby's advice and took the day off. In the morning I took my usual walk with Wainwright to the beach and back. After Greg and Wainwright left for the office, I played with Muffin, getting in some rare one-on-one time with my furry baby girl. Then I picked up the house a bit, after which I placed the call to Simon Tobin on his private cell.

"Simon, it's me, Odelia Grey," I said starting out the conversation as if he couldn't read the display on his phone.

"You must have had quite a chat with Ms. Fox yesterday," he said instead of hello. His voice sounded pleased and surprised. "Did you threaten to have her killed if she didn't disappear?"

My heart nearly stopped. "Why?"

"My mother said Eudora went to the ladies' room, then returned to the table and excused herself, saying she didn't feel well.

When my mother called her last night, her phone number was no longer working."

"I found out that Eudora Fox and her company were fakes. She probably preys on other elderly people by bilking them out of their money."

"I'm not surprised," Simon said. "It's what I suspected."

"I confronted her when she went into the ladies' room and told her to back off your mother or I'd turn her in."

"I wish you had turned her in," he said. "Now she'll move on to other unsuspecting people."

I had to think quickly to come up with an excuse why I didn't call the authorities on Eudora Fox. *Um, because I didn't want to be found dead, shot execution-style.* Would Simon believe that?

Instead, I said, "I didn't want to cause a fuss and embarrass your mother, Simon. Calling the police might have put her back into the public's eye. I thought you wanted it handled discreetly."

"True, I did." He paused. "Excellent job, Odelia. You handled it perfectly. My mother was very concerned about Eudora. She was worried that she'd become very ill. She called Eudora's hotel this morning to see if they would look in on her, only to find out

283

that the woman had checked out yesterday afternoon."

"I'm sorry Mrs. Tobin got her feelings hurt and worried unnecessarily," I said, but silently I was applauding Elaine for not only sticking to her promise, but being so quick about it.

"Oh, don't worry about that," Simon said with a chuckle. "Today Mother is heading to the top spa in town to have her feelings massaged and her ego given a facial. By tomorrow she will have forgotten all about Eudora."

*Hmmm, rich people.* "I hope you don't mind, Simon, but although this matter is over, I'm not going into the office today. I have some personal things to take care of."

"As far as I'm concerned, you've earned it."

*Earned it* — the same words Ann Tanaka had used.

"I will be checking in on Steele a bit later to make sure he doesn't need anything."

"It's nice to see that you are as conscientious as I've been told." I could hear him smiling through the phone. "But don't worry about Mike. He called me this morning to say he would definitely be back on Monday. His speech was even much clearer today than yesterday."

The day with his buds must have done Steele a world of good. "Still, I'll give him a jingle," I told Tobin. "Just to make sure."

After saying goodbye to Simon, I showered and dressed, then called Steele. "How are you doing this morning?" I asked my boss.

"Not bad," he answered. Simon was right. Steele's voice was much improved. "I'm actually thinking of not doing a lick of work today."

"Are you still on drugs?"

He laughed. "Actually, Grey, I haven't had a pain pill since Wednesday night. I've just decided after everything to stop and smell the roses before I jump back into things on Monday. What about you? Are you still on that top-secret project for Simon Tobin?" The question was delivered with his signature sneer, letting me know the old Steele was indeed back.

"I finished it up yesterday and just called in a report to him on it. He gave me the day off."

"Nice. So you can spend time working on the Henderson matter. Do you have anything more for me to do?"

"Not right now. In fact, we've hit a bit of a brick wall." I brought him up to date on what Greg and I had found out at the Tanakas and on what Dev had told us.

"I know that's not what you wanted to hear, Grey, but it makes sense now that we know more about Miranda."

"Yeah, I guess it does," I said with reluctance.

"Why don't you just relax today. You and I will both have a lot to do in the office on Monday, and I'll expect you there bright and early."

"Okay," I said with less eagerness than he probably wanted to hear. "What's happening with your car?"

"I called the dealership yesterday morning and told them what I wanted as a replacement. They're bringing by the paperwork and dropping off the car sometime this weekend."

"The car dealership is coming to you?"

"Considering the money I've spent there over the past two decades, why not?"

*Why not, indeed?*

I hesitated, then jumped into the deep end. "Are you ready to tell me what happened in Perris?"

"Nope, and I probably never will."

"I can live with that, but just promise me this: stay out of Perris, California, in the future, will you?"

"No fears there, Grey. As far as I'm concerned, the place doesn't exist."

After talking with Steele, I moved on to my next call. It was to Jill to let her know I wouldn't be in until Monday.

"Sounds good to me," she said. "Steele called and said I was to gear up for a hurricane on Monday when he returns, and to get my butt in early."

"Yeah," I said, "he told me the same thing. How's Jolene doing? Is she still waddling around the office?"

"Sure is. I think she's determined to work right up until her water breaks."

I laughed. "Then you have your hands full today without me and Steele." I paused, remembering something. "I got another call from that Michelle Jeselnick this morning, but she still didn't leave a callback number. Still no luck on figuring out who she is?"

"None," Jill answered. "Maybe she'll get tired of getting voice mail and finally leave a number."

"Well, if she calls back, will you please give her my cell number, and tell the front desk to do the same?"

"Will do. Hey, do you think Steele would be able to eat bundt cake if I brought one in for him on Monday?"

"Steele loves your bundt cake. If his mouth isn't healed enough by Monday, he'll probably puree it in a blender so he can drink it."

After saying goodbye to Jill, I couldn't get Michelle Jeselnick out of my mind. Firing up my laptop, I went to my favorite people-finder website and searched for a Michelle Jeselnick in California. There were five listed for the whole state. As I read down the short list, one name jumped out at me like a jack-in-the-box: *Michelle Jeselnick, M.D. — Perris, California.*

A doctor? My first thought was that she was the doctor who treated Steele at the ER after his beating. But if so, why was she calling me? I knew I was one of Steele's emergency contacts. So were Jill and Marvin Dodd, one of his long-time pals. Except for some distant cousins somewhere in the Northwest, Steele didn't have any family. But Dr. Jeselnick had been trying to reach me for a couple of days, and I'd just spoken to Steele. He was not only holding his own but getting better each day. Then again, maybe Dr. Jeselnick wasn't the same Michelle Jeselnick trying to reach me. Maybe the fact that she was listed in Perris was just a coincidence.

In the back of my mind I heard Dev Frye's voice — *coinkydinks,* he called them, and he did not believe in them. But wasn't it a coincidence that Eudora Fox turned out to be

Elaine Powers and she was trying to put the squeeze on the mother of one of my bosses? Or was there some cosmic prankster up above having the last laugh and trying to make my life overly complicated?

No, this was not a coincidence. Whoever Michelle Jeselnick was, whether or not she was this doctor in Perris, she knew Mike Steele well enough to know my name. Well, there was only one way to find out. I'd call every Michelle Jeselnick on the list if I had to, but I was starting with the doc.

I called the number listed for Dr. Jeselnick. A professional voice answered, "Perris Pediatrics."

*Pediatrics?* Well, that made sense. Steele often acted like a child.

"Dr. Jeselnick, please," I said to the woman on the phone.

"Dr. Wesley or Dr. Michelle?" the receptionist asked.

"Excuse me?"

"Did you want Dr. Wesley Jeselnick or Dr. Michelle Jeselnick?" the woman clarified.

"Oh," I said, slightly taken back. I didn't expect to have a choice. "Dr. Michelle Jeselnick, please."

"Dr. Michelle is not in today. Is this an emergency? Perhaps Dr. Wesley can help you?"

"I'm actually returning Dr. Michelle's call," I told her. "We've been missing each other. May I leave a message?"

"Of course. She checks in regularly. Your name and number, please?"

I gave the woman my name and my cell phone number. "Please let her know I'm not in my office, so she should call my cell phone."

"I certainly will."

I looked at the rest of the Michelle Jeselnicks on the list. Should I start calling them or wait until the one in Perris called me back? I decided to wait, putting my money on hitting the jackpot with my first try. Next I called up Google and did an image search for photos of Dr. Michelle Jeselnick. There were a few. She was very attractive but not uncommonly beautiful, trim, and rather bookish behind fashionable glasses. Her honey-colored hair was worn shoulder-length. There were photos of her in running clothes participating in charity runs and photos of her with children in a hospital. In most of the photos she beamed with a warm, welcoming smile. She looked like someone I would like.

What I didn't like was waiting. I felt adrift and wished I'd gone into the office. I'd planned on spending today looking into the situation with Miranda and Peter, but it looked like that was coming to a close, even if not to my satisfaction. Looking around the house, I sighed. It wasn't like I didn't have things to do around the place, but I didn't want to do them. It was just past ten and I was restless, with the whole day before me like a yawning maw. Grabbing my car keys, I headed out the door, deciding to check on Mom's plants. Mom had emailed saying they'd arrived and reminding me to check her place. After, I'd go to the grocery store. I would be a good wife and make one of Greg's favorite meals for dinner, maybe even a key lime pie. He loved key lime pie. Well, he loved my mother's key lime pie. On the way to my car, I thought I might also start cleaning out my clothes closet. It needed attention in a big way. Greg always claimed I could clothe a small nation with the clothes I never wore, and he was probably right — if those people wore size 20. Or maybe they could cut them down and make two dresses out of one of mine. Either way, I really did need to start that project.

Following my plan, I stopped by Mom's and picked up her mail and checked the plants. She must have watered them right before she left because they didn't need it. I checked the fridge and disposed of any food that would go bad before Mom returned.

My mother's condo at the retirement place was cute and tidy. Before she'd moved in we'd painted the walls with soft but cheerful colors and hung new blinds. On various shelves and tables were photos of Clark's kids and grandkids at various ages. There was one particular photo that always tugged at my heart. It was of Clark and our deceased half brother Grady, both in their police uniforms. All three of us had had different fathers, yet Clark and I looked alike in the face. Grady, with his blond golden boy good looks, had resembled neither of us, making me wonder what his father had looked like. He was the man my mother had left with when she'd abandoned me as a teen.

There were two photos of Greg and me. One was a wedding photo that I'd given Mom after we'd reconnected. The other one was taken last Christmas with Wainwright and Muffin. And on the table next to her favorite chair was a photo of Seamus, our beloved elderly cat who died last November. Mom kept us all gathered around her. The only thing missing were photos of the three men who'd sired each of us kids, making it feel like we'd been dropped from the sky or were, in fact, delivered to Mom via a stork, with no human contact used in the process.

With nothing more to do, I took a deep breath and headed out the door. Maybe I could grab an early lunch at a cute café before heading to the grocery store. I was just about to lock up when my cell phone rang. I didn't recognize the number on the display.

"Hello," I said, after punching the answer button.

"Odelia Grey?" asked a woman.

"Yes, this is Odelia."

A big sigh of relief, followed by, "This is Dr. Jeselnick."

I took a seat in my mother's chair. "Are you the Michelle Jeselnick who has been trying to reach me?"

"One and the same," confessed the strong but pleasant voice.

"I looked up Michelle Jeselnicks in California," I told her, then followed it up with a lie just in case this had nothing to do with Steele's altercation in Perris. "I called them all. I've been out of the office, so I had to get creative when you didn't leave a call-back number."

"You didn't tell Mike about my calls, did you?" The confident voice suddenly sounded worried.

"No, I didn't. What is this about, Doctor?"

"I'm worried about him." She hesitated. "The last time I saw him, we didn't leave off very well between us, and now I can't reach him. Is he okay or just avoiding me?"

*Huh?* An attractive, active, and socially responsible lady doctor practicing in Perris. A woman Steele didn't tell us about and who, when he last saw her, presumably shortly before getting the crap beaten out of him, parted with something negative brewing between them. Steele's mysterious event was clearing in my brain like frost hitting a warm window.

"When was the last time you saw Mike Steele, Dr. Jeselnick?"

"Please call me Michelle," she told me. "I last saw Mike on Sunday morning. We had brunch at my parents' house, followed by a bit of an . . . well, an argument. He left abruptly."

The timeline certainly fit. "Do your parents live in Perris?"

"Why, yes, they do. Our medical practice is here, too. My father and I have a pediatric practice."

The question was, how much to tell Michelle? I made a quick decision. "I'm sorry to tell you that Steele was in a car accident on Sunday." I heard the sharp intake of breath on the other end. "Don't worry," I said quickly. "He's going to be fine. He's been at home recovering this week and hasn't been much for company or calls." Another lie. They were stacking up like cords of wood, but I didn't want to give away too much before I could talk to Steele.

"Oh my God!" Michelle said, clearly upset. "I need to go to him. I'm going over there right now."

"Hold your horses," I told her. "If he's not taking your calls, I'd suggest you wait a bit before showing up on his doorstep. Give him time to get better. Allow me to tell him you called and are concerned. I have a way with him." Another lie.

"Yes," she agreed after a pause. "That might be best. He does think the world of you."

*But not enough to tell me about you.*

I made it to Laguna Beach in record time, in spite of midday traffic.

"So," I said to Steele, standing over his recliner, with him trapped in it. "Who is Dr. Michelle Jeselnick, and why have you been hiding her away?"

"I'm not hiding anyone, Grey. I simply hadn't told you about her yet."

"More to the point," I pressed, "what does

she have to do with what happened to you in Perris?"

"She has nothing to do with my injuries."

"Bullshit, Steele. This woman is frantic with worry about you. She was about to land on your doorstep when I convinced her to let me talk to you first."

He shifted in his seat, the majority of his bruises now reduced to green and yellow. "Anyone ever tell you, Grey, that you have all the charm of a cement truck?"

"Actually, yes," I confessed. "But this isn't about me." I took a seat on the sofa close to him. "Listen, Steele, I'm sorry I'm coming on strong, but I'm worried about you. I'm worried about Michelle. She's very distraught."

"She's a she-devil," he spat out.

"Uh-huh. A she-devil — right. Someone so odious you went to Perris to have brunch with her parents. You almost never meet the parents of the women you date. My nose tells me this Michelle is someone pretty special."

He got up out of the chair and walked stiffly to the wet bar, where he poured orange juice into a squat crystal glass and took a sip. I noted he was no longer needing a straw or squeeze bottle to drink.

"What happened, Steele? Come on, talk to me."

"What did you tell Michelle?" He took another drink of juice, then offered me some. I shook my head, and he stashed the container back into the mini fridge.

"Our story that you were in a car accident. Then she started ranting and raving, saying it was all her fault." I eyed Steele. "Why would she think it's her fault? Is it because you two had a fight?"

"We didn't have a fight."

"Well, that woman — who, by the way, sounded lovely on the phone when she wasn't crying hysterically — said you two didn't leave off Sunday on the best of terms."

I got up and went to lean on the wet bar in front of him. "Let's recap, shall we? You went to brunch at her parents' house on Sunday. Something happened, and you stormed off and headed for the nearest dive bar, where you had a few drinks and provoked some Neanderthals into beating the crap out of you and your Porsche. So far, so good?"

"Don't you have a murder investigation to stick your big nose into?"

"Don't try to change the subject, Steele. Like it or not, you're important to me, and

I think it's important for you to face whatever this is, and the sooner the better. Or should I call Dr. Michelle and have her drop by with her stethoscope and rubber gloves?"

He put the glass down on the bar with a heavy thunk and turned to one of the bookshelves behind him. From a wooden box he took another box, a smaller one of velvet, and handed it to me. I opened it and gasped. Inside was a diamond engagement ring the size of a kiwi.

"I was lucky," Steele said, "that those goons didn't riffle my pockets when they were beating me and find that."

"You asked Michelle to marry you, and she got mad?"

"I asked Michelle to marry me, and she said no." He picked up his juice and returned to his recliner. "Happy now?"

"So you left in a huff," I said, still eyeing the rock, "drove to a bar, and behaved like a prize ass until you nearly got yourself killed?"

Without looking at me, he raised his glass in my direction. "That is an accurate statement."

Steele wasn't used to rejection, so I knew Michelle's refusal didn't go over well. He'd been married before — years before I knew him — but in all that time he'd never gotten that close to a woman again. At least not that I knew of. Greg and I often wondered if it was because he was afraid of being hurt. Date 'em and dump 'em before they could get close seemed to be his MO. He dated women he would never consider for the long haul or women who were unavailable, like married. But remembering the photos of Michelle Jeselnick, this made sense. His ex-wife, Karen, had been a woman of intellect, a lawyer with a social conscience, and although attractive, she was not a bombshell like most of the women he tended to date. Michelle was a lot like Karen in that regard. Steele might dally with fluffy women, but he fell in love with substantial ones.

I took my seat on the sofa again. Reaching over, I placed a hand on Steele's arm in comfort. "I'm sorry, Steele. Really, I am."

He didn't look at me, but he didn't shake off my touch either. His jaw was clenched and his eyes were shut tight. I thought for a moment he might cry.

"No matter what happened between you and Michelle," I told him in a gentle voice, "you need to at least call her and let her know you're going to be okay. She obviously cares about you a great deal and is worried sick." I put the ring box down on the end table.

"You know why she said no?" He opened his eyes and looked at me. When I didn't answer, he said, "Because she was afraid I'd never be faithful to her. She'd heard the stories about my catting around from mutual friends and said she couldn't trust me."

"You do cat around, Steele." When he started to protest, I held up a hand to stop him. "But if there's one thing I do know about you, it's that you're true blue and one-hundred-percent loyal to the people you love and care about. I have no doubt that if you love Michelle enough to want to marry her, you'll be as faithful as the day is long and then some. Michelle doesn't know that yet. When she does, she'll come around."

"We've been dating exclusively for almost a year. How long does it take for someone to learn that?"

"A year? Where have I been?" I paused as it came to me. "Wait a minute. Is Michelle the reason you unexpectedly dashed off to Switzerland for Christmas last year?"

He nodded and gave me a weak smile. "We met shortly before last Thanksgiving. When friends said they were skiing in Switzerland for the holidays and Michelle was going along, I finagled an invitation. I haven't thought of or dated anyone else since."

"Huh! Jill and I thought you weren't seeing anyone because you were so busy with work." I narrowed my eyes at him. "And just why did you keep Michelle a secret from us?"

"Because she was so special," he answered. "I didn't want to jinx it until it was a sure thing."

I picked up his cell phone from the side table and held it out to him. "Call her, Steele. Man up and call her. Tell her you're fine. Tell her she's not to blame for the accident. Tell her she has nothing to worry about. Tell her to call me for character references. Beg that woman to marry you or I'll do it for you."

He took the phone and gave a nervous laugh. "Okay, boss. I'll give it another shot, but if she says no again, I'm shaving my head and joining a religious cult."

I stood up. "If she says no again, then it's her loss, and you'll pick yourself up and get on with your life until you do meet the right one." I bent down, kissed my boss — no, not my boss, my long-time dear friend — on the forehead, and left.

# TWENTY-ONE

"So do you think he called her?" Greg asked me the next morning over breakfast.

"I think so," I said between bites of cereal. "I received a text very early this morning from Michelle. All it said was 'thank you,' in all caps."

Greg grinned. "Do you think the wedding will be soon or will it be a long engagement?"

"I'm betting soon. I'm thinking if she does change her mind about marrying him, Steele isn't going to let her have a chance to change her mind back."

"Mike Steele married," Greg said, more to his coffee than to me. "Hard to believe."

"Yes, honey. Our little boy is growing up."

Yesterday, on the way home from Steele's, I finally made it to the grocery store. When I got home I put a pot roast and veggies in the slow cooker and set about making that key lime pie — from scratch, no less. I even called my mother to see how she was doing and to get a couple of pointers on the pie. It was still early afternoon when I finished, even though I felt like I'd put in a full day.

After grabbing a quick peanut butter and jelly sandwich for lunch, I got down to tackling that closet. Pulling out one article of clothing at a time, I separated them into categories: keepers, charity donations, needs mending, and rags. The rags were just that — torn and threadbare favorite clothes that I wore around the house until they were so ragged they were indecent. I tossed most of them into a big cotton bag to be used when we needed rags for painting or in the garage or for other messy jobs around the house. My mother always had a rag bag when I was growing up, and it was a tradition I maintained when I got my first apartment. When I married Greg, he had laughed at the notion of a rag bag, but over the years he's gotten onboard with the old-fashioned concept and uses the rags quite often for his chores.

The hours flew by as song after song played on the radio. Muffin had made a bed out of the mending pile, and I didn't have the heart to shoo her off the clothes. When I finished, I was quite proud of my tidy closet and couldn't wait to show it off to

Greg. I showered and waited for him — a smile on my face and a fresh beer in my hand, ready to hand it to him when he came through the door — like any good 1950s housewife.

Over dinner we made a pact not to discuss anything about death of any kind. It had been on our mind for six days straight and we were mentally exhausted and needed to reconnect. After dinner, we made slow, sweet, selfish love.

The truce about murder and mayhem lasted throughout most of breakfast the next morning, but over the last of our coffee we talked about Rocky.

"I may go to the hospital today," I told Greg, "and see if there is anything I can do to help Rocky's parents. They must be exhausted."

"Good idea, sweetheart," Greg said. "Now that the San Diego police have determined Miranda's death to be a suicide, they might release the body soon for burial. I'm sure the Hendersons would appreciate some assistance with that, even if it's just letting friends know."

Since we'd been out of town the Saturday before, Greg was off to his shop so that Chris could have the day off. As a rule, they took turns working Saturdays to give each other a break and a full weekend. I had just kissed my husband and patted Wainwright goodbye when my cell phone rang. I didn't recognize the number.

"Hello," I answered, the greeting filled with curiosity.

"Put your sneakers on and take a walk," the voice ordered. "We need to talk."

I stopped breathing. It was Elaine Powers. "Talk about what?"

"Just get your ass out the door and to the beach, Odelia, and don't even think about calling your cop pal on me."

*I wouldn't dream of it.* "Where should I go?" I asked.

"Sit on one of the benches facing the ocean where you usually sit when you walk your dog," she directed.

"The dog isn't here."

"I know that. I just saw your husband leave."

The knowledge that Elaine Powers was watching my home tongue-tied me for a moment. "I'll be there in five minutes," I finally squeaked out.

I was still in my usual walking clothes — black stretch capri leggings and a tee shirt — since I'd taken Wainwright for a walk before breakfast. As I slipped back into my walking tennies, I thought about calling

Greg and telling him where I was heading. He'd go ballistic later if I didn't, but he would worry himself sick if I did it now. I was still contemplating the call as I shrugged on a light jacket and hit the sidewalk heading for the beach. Two seconds later, I returned to the house and rummaged through my tote bag to snag some cash and my ID, which I stuck in the pocket of my jacket along with my house keys. Just in case I wound up as fish bait, I wanted them to be able to identify my body. The cash was for a stiff drink in the event I needed one after my chat with Elaine.

I wasn't even back out the door when Greg called. "Hi, honey," I said tenuously, "I was just about to call you."

"I just heard from Lance," he said, his voice low and solemn. "No need to go to the hospital today, sweetheart. Rocky died in the middle of the night."

My heart sank as I staggered to the sofa to sit before my knees collapsed. "Oh, Greg" was all I could say before the tears started.

"We knew this was probably coming," Greg said. "I'm not at work yet. Should I turn around and come back to the house?"

"No, honey, there's nothing we can do except pace our living room at this point, so why don't you keep occupied at work." I swept away my grief long enough to remember that Elaine was waiting for me. "Besides, I'm meeting someone at the beach in a few minutes."

"Who?"

I swallowed hard and got up to fetch a tissue. "Elaine Powers."

"Mother?" he asked in a high pitch. "You're meeting Mother?"

"She called and said she needs to speak with me right now."

While I wiped my eyes and blew my nose, Greg ranted, "No way in hell are you meeting her!"

"I'll be fine, Greg," I assured him. "It's in a public place. I'll call you as soon as we're done so you'll know I'm okay."

"Don't go anywhere. I'm coming back."

"No, don't. And don't call anyone and tell them either. I really don't think she'd ever hurt me, but if she felt cornered or betrayed, my safety might be jeopardized; remember that." After ending the call with numerous promises to call Greg back as soon as possible, I hit the trail for the beach.

I didn't see Elaine when I got there. Even though it was a Saturday, there was almost no one at the beach and just a few strolling the pier. It was cool today, and the air was heavy with the possibility of rain. I pulled my jacket tighter around me and walked to one of the benches at the edge of the grassy area. Directly in front of me was the parking lot. Just beyond that was the sand and sea. To my right was the pier. After making sure the bench was dry, I sat down and waited. I fought the urge to look anxiously around by concentrating on the waves, using their ebb and flow to calm my nerves and soothe my grief over Rocky.

"Morning, Odelia."

I looked up at the familiar voice to find Elaine standing there with two steaming cups of coffee. She handed one to me.

"Thanks," I said with some hesitation.

"Don't worry," she chuckled. "It's not poisoned." She was dressed in jeans, a white turtleneck jersey, and a blue jacket, and she looked more like her old self than she had when I'd last seen her at Bouchon. Out of the pocket of her jacket she produced some powdered creamer and sugar packets. "I didn't know how you take it."

"Black is fine," I told her. "I only like sugar and cream in iced coffee."

"I'll remember that for next time," she said dryly as she sat down next to me.

I smelled the hot brew, which I knew from the logo on the cup came from my favorite local coffee shop. "Thanks." I took a sip but didn't look at her.

"You look like shit," she announced, staring at me.

I wiped a still-wet eye with the back of one hand. "Greg just called to say that our friend Rocky died."

"I'm sorry to hear that," Elaine said in a voice that sounded sincere, "but in a way that ties in with what I want to talk to you about. I have some information on your friend's murder."

"Miranda?" I asked.

"You have any other murdered friends at the moment?" Mother's voice was calm and sober, even if her words were sarcastic.

I shook my head. "We were told that the police are considering Miranda's death a suicide. They said the evidence points to her shooting herself, just like her husband. A murder-suicide is how they see the whole thing with Peter Tanaka and Miranda Henderson."

"That's not what I hear."

I snapped my head in her direction and sniffed. "It was a hit after all?" I pulled tissue from my jacket pocket and wiped my runny nose.

"I'm not sure if it was a professional hit," Mother said, "but someone killed that woman."

"So you think the police are covering it up?"

"No," she said between sips of her coffee. "They just aren't asking the right questions of the right people."

I shook my head to clear it and looked at her. "So why are you asking the right questions — or any questions?"

"For selfish reasons," she answered, her eyes moving, shifting, and combing the area for any threats to her safety. "If it was a hit and not mine, I wanted to know which of my competition was involved. My people poked around and found out none of the usual crews knew anything about it. Other poking around discovered that it was not drug related."

"So it was a suicide."

"No." She shook her head. "It wasn't. One of my people found a witness who saw it."

I stared at her slack-jawed. "A witness? Why didn't this witness come forward during the police investigation?"

Elaine looked at me like I was short on brain cells. "People have all kinds of reasons not to go to the police, Odelia." She took several big gulps of her coffee, draining it, and stood up. "Come on, we're going on a field trip." She tossed her empty cup into a nearby trash can.

"A field trip?"

"You got wax in your ears, Grey?"

Hearing her call me Grey reminded me of Steele, and I wondered what was happening with him and Michelle. I had to think about them. I couldn't think about going anywhere with Elaine Powers, a killer and a fugitive. If I did, I'd collapse in fear.

"But I can't. Greg will be worried." I hesitated. "He knows I was meeting you." I readied myself for a barrage of threats, but none came.

Instead, she smiled. "Glad to hear you're smart enough to tell someone, but I hope he's smart enough to keep his trap shut."

*Me too.*

"He is," I assured her. I seemed to be assuring everyone but me.

"Give him a call and let him know you're chasing a lead and you'll call him back later."

Pulling my cell out of my jacket pocket, I called Greg. While it rang, I tried out several upbeat explanations for my losing my mind and getting in a vehicle with Elaine. "Hi, honey," I said when he finally picked up after several rings.

"Sorry, sweetheart," he explained. "I left my phone on my desk while I was in the workshop. Is your meeting over?"

"Not exactly." I paused. "Elaine just gave me a hot lead on Miranda's death. She says she has a witness who knows it's not a suicide." I paused again. "Um, I'm going with her to check it out."

When Greg let loose with a flood of swearing, I pulled the phone from my ear. His tirade was loud enough for Elaine to hear it without the benefit of the speaker feature. She held out a hand for the phone. I grasped it tighter, worried she'd toss it into the trash and really send Greg into a fit of worry. She wiggled her fingers, indicating to hand it over. With reluctance, I did.

"Greg," she said into the phone. "This is Elaine." He must have screamed louder because she held the phone away from her own ear for a second or two. "Greg, calm down before you have a stroke. I mean it," she said in the voice of a parent running out of patience. "Calm down or I'm hanging up."

He must have finally quieted down because Elaine's face softened and I couldn't hear him yelling anymore.

"That's better," she told him. "Now here's how this works. You listening?"

He must have said yes because Elaine continued. "Odelia and I are going on a drive to meet the witness. For obvious reasons, I can't go to the police with the information, and I'm sure the witness won't either. If you want your friend's murder to be solved, you'll have to trust me."

She stopped and listened. I was dancing from foot to foot, wanting to hear what was going on.

Finally, she looked me directly in the eye and said into the phone, "Because she reminds me of my dead sister."

# TWENTY-TWO

We were driving south on the 405 Freeway in an older white SUV. Elaine was at the wheel; I was riding shotgun. Since we left the beach she hadn't said much to me except to say no when I asked if we could swing by my house so I could pick up my purse and change into something else. I also didn't have on any makeup and hadn't even taken the time to brush my hair before leaving the house.

For miles I watched the familiar scenery of Orange County fly by. Shortly we would be at the intersection where the 405 melted into the southbound 5 Freeway, also known as the San Diego Freeway. That meant we were almost to Lake Forest.

"Are we heading to San Diego?" I asked.

"Considering that's where the crime scene is," Elaine answered, not taking her eyes off the road, "don't you think that's where the witness will be?"

"Not necessarily," I said. "They could be anywhere."

"But they're not," she said curtly.

I looked straight ahead and sniffed. "You could have at least let me say goodbye to my husband." After speaking with Greg, Elaine had shut off my phone and pocketed it. She still had it.

"You can call him when we're done." She glanced over at me and smiled. "And if you're a good girl, I might even take you for ice cream after."

"Just get me home and I'll be happy," I told her, not one bit amused. "We have ice cream in the freezer."

We rode along a few more miles in silence. When we reached San Clemente city limits, I said, "We need to stop and find a ladies' room." When Elaine looked at me with raised brows, I added, "I've had several cups of coffee this morning. It's running right through me."

"Yeah, me too," she admitted after some thought. "It's a bitch getting old. It's more of a bitch when your bladder gets old."

"Tell me about it," I said with a little chuckle. "Do you pee when you sneeze?"

"Sneeze, cough, laugh, yawn — hell, even when I think too loudly."

We looked at each other, and Elaine gave

me a genuine smile.

After putting on her turn signal, Elaine moved the SUV into the far right lane and took the first exit we came upon. We pulled into a fast food restaurant right off the exit and went inside together to use their restroom. In less than ten minutes we were back on the road — Elaine with another coffee, me with a bottle of water.

"You need to pee again," she told me, looking at the water, "you can just do in your pants. Pretend you sneezed."

After a few more miles, I asked, "So I remind you of your sister?"

She was silent until we hit Carlsbad. "Yes," she finally said. "You do."

"Do I look like her?"

She looked at me, then shook her head. "Not much, but your personality is a lot like hers." With her right hand, she picked up her coffee from the cup holder and took a long pull. "Her name was Dottie. She was short and squat, like you, and just as pigheaded and stubborn. Always going headfirst into messes without a thought to her own safety." She took another slug of coffee. "Like you, she was a fixer."

"A fixer? On TV that's someone who cleans up after the rich and famous when they've screwed up."

Elaine smiled to herself. "In her case, and in yours, it's someone who's trying to make things right. You know, hell-bent on justice at all costs. In the end, it's what killed her." She turned to me, her face dark. "I don't want that to happen to you."

I took a deep breath. "How did she die?"

"Do you remember that big scar on my right side?"

"Yes," I answered, remembering the long, ugly scar I saw when I'd once seen her naked. "You said your husband gave it to you with a saw or something."

"Yes," Elaine replied, her voice dull with matter-of-factness. "It was a hacksaw."

"And later you killed him for doing it, right?"

She took a deep breath. "Yes, but what I didn't tell you is that Dottie was in the house when the fight started between me and my husband. After he sliced me open the first time, he tried again, hell-bent on killing me once and for all. Dottie got between us, and he caught her across the neck with the saw. He took off once he saw what he'd done. I survived; Dottie didn't. I caught up with the bastard a year later."

I was speechless for a full minute. "I'm very sorry, Elaine. That's truly horrible and tragic. But trust me, I'm no hero like that."

"You killed someone once, didn't you?"

I looked at her with surprise. "You know about that?"

She nodded. "I did my homework after we first met. I heard you saved your life and someone else's by putting a bullet into an attacker. The life you saved was Willie Proctor's right-hand man. No wonder he's so loyal to you." She glanced at me again. "And yet you still go after killers armed with only your wit and dumb luck." She paused. "I know you'd pull that trigger again if you had to. You're a gutsy lady, Odelia Grey, just like Dottie, but one day you'll pay for always being on the side of what's right."

Borrowed time, that's what Dev called it.

Again, we rode along in silence until I broke it. "Do you have any children, Elaine?"

"No," she answered. "And considering my lifestyle, that's a good thing."

Entering San Diego, we stayed on the 5, then merged onto the 94, finally exiting a few miles later. The further we drove, the more poor and unkempt the neighborhoods became until we finally pulled up in front of single-story stucco house with faded turquoise paint surrounded by a chain-link fence with a broken gate. The yard was mostly dirt with brown scruffs of grass and littered with dirty toys. In the driveway were a couple of old cars, one obviously not in working condition. The other houses in the neighborhood looked about the same.

Elaine pulled out her cell phone and made a call. "We're here," she said into the phone. She listened, then said, "Got it." Opening her door, she got out of the SUV. "Come on," she told me.

As soon as we were out of the vehicle, the front door opened and a figure emerged. It was a small woman wearing all black. She was toting a gun, held down close to her thigh. Recognizing her, I held my breath.

"You remember Lisa, don't you?" asked Elaine as we walked up the cracked sidewalk.

I did, and it wasn't from book club. The last time I'd seen the petite gunslinger, she'd just killed someone. "Yes, I do." I looked at her and the gun with wariness. Lisa hadn't liked me when we'd met, and from the look on her face, she hadn't changed her opinion.

"Where are they?" Mother asked Lisa.

"In the back," Lisa answered, indicating for us to enter. Elaine went first, then me. As I passed, I felt Lisa's cold killer eyes on me. She brought up the rear — the caboose toting firepower.

We entered the house, which was dark due to most of the curtains being drawn. It was tidier inside than out. Toys were stacked neatly in a corner of the living room, newspapers and magazines were in order on the battered coffee table, furniture was dusted, and the thin carpet looked newly vacuumed. In spite of the poverty of the place, someone was taking pride in its cleanliness. My nose caught the aroma of something savory and yummy coming from the kitchen.

The three of us made our way through the kitchen single file, like ducklings crossing a road. A thick-set older woman with brown skin and long gray hair pulled back at her neck was stirring something in a big pot on the stove. She was wearing an old-fashioned house dress and apron. She nodded to us without smiling and went back to her work. On the kitchen table, boxes of cereal were lined up like soldiers next to a big bowl of bananas, apples, and oranges. Freshly washed bowls, glasses, and mugs were drying in a rack next to the sink. Even with its worn linoleum and ancient appliances, the kitchen was homey and well-tended.

Lisa had stashed her gun and now led the way into the back yard, where a man was seated at a plastic table reading a newspaper, a coffee mug in front of him. A woman sat at the table next to him. She was young and wore worry like an ill-fitting suit. She never took her eyes off a boy kicking a ball around the yard. The boy was thin but sturdy and looked about eight or nine.

Seeing us come through the back door, the man put down the paper, took off his reading glasses, and got to his feet. He was nearly six feet tall and slender. He smiled at us, his face lined, his eyes dark with concern but not hostile in any way. He shook my hand and Elaine's, but no names were exchanged. When I offered mine, he smiled politely but still did not offer his or that of the woman with him. I took the hint.

"Carlos," he called to the boy once we were all seated — all except for Lisa. She stood behind me and Elaine, her feet planted military style, keeping watch.

The boy stopped playing and jogged to the table. The man said something to him in Spanish and pointed at us. Carlos went to the woman's side, his dark eyes round with fear. The man said something again to the boy and the boy relaxed a bit, but the woman, who I assumed was his mother, did not.

Then it dawned on me — the boy was the witness. He was the one who'd seen Miranda murdered. I closed my eyes tight, wishing it were not so for his sake.

The interview was conducted with the man acting as interpreter, translating our questions and the boy's answers.

"He heard a shot," the man told us, going over the story again to sum it up. "Then someone hopped out of the van and took off running."

"Can he tell us more about the person who fled?" I asked.

"It was either a small man or a woman, thin and possibly white, dressed in jeans and sweatshirt." He turned to the boy and asked him something. The boy responded. Turning back to us, the man relayed, "He said he didn't see the face, but the sweatshirt was gray with a hood, baggy and long."

The boy pantomimed something, accompanied by a barrage of words in Spanish. He was becoming more relaxed with the telling. The man said to us, "He says the hood was up, covering the head and the face."

"I understand," I said, "that the van was behind an old, abandoned warehouse. How did this little boy see it?"

The man and Elaine exchanged glances, then Elaine nodded to him as if giving him a green light. "You can tell her. She's okay."

"Carlos and his mother were in the area . . . traveling . . . and stopped for a bit at the warehouse to rest. Carlos was a bad boy." Here the man looked at Carlos, who obviously knew enough English to hang his head at the words. "He slipped out, and that's when he saw what happened."

"But what were they doing down there?" I asked, confused. "I understand that area can be dangerous."

Behind me I heard Lisa say half under her breath, "Dumber than a box of rocks."

Elaine shot Lisa a stern look, and she went back to being a sphinx.

When the answer occurred to me, I did feel dumber than a box of rocks. "They're illegal." I said it softly, as if someone might have the place bugged.

"Yes," answered the man. "Carlos's father is deceased. They were being helped across the border, and that warehouse was a stopping place until they could be brought here. They are on their way to join family in the Central Valley."

"Of course, and that's why they can't go to the police," I said, more to confirm it for myself.

"My home is a safe house until people crossing the border can be united with family members," the man told me, locking his dark eyes onto mine. "If you tell anyone, you will put many in jeopardy, including my own wife and children."

I nodded my understanding. "You have no worries here. You and this place are already erased from my memory."

When driving south in Southern California you can always tell when you are getting close to the Mexican border. Along the highway are yellow caution signs depicting a family of three — dad, mom, and child, with mom holding the child's hand — running across the highway. Californians, including me, make a lot of jokes about those signs, but to the people running they are no joking matter. Many illegals have been struck and killed while running for a better life. Now Carlos and his mother had another worry. Depending on who killed Miranda Henderson, they may be running for a different reason.

I reached out and touched the young woman's arm and gave her a smile that I hoped conveyed assurances that I was no snitch and understood her plight. She gave me a shy, tight-lipped smile in return.

The man said something to her. She looked at me with sadness and said something in Spanish, pulling her son closer to her. "I told her," the man said, "that you were a friend of the woman who died in that van. She said she is very sorry, but her son cannot help you."

"He's already helped a great deal," I said to the woman. The man translated my words to her.

*"Muchas gracias,"* I said to her and smiled. Reaching into my pocket, I pulled out the cash I'd taken from my wallet before meeting Elaine. It wasn't much — about thirty dollars. I held it out to her. *"Por favor."*

She looked at but didn't touch the money. She turned to the man. He smiled and said something. Quickly the cash disappeared from my hand into one of her pockets. *"Gracias,"* she said to me and looked down.

I looked at the man. "What else can we do for her and the boy?"

"That's been taken care of," Elaine said to me. "We're giving her and Carlos a lift to her family. They're leaving with us right now."

*"Bueno,"* I said and smiled at the boy and his mother.

With Carlos and his mother packed into the back seat of the SUV along with their meager belongings, Elaine and I left, but instead of heading for the 5, she took a smaller, less-traveled highway north. Lisa was riding a motorcycle behind us.

"How did you find Carlos?" I asked Elaine in a quiet voice.

"My people asked questions about the van and the shooting. One thing led to another and eventually to him."

"But if you found them, so could the police."

"Like I told you, the cops weren't asking the right people," she said. "My people went into the shadows, asking people who would never tell anything to the police." She paused, then added, "Somebody always knows what happened, Odelia. You just have to know where to ask and have the right credentials to gain access to those people and their trust."

I thought about Willie and how he could magically conjure up information authorities would take weeks or even months to discover.

"Does the description of the killer sound like anyone you know?" I asked.

"Nope," Elaine answered. "That was a pretty general description, but I'm confident it wasn't a professional hit or a random crime. Mark my words: that was personal. Your friend Miranda probably knew her killer. But at least now you know it wasn't a suicide."

"But I can't go to the police with what

I've just found out. They'd never let up on wanting to know how I learned it."

"True." She looked at me. "I have faith that you and that good-looking husband of yours will figure out a way to ferret out the killer without jeopardizing innocent people. If I didn't, I would never have taken you there today." She laughed. "Lisa may think you're dumber than a box of rocks, but I know better."

After several miles, Elaine pulled into the parking lot of a small strip mall and parked on the far end. Lisa pulled in behind us and waited.

Pulling out my cell phone, she handed it to me. "Get out and call someone to come get you," she told me. "You can't come with us, and I can't risk driving on the 5 with them, especially with that checkpoint just north of here."

I looked over my shoulder at the back seat. Carlos was playing with some action figures while his mother looked anxiously out the window. I knew she wouldn't relax until she reached her family.

"I want to argue with you," I said to Elaine, "but I know you're right." I looked into her eyes. "Thanks for everything — not just for what you've done for me, but for what you're doing for them." I jerked my chin toward the back seat.

She gave me a half grin. "Just stay out of my business in the future, okay? I'm getting used to doing you favors, and that's not good for my reputation." She pulled a five-dollar bill out of the middle console and handed it to me. "I know you gave them all your cash, so here — buy yourself a cup of coffee while you wait. If you go to that fast food place over there, you might even be able to buy yourself lunch."

While I watched, the SUV exited the parking lot, with Lisa guarding the rear. I fired up my cell and called Greg. Before I could even say hello, he was all over me. "Where are you, and are you okay?" His voice was high pitched with worry and stretched to breaking.

"I'm fine, honey," I assured him. "But I need a lift."

# TWENTY-THREE

When Greg's van pulled into the parking lot of the burger joint ninety minutes later, I almost leapt into it before it had come to a complete stop. We'd been in touch by phone during his drive, but I'd refused to discuss what'd I learned until I saw him in person. Instead, I used the time to grab an iced tea and think about who might have killed Miranda. Borrowing a pen from the girl at the counter, I scribbled notes and possible suspects on a bunch of napkins while I waited for my honey.

"I'm sorry I pulled you away from work," I said to Greg after giving him a hard kiss on the mouth and patting the dog. I was so happy to see the two of them.

"I wasn't getting much done worrying about you," he said, his voice strained. "Besides, it was kind of quiet today."

He didn't make any attempt to put the van into gear and leave. Instead, Greg stared out the windshield, his jaw taut, and I knew I was about to get an earful. "You nearly gave me a heart attack today, Odelia," he finally said, straining to keep his voice even. "What were you thinking, meeting that woman like that?"

"She said she had information about Miranda's death, Greg. And I really didn't think she'd hurt me." I paused. "She says I remind her of her sister."

"Yeah, that's what she told me when I asked her why she was helping." He looked at me. "Do you believe her?"

"Yes," I said, then told him about Dottie.

"It explains a lot about the woman, doesn't it?" he finally said after thinking about what I'd just told him. "But most people still wouldn't turn into contract killers. You have to be pretty bent to do that."

After another moment, he put the van in gear and asked, "You hungry? Or did you eat lunch while you waited?"

I shook my head. "Just an iced tea." I looked at the clock on the dashboard. "You can drop me off at home," I told him, "then head back to work. No sense you losing a whole day because of me."

"It's really okay, Odelia. I told Emily to close up if I don't come back."

"Then let's grab something, and I'll tell

you what I learned."

After consideration, we decided to eat closer to home and headed for The Gull in Huntington Beach. It was a café on Pacific Coast Highway across the street from the beach. It was also the place where Greg and I had had our first meal together. We still frequented it. I didn't know if he suggested it today out of sentimentality or because it was close to his business and he could check up on things on the way home. Emily could close up, but Greg would feel more comfortable if either he or Chris battened down the hatches for the evening.

"So who do you think the killer is?" he asked after I filled him in during the hour-and-a-half drive back to our neck of the woods.

"I'm still not sure. Elaine thinks that it was not drug related. She thinks it's personal and that Miranda might have known her killer."

"How about that sister of his?" Greg asked. "She could pass for a small man."

"I thought about her, then remembered Dev saying that the police had looked into her already — she had an alibi for that day."

"They were wrong about how Miranda died. Maybe they're wrong about Ann Tanaka."

"But she wasn't at the tournament, so she wouldn't have been anywhere near Tanaka's drinks that day."

"By the way," Greg said, "I heard from Rob Rios, the coach of the Vipers."

That got my attention.

"He confirmed," Greg continued, "that Peter usually brought and drank his own sports drink during games and practices, sometimes supplementing it with water supplied by the team but always using his own drinking bottles."

"Who filled them for Tanaka?"

"Coach Rios said Tanaka usually brought a few pre-filled bottles and if he ran out, he refilled them himself from a larger jug in his van."

"Which we already knew."

I looked out the window, watching scenery fly by that I'd watched going in the opposite direction just a few hours earlier. "So both Ann and June Tanaka would have had access to the jug and water bottles, but not on the last day of the tournament."

"The mother is definitely on my list," Greg said dryly. "I'd bet if both Ann and Peter are out of the way, she'd get all their money. She could have hired someone to put the poison in the jug."

I shivered. "I know mothers have been

known to kill their kids before, but she seemed obsessed with Peter. It's hard to believe she'd remove him from her life permanently, considering she was having trouble cutting the apron strings. Besides, Dev said Martinez looked into both of them."

"If they're clean, then my money is on someone else Tanaka might have been blackmailing, and Miranda got in the middle of it somehow."

"That's a good possibility, honey, but he could have been blackmailing most anyone. Maybe we can ask some of the players to-morrow."

Greg nodded his agreement, then said, "I found out something else from Coach Rios."

Again I looked at my husband with inter-est.

"Seems he and many of the players weren't happy with Tanaka's unsportsman-like behavior during the tournament. Rios told me he was going to call a team meeting to vote him off the Vipers."

"Maybe one of his teammates took things into their own hands."

"Could be, but when I asked how Tanaka got along with the other Vipers, Rios said in general Tanaka was well liked and made an effort to get along, almost like he was trying hard to make it work."

I snorted. "Tanaka probably realized if he failed on the Vipers, he'd have a lot of trouble playing for any team again."

"He did love the sport," Greg commented. "Not being able to play would have really been a big blow to him. He would have to move someplace that had a team where he wasn't well known."

Still holding my cell phone, I scrolled through the photos taken last weekend. Tears welled in my eyes when I reached one in particular.

"What's the matter, sweetheart?"

I sniffed back the tears. "I was just looking through photos from last weekend." I showed him the one that had stopped me cold. It was of Miranda and Rocky together, smiling for the camera. "It's so difficult to believe that they are both gone in such a short time."

Greg reached over and patted my knee softly. "I know, sweetheart."

Lunch was great, if somber. We both wolfed down burgers and sweet potato fries along with cold beer. After, we sat sipping espresso while holding hands and watching the ocean across the street. It was chilly outside, but we'd opted for dining on their patio near one of their outdoor heaters so we could do just this and so we wouldn't have to leave Wainwright in the van. The loyal dog was currently sleeping under our table.

Our peace and quiet was short-lived when Greg's phone rang. "I'll bet that's the shop," I said, with the realization that our slice of quiet was coming to an end.

"It's not the shop's number," he said, looking at the display. "It's Lance." He answered and soon after said, "See you soon."

When the call ended, Greg paid the check. "Lance wants to talk. He's coming to the shop around closing time," he told me. "Do you want to go home or sit in on the meeting? I'm sure he won't mind, but I know you're exhausted."

Exhausted, still not showered, and wearing my morning walking getup, I felt grimy and disgusting but said, "Wild horses couldn't keep me away."

Greg winked at me. "I knew you'd say that."

Ocean Breeze Graphics closed at four on Saturdays. I holed up in Greg's office until then, playing with my scribbled notes and trying to fit together the pieces while Greg finished his workday.

Another possibility that came to my mind

was that Miranda was killed by whoever handled her call-girl bookings. Dev had told us that the evidence had suggested she worked alone, but if that was true, how did she make contact with potential clients? Prior clients could be booked as repeat business, but what about the marketing end of things for new clients? I wrote *contacts?* under Miranda's name on the sheet I was scribbling on. She might have been killed by her competition or by the competition's handlers. But if so, who killed Peter Tanaka, and were the two deaths connected? Maybe someone was watching Miranda, looking for a chance to find her alone and vulnerable. After fleeing the game, she might have been distracted long enough for someone to stalk and kill her.

Around four o'clock Greg wheeled into his office with Lance Henderson. He looked even more haggard than he had when we'd last seen him a few days before. I got up and went to him, giving him a warm hug. "I'm so sorry," I said in a soft voice.

He hugged me back. "Thanks, Odelia. And thanks for letting me come by. I wanted to talk to you guys and needed to get out of the house for a bit."

"Take a seat, Lance," I told him, indicating one of the chairs Greg kept for visitors.

I took the other. "How are your parents doing?"

"As well as can be expected," Lance said, running a hand over the stubble on his face. He looked like he hadn't shaved or showered in a week. "My mom had to be sedated after Rocky died. My dad just stares into space. You know, after Rocky survived his accident, the last thing they expected was for him to die like this."

There was a moment of silence, then Greg asked, "Can I get you something, Lance? I have some beer, soft drinks, and water."

"No, thanks," Lance said. He fidgeted, then asked, "Have you heard that they've ruled Miranda's death a suicide too?"

"Yes," I told him, "but we're still not sure that's true." I didn't want to tell him about what Carlos had seen, at least not yet. I exchanged looks with Greg, noticing he seemed to be on the same page. "We both have a gut feeling something's missing."

"Yeah, me too," Lance said, looking down at his shoes. "Like maybe why she was working as a hooker?" He looked up. "That just about killed my folks when they found out. All this has been way beyond their understanding."

"What about *your* understanding?" Greg asked. "I'm sure the cops told you they found a stash of money and travel information in Miranda's car, along with suitcases of expensive, flashy clothing."

"I knew Rocky and Miranda were having a rough time of it and had been for a while," he told us. "Rocky's business was failing. He was moving heaven and earth to keep it afloat."

"We heard that," Greg said. "He had asked to speak with me after the tournament, but we never got the chance. Do you think it was about that?"

"Yeah, it was," Lance said. "I had suggested that he pick your brain for advice since you've been so successful with Ocean Breeze."

I had a delicate question to ask and swallowed before voicing it. "Do you think Rocky knew anything about Miranda's side business? Maybe she was doing it to get them over their financial problems."

"No way," answered Lance. "I know he'd asked her to try to pick up more hours at the dental office or to find another job with more hours, but she never did." He looked at each of us. "Did you know that they separated several months back?"

"No," I answered for the both of us.

"It didn't last long, but it was longer than the other times," Lance told us. "They'd actually split up several times before, just for a few weeks at a time, but kept getting back together. They kept it pretty quiet; even my folks didn't know. I kept telling Rocky that Miranda was no good for him, but he loved her and kept taking her back."

"What was the problem?" Greg asked.

"Miranda was never satisfied," Lance said. "She was always wanting bigger and better. They got underwater in their house because she wanted a fancier place than they could afford. They were about to lose it when this happened. They were going to move in with me until they got back on their feet. I'll bet Miranda was going to leave before that ever happened. It would be like her to cut and run when Rocky needed her most. Even my mother told him before he married her that she thought Miranda was immature." Lance ran a hand through his hair. "Hell, from what the cops told me, the money she had stashed in her car would have been enough to keep the wolves from their door. She must have been working on her back a long time and saving almost every penny. But did she give any of that to help my brother? Not a damn cent that I knew of."

It occurred to me that maybe losing Miranda wasn't Rocky's only reason for wanting to check out. His business and his marriage were failing. He was losing his home, and Peter Tanaka had probably landed the final blow by telling him his wife was a call girl. I shut my eyes, thinking of all the pain and stress Rocky was shouldering in silence.

"Did you know that Peter Tanaka was blackmailing Miranda?" Greg asked.

He nodded. "The police told me they think that was the case. Their theory is that Miranda had arranged to meet Tanaka at his van between games for a payoff, and she took the opportunity to slip him the poison. But when Tanaka used her secret to get the upper hand in the game, she fled, then killed herself."

That made no sense to me, even if I didn't know about what Carlos had seen. "But why kill herself?" I asked. "I would have just driven home as fast as I could, grabbed my own car with the cash and my stuff, which was already packed, and hit the road."

"Guilty conscience, maybe?" suggested Lance.

I knew better. If Miranda felt guilty it was because her husband might have found out her secret. I still wasn't buying that she killed Peter Tanaka.

"And what if Miranda didn't commit suicide or kill Tanaka?" asked Greg.

Lance gave a shrug that was slow and heavy. "So what? It won't bring my brother back, will it? As far as I'm concerned, both Miranda and I have Rocky's blood on our hands. I let him know I had a gun in the house, and she gave him a reason to pull the trigger."

"This was not your fault, Lance," Greg told him with conviction. "Not your fault at all."

Lance gave a half shrug that let us know he didn't believe it. "What I really wanted to talk to you about," Lance said, "was the funeral — or, rather, funerals. We're contacting as many people as we can, but it's tough. Could you guys contact Rocky's team and any other athletes you think would want to know and tell them? The service for both Miranda and Rocky will be held at the Congregational Church in Corona del Mar at ten o'clock on Wednesday morning." He got to his feet like an old man. "I'll text you the exact address and details tonight."

Greg rolled over to him, his hand extended. "Don't worry, Lance. Odelia and I are going to see the team tomorrow. We'll make sure everyone knows about the service, including those not there tomorrow."

Lance took his offered hand and shook it, covering Greg's hand with both of his.

"Thanks. My family and I really appreciate it."

Before he left, I gave him another hug and told him to call if he needed anything.

After Lance left the shop, Greg locked the door behind him and returned to his office. I had pulled up my chair closer to Greg's desk and was poring over my notes again with the fervor of a mad scientist.

"What are we missing?" I said, not looking up from the scraps holding my scribbles.

"Sweetheart," Greg said with tenderness, "let it go. Like Lance said, nothing is going to bring Rocky back."

"But we know that Miranda was murdered." I looked up at my husband with surprise. "Don't you want to find out who did that and who killed Peter Tanaka?"

"Not tonight. I'm too exhausted and sad to even think about it anymore."

I studied Greg, feeling my brows bunch over my eyes like small, tight fists. "Did what we're finding out about Miranda dampen your interest in finding her killer?"

He rolled over to me and looked me in the eye. His were sad yet steely with anger. "To be honest, it did. She was deceiving Rocky and hoarding cash while he was trying to hold their life together. Right now I don't care if we do find her killer. Lance was wrong about him being partially to blame because he had a gun in the house, but he was right about Miranda giving Rocky a reason to pull the trigger." He rolled behind his desk and started locking his desk and shutting down his computer for the night. "Let's go home and have another peaceful evening. It's going to be hard seeing all the players tomorrow."

I gathered up my notes. "Sounds good, honey. I think I'm going to have a good long soak in my tub tonight."

"And I'm going to drown myself in a few beers and the rest of that key lime pie."

"The rest?" I asked. "There's more than three quarters of it left."

"Don't worry," he said to me with a half smile. "I'll save you a sliver."

# TWENTY-FOUR

After a late breakfast, the next morning Greg and I were back on the 5 Freeway heading south with Wainwright in the back of the van. We were on our way to Ocean-side and the Lunatics' quad rugby practice. Greg didn't seem any more inclined toward finding Miranda's killer this morning than he'd been last night. I, on the other hand, was biting at the bit to find out who Carlos had seen running from the van. I under-stood Greg's feelings. I wasn't feeling so warm and fuzzy toward Miranda myself these days, but it didn't change the fact that I wanted — needed — to get to the bottom of things. To not do so felt like unfinished business, and I'm one of those people who cannot leave something half-assed. Unless Greg changed his mind, I might just have to see this to the end on my own. Maybe I was a fixer like Elaine said.

When we arrived at the practice place,

most of the Lunatics were there warming up, circling in their rugby wheelchairs, loosening up their muscles, and getting their minds ready to play. I'd been to many of their practices over the years, and usually they were boisterous and high spirited. Not today. This morning a shadowy, heavy feeling hung over the place like a shroud. It was a shroud — the shroud of their fallen friend and captain.

Practices were held in the gymnasium of a small community center. When we arrived, I took a seat on the set of retractable bleachers next to Cory Seidman while Greg went to speak to Coach Warren. Wainwright was at his heels. Not many friends and family members ever showed up for the practice sessions, but I saw a couple of women sitting together and chatting. I recognized one as Samantha Franco. The coach stopped the warm-up and gathered the team around, then he turned it over to Greg.

"I understand you all know that Rocky Henderson died yesterday," Greg began, his voice straining to stay even. "His brother, Lance, wanted me to let everyone know when and where the joint service for Rocky and Miranda will be held. It's this Wednesday at ten at the Congregational Church in Corona del Mar. My wife has the details about it, including the location of the grave-side service and the reception after." That was my cue to hold up the half-sheet flyers we had made up early this morning. I waved them in the air. Cory immediately held out a hand for one. Samantha left her spot on the bleachers and came down to me to get two, then returned to sit with the other woman.

"Who's that?" I asked Cory.

He glanced up the few rows behind us. "I don't know her name, but I think she came with Kevin. Probably his latest conquest."

In spite of the gravity of the day, I smiled. Kevin Spelling had the reputation of being a ladies' man — something he and Peter Tanaka had in common — but Kevin, one of the Olympian players, was known for being a full-blown charmer, not a batterer. And to my knowledge, Kevin kept his hands off of other players' ladies.

"He had a different woman with him at the tournament," Cory whispered to me with a grin.

"Really? I didn't notice him with anyone."

Cory nodded. "I don't think she stayed long. I saw them briefly together in the parking lot on one of my smoke breaks. I didn't see her with him before that, though. It looked like they were having a spat, then

she left and didn't come back into the gym."
Cory shook his head and grinned. "I never
got that much action when I was single."

"Cory, did you notice if Peter Tanaka ever
brought anyone to the games or scrimmages?"

He gave it some thought, pursing his lips
and rolling his eyes upward as if looking for
the answer in the top of his head. "Nope,
not that I can recall. He always came alone."

"So you've never met his sister? Her name
is Ann."

"No. I didn't even know he had a sister."

I nodded. "A twin, no less."

"Wonder if she's a jerk too?"

Coach Warren called for a full minute of
silence in honor of Rocky Henderson. The
few of us on the bleachers stood up, and
everyone bowed their heads in respect and
some in prayer. When the minute was up,
Coach gave the team a pep talk and announced that Kevin Spelling would be the
new team captain. The other players nodded in agreement and welcomed Kevin as
their new leader. As his first act as captain,
he announced that the rest of the season
would be dedicated to Rocky and that they
should honor him by playing their best and
holding back nothing.

Cory and I watched the practice together.

"Mona has greatly improved over last year," I said to him.

"Yes, she has," Cory answered with pride. "She's been working with a personal trainer to build her upper body strength and utilize her arms and hands more. The same trainer worked with me after I had knee surgery last year. He's amazing." Suddenly, Cory smacked his forehead with the palm of his right hand. "Damn it. I told her trainer I'd take some video of Mona's practice so he can see how she's doing, but I left the video cam at home on the table." He pulled out his phone, then swore again, this time under his breath. "And this thing isn't charged enough."

"Don't worry," I told him. "I'll take some video. My phone's fully charged."

"Can you email it to me later?"

"Sure. Happy to do it."

I pulled out my cell phone and discovered that Steele had sent me a text. DON'T FORGET, it said, TOMORROW: BRIGHT EYED, BUSHY TAILED, AND EARLY.

I texted back: NICE TO HAVE THE OLD STEELE BACK . . . I THINK. DID YOU AND MICHELLE RECONNECT?

In an instant came the reply: MYOB! BTW, DON'T BOTHER ME TODAY. I'M BUSY.

I laughed to myself, remembering the

enthusiastic thank you text I'd received from Michelle yesterday and a promise to get the four of us together soon for dinner that I received this morning. If I had minded my own business, Steele wouldn't be getting busy at all.

I started to take the video, then saw Mona sitting on the sidelines next to Greg while the coach and Kevin helped a few of the other players with some moves. Wainwright had wisely found a place to lie down away from the rolling wheels. Both Greg and Mona watched and listened intently, picking up pointers. Greg had already mentioned that he'd like to coach a wheelchair sport one day, and I wondered if maybe he'd like to coach quad rugby instead of basketball. I was sure he'd be great at either. He already helped out on occasion with wheelchair sports for young people.

I stopped the camera to save juice. While I waited, I started flipping through the photos on the phone, especially those taken at the tournament just a week ago. I stopped short again at the one of Miranda and Rocky, taking note of Miranda's smile. Upon inspection, it did look forced, and while Rocky had his arm around her waist, she wasn't touching him at all. Greg and I always had our hands on each other in photos. The signs were there; we just hadn't seen them.

I kept scrolling through the photos from the weekend before, looking each one over more carefully than before while keeping an eye out for Mona to return to the court. I enlarged a few of the photos as I viewed them. There were lots of action shots of various games and many of the players with girlfriends, spouses, friends, and family members. There were several that included Kevin Spelling. I'd been around Kevin quite a bit over the years and had found him charming, intelligent, and fun. Chair or not, it was little wonder why women flocked to him.

The clash of metal caused me to look up from my phone to watch the practice. Kevin was on the court, in the thick of things, using his powerful body and wheelchair to block his opponent. The Laguna Lunatics were looking good in spite of their shared grief.

Going back to the photos, I kept scrolling and reviewing the ones from the prior Sunday. None of the ones with Kevin showed him with any women. About a dozen photos in, something caught my eye. It wasn't a photo of Kevin but one of Greg taken outside the gymnasium shortly after our encounter with Peter Tanaka and shortly before the playoff game started. Turning my phone, I viewed the photo in landscape mode, then enlarged it. In the background was a Lunatic in uniform, and I was pretty sure it was Kevin Spelling but couldn't be positive because I couldn't see the number on the jersey. With him was a woman, and from the expressions on their faces it looked like they were arguing.

I scanned the photo again and saw another figure I also thought I recognized. Off to the side of the building, near the back, was someone leaning against the wall, smoking.

I nudged Cory. "Is that you leaning against the wall in this photo?"

He looked at the photo, squinting at it. "Caught me with my filthy habit."

I pointed at the player. "And that's Kevin and the woman he was arguing with?"

"Yep."

"But I thought you saw Tanaka arguing with Miranda when you took your smoke break."

"I did," he answered, "but that was earlier in the break. If you'll remember, before the final playoff games, there was a long break so that the players could rest up and get something to eat."

He was right. That break was longer than the others. It was during that break that I'd spoken with my mother and bumped into Tanaka.

"Could you hear what they were saying?" I asked. "Or see her face?"

"Not a word," he answered. "I was too far away. Couldn't see her face either." Cory laughed and shook his head. "Seems like no matter where I went during the break, players were having fights with women."

I looked again at the photo. The woman had her back to Cory. All he had seen was a slender woman with a hoodie pulled up over the back of her head — a long, baggy, gray hoodie worn over jeans.

Looking down at the photo on my phone again, I shuddered. Although in the background and when enlarged the picture was very fuzzy, the woman with Kevin looked familiar. I was almost positive it was Ann Tanaka.

I nearly fell in my rush to climb down from the bleachers and get to Greg. If it hadn't been for Cory, I just might have landed with a big face-first splat on the hardwood and ended up looking like Steele, but he caught my arm and helped me down.

"What's the matter, Odelia?" Cory asked, steadying me.

"Something," I gasped, wondering what

to say. "An important message on my phone."

When I got to Greg, I grabbed his arm and tugged him away from the players. "You've got to see this."

I made my way to a far corner, and Greg followed. Wainwright faithfully trotted along next to him. When we were out of earshot I showed him the photo on my phone. "I'll bet that's Ann Tanaka with Kevin Spelling," I said, pointing at the two figures behind him in the photo. "And look at what she's wearing."

Greg took out his reading glasses and studied the photo closer and for a long time. When he looked back up at me, his jaw was clenched. "I hope Kevin had nothing to do with this," he said, keeping his voice low. "Because if he did, I'll beat him to a pulp."

"Honey," I cautioned. "That won't solve anything. I think we need to be very careful how we handle this or it could blow up." I paused for my words to get past his anger and penetrate his brain. I knew when they did because Greg's shoulders relaxed a tiny bit.

"Do you recall," I continued, "if Dev said what Ann's alibi was or who provided it?"

He shook his head. "No, just that Martinez told him she had one and it checked out." He blew out a gush of air. "You're right, we need to handle this delicately."

"So you're on board again with finding Miranda's killer?"

"I'm on board with finding out what happened, once and for all." He rolled his chair back and forth as he thought it through.

# TWENTY-FIVE

Our story for our abrupt departure was that my brother had texted that my mother, who was visiting him, wasn't feeling well and I might have to fly to Arizona to be with her if she didn't improve.

After giving Wainwright time to pee, Greg and I sat in the van and brainstormed about where to go with our new information.

"Should we call Dev?" Greg asked. "Or Martinez?"

"We're in Oceanside," I pointed out, "almost in Bill Martinez's back yard, and I have his card." I fished around in my tote bag until I found the business card the detective had given me the day Tanaka died. "Or we could go it alone and see if we find out anything."

Greg shook his head. "Not this time, sweetheart. I vote for letting the police handle this."

"But I can't tell them how I knew to look

for someone in a gray hoodie."

"You don't have to." Greg turned to me and patted my knee. "Just tell Martinez that Dev told us Ann Tanaka had an alibi, yet here she is just minutes before her brother died and she didn't stick around. That should be enough for them to investigate further. If they don't listen, then we'll strike out on our own."

Once in agreement on our story and our agreement not to say anything about Elaine Powers or Carlos and his mother, I placed a call to Detective Martinez's number and reached voice mail. I left him a message that it was about Miranda Henderson's murder, along with my callback number. Greg started the van and began driving.

"Are we going home?" I asked. "Why don't we wait a bit to see if he calls back."

"That's what I was thinking, sweetheart, but we need to get out of this parking lot before someone comes out of the gym and gets suspicious."

"You mean like Kevin?"

"Yes. He may or may not be involved in this mess, but until we know for sure, I don't want him wondering what's going on if he sees us lingering in the parking lot after leaving in such a rush."

We didn't drive far. Greg pulled into

another lot just a block away from the gym. He backed into a space so that we were staring out and could make a speedy departure if needed. Then we waited. From where we were, we could see the community center but were somewhat covered on both sides by other vehicles. Our old van, the larger one, would have stuck out like a sore thumb. Only someone we knew well, staring directly at us, would know it was us in our new minivan.

"Why here?" I asked.

"Why not?" Greg answered. "We don't want to go too far afield unless Martinez calls and wants to see us, and my gut is telling me to keep an eye on the community center."

"It's usually my gut that's talking."

"What can I say, sweetheart," he said with a smirk. "Your gut is rubbing off on my gut."

"That sounds dirty."

He laughed his throaty laugh. It was suggestive and usually signaled fun times ahead, similar to my wearing negligee instead of a long tee shirt at bedtime. But the fun times would have to wait, no matter how expertly that laugh played my spine like piano keys, running scales up and down at will.

It wasn't long before one of the things we

were waiting for happened. It took the form of Kevin Spelling's car — a Jeep Grand Cherokee the color of an expensive granite kitchen counter. His vehicle spilled out of the community center parking lot onto the street, nearly hitting a kid on a skateboard. The kid yelled an obscenity and flipped Kevin off, but Kevin never even slowed down. Greg saw the Jeep a split second before I did and had already started the van and put it into gear. He pulled out of our space, following Kevin.

The Jeep might have gotten off to a quick pace, but we quickly caught up to him, staying a few car lengths behind, as it slowed to make its way through the streets of Oceanside.

"I think he's heading for the freeway," I said to Greg, not taking my eye off of the Jeep up ahead.

"I think you're right," he answered. "Practice had just barely started when we got there, so unless his mother is also ill, something spooked him."

"Something like Cory mentioning the photo of Kevin with Ann?" I suggested.

"Could be. If Kevin was feeling guilty about anything, he might have asked Cory what you two were talking about." Greg glanced over at me, his face sagging with disappointment. "I would have given anything to have not seen that vehicle leave that parking lot on our heels."

"I know, honey. I'm sorry." An alarming thought occurred to me like a slap across the face. "Do you think Cory might be involved too?"

"At this point, anything is possible."

I didn't want my brain to go down that path. I couldn't think of Cory Seidman and possibly Mona being involved in this mess, but as Greg said, anything was possible.

As we suspected, Kevin's vehicle was heading for the 5 Freeway. We followed it onto the northbound ramp, glad for once for the heavy traffic that provided us with great cover.

"He looks to be alone," I said. "I wonder what happened to the girl at practice?"

Greg shrugged. "Who knows?"

"Where do you think he's heading?"

"Kevin lives in Huntington Beach, not far from Ocean Breeze," Greg told me, not taking his eyes off the Jeep we were pursuing. "Maybe there. If he's in cahoots with Ann Tanaka, maybe he's meeting up with her, though I doubt he'll drive all the way to Altadena." He looked at me. "We need to know what happened at practice after we left."

"We can call Cory, or maybe Coach War-ren," I suggested.

"Both numbers are on my recent calls list," Greg said. "We just have to pick the right one."

I looked at Greg's phone. When he's in his van it's always hooked up to the hands-free feature. "I have an idea," I told him. "We'll call Cory. Follow my lead."

Greg made the call and put it on speaker. When Cory answered, I said, "Cory, it's Odelia and Greg. Can you do us a big favor?"

"Sure, guys," came his affable voice with no hint of hesitation. "Name it."

"We don't want to disturb Kevin while he's at practice," I lied, "but we need him to call us. Would you ask him to give Greg a call after he's done?"

"Sure, but I can't," Cory said. "Kevin left practice shortly after you guys did."

"He did?" I asked, faking surprise.

"Yeah. He was on the sidelines and I told him about the photo you had of him and that chick. I was ribbing him, asking if she was a done deal or just on the sidelines for now." He laughed. "You know, guy ribbing."

"He left because of that?" Greg asked.

"No, I'm sure he didn't. Kev isn't sensi-tive about stuff like that. But shortly after, he was on his cell, then he told Coach he had to leave, making apologies to the team and saying he'd see all of us at the funeral on Wednesday."

Greg and I exchanged silent looks, then Greg looked ahead, keeping his eyes on the Jeep. "Okay," he said into the phone, "then I'll give him a call a little later. Thanks anyway."

"No problem," Cory said. "See you two on Wednesday."

"Hey," I called toward the phone, hoping to catch Cory before he hung up. "Did Kevin take his girl du jour with him?"

"No. I think she came in a separate car. He said something to her about calling her later right before he left. She waited a few minutes, then left herself."

"Cory may be playing us," Greg said after the call, "but I don't think so."

"Neither do I, honey. But that photo definitely kicked Kevin into action."

We travelled along, both of us watching the Jeep for any signs that it might take an unexpected exit ramp, but it kept to its course, not speeding or moving erratically, keeping with the movement of the traffic. We were getting closer to Huntington Beach with every mile.

"I thought you said Kevin Spelling and

Peter Tanaka were friends," I said, finally breaking the tense silence.

"They used to be tighter than ticks years ago," Greg answered. "Maybe they had a falling out, although Mona said Kevin fought to get Tanaka back onto the Lunatics."

"Well, being with Ann doesn't make Kevin a murderer," I said, mindful of the hope in my voice. I liked Kevin and, like Greg, was heartbroken when I saw his vehicle follow us out of the community center parking lot.

"No, it doesn't," Greg agreed, "but it does make you wonder what he was doing with Ann. I don't recall ever seeing them together, not even years ago. In fact, I never even knew Tanaka had a sister until the night we met her."

The Jeep finally put on its turn signal and merged onto southbound 55. It certainly did look like Kevin was heading for home. We followed.

"What are we going to do once he stops?" I asked.

Greg shrugged. "I guess we'll see what he does."

When Kevin pulled into the driveway of a condo complex not far from the beach, Greg kept going. "That's his place," he told me. "He has a nice two-bedroom ground floor condo back by the pool." We circled the block, then parked on the street just a few car lengths from the entrance. "If I recall correctly," Greg said, "that's the only way in or out of this gated complex. And most of the visitor parking is in the front right as you drive in."

He cut the engine, and we waited. Wainwright was trained to lie still while the van moved. Now he got up and made his way forward to push his nose between the two front seats. We both gave him several pats and assurances that he was a good boy. I got out his travel bowl and poured some water into it, which he immediately lapped up.

Then we waited.

Just over fifteen minutes later, my cell phone rang. It was Detective Martinez. I put him on speaker.

"So," he said, after squaring away the greetings. "You have new information on the Tanaka/Henderson deaths?"

"We sure think so, Detective," I told him. "We think Peter's sister, Ann, had something to do with both — at least something is fishy about her. Detective Dev Frye is a good friend of ours, and he told us that she had an alibi for the day her brother was murdered."

"That's right," he said, his voice swelling with amusement. "You're the two who think they're a modern-day Nick and Nora Charles. Don't you even have a dog?"

I glanced at Wainwright, who was five times the size of Asta and now snoring away in the back.

"We have proof," I said, ignoring his dig, "that Ann Tanaka was at the gymnasium the day her brother died."

There was silence on the other end. "Proof, you say?"

"Yes, a photo taken just outside the gym in San Diego less than an hour before he died. It's on my phone. I can send it to you, if you like."

"Please do. Text it to this number. It's my cell."

Quick as a bunny, I sent the photo of Greg with Ann and Kevin in the background. "Sent," I said to Martinez once the photo had been sent through space. "The photo is of my husband, but if you enlarge it you'll see Ann in the background arguing with Kevin Spelling. Off to the side you'll see Cory Seidman standing next to the wall, smoking. Cory didn't know that was Ann Tanaka, but he can confirm that he saw this woman with Kevin and when."

"Hold on," Martinez said. A minute later

he came back on. "Why didn't you say anything before now?"

"Because we didn't notice this photo until today," I said, getting a bit defensive. "I'd taken quite a few at the tournament, but with all the craziness after Tanaka died, I didn't go through them until today."

I could tell from the additional silence that this cop wasn't going to be as forthcoming with information as Dev would be in similar circumstances.

"What was Ann's alibi?" Greg asked.

"She was playing tennis with a girlfriend, she told us. The friend confirmed it. Where are you two now?" Martinez asked.

Greg and I exchange looks. Should we lie or tell Martinez the truth? "We're in front of Kevin Spelling's place," he answered, making the decision for the two of us.

"What in the hell are you doing there?" snapped Martinez.

"When Kevin found out about the photo we had of him and Ann arguing at the tournament," I answered, taking my turn, "he left rugby practice like he was shot out of a canon. We followed him and wound up at his place in Huntington Beach."

"Does he know you're there?"

"Not that we know of," I told him. "According to Cory Seidman, as soon as he told him about the photo, Kevin made a phone call and lit out of there."

"What does Seidman have to do with this?" asked Martinez.

"Nothing that we know of," said Greg. "Odelia showed him the photo, and it seems he told Kevin. Cory appears to be in the dark as to who the woman is in the photo or any possible connection to Peter and Miranda's death. He's under the impression that Ann is just another of Kevin's romantic conquests who got hot under the collar at the game."

"I want to thank you for calling with this information," Martinez said. "Seems we'll need to be asking Mr. Spelling and the Tanaka ladies a few more questions. I'll probably be asking you two some more questions, too. So don't go anywhere."

"Do you want us to wait here for you?" I asked.

"At Spelling's? No. I want you to please get the hell out of there and go home. Leave the police work to us, thank you very much." He voice was edgy, like a serrated knife, and not at all in league with *please* and *thank you.*

# Twenty-Six

We didn't go home. Instead, we stayed put, agreeing that it seemed unlikely that Kevin left the game just to sit on his butt at home. Either he was packing and about to hit the road or maybe he was waiting for whomever he called. Maybe it was both.

"My money is on Ann Tanaka showing up," Greg said, taking a sip of water from the bottle he kept in the console's cup holder.

"Who will show up first?" I asked my hubs. "Ann or Detective Martinez?"

"If it was Ann who Kevin called and she left Altadena immediately, she should be here soon." He opened his door and grabbed for his wheelchair, which was stashed behind his seat.

"Where are you going?" I asked.

"To talk to Kevin," he said, setting up the chair and swinging his butt into it. "I'm getting to the bottom of this once and for all."

"Not without me you're not." I started to get out of the van.

"No, stay here," he told me, talking across the front seat of the van. "See if Ann shows up or Martinez."

"Not on your life," I told him. "If Kevin is involved with Peter and Miranda's murders, I'm not letting you go in there alone."

"And if he is," Greg snapped back at me, "I'm not letting you near him."

"Let's not forget that I took a ride with a contract killer yesterday."

"Yeah, and your luck is running out, Odelia. Let's not press it any more than we need to."

Ignoring him, I got out of the van, but as soon as my feet hit the curb I heard Elaine telling me that one day I'd pay for being on the side of right all the time. Maybe she was right. Maybe Greg was right.

"What if he pulls a gun on you?" I asked Greg.

"He could pull a gun on both of us," was his response. "I'd rather he only have one target."

"No sale." I stuck my cell phone in a pocket, then lowered my window a few inches to give Wainwright air and shut the door behind me. I stood on the curb waiting for Greg, clearly not budging until he gave in on the matter.

Greg took a deep breath and said something under his breath, then something to Wainwright. After closing his door, he locked the van and set the alarm. The beep of the alarm sounded like a final high-pitched swear word.

The complex Kevin lived in was large and nicely landscaped and made up of both single and two-story buildings. It had to be an older complex. Newer ones weren't being built with this much green space or in single stories. With Greg leading the way, we moved along the wide sidewalk until we reached the pool area. Greg stopped and looked around. "It's one of these along here to the right," he whispered. "The carports are in the back."

I trotted ahead, looking over the front doors for clues or names, finally pointing to one that had a ramp built where normally a few steps up to the entrance would be.

"I think you're right," Greg said, joining me.

"If we ring the bell," I asked, "what are the chances he'll make for the back and get away while we stand here?"

"Could happen," he said.

"Why don't I go around back so he can't escape that way?"

I could tell Greg didn't want me out of his sight. He didn't mind if I was out of sight in the van, just not out of sight nosing around. Finally, he said, "Okay, but if he does come out the back, don't get in his way if he's armed, and keep your cell phone on."

"Give me a minute before you ring the bell," I said, taking off down the sidewalk to the end of the building. I went around the back to the driveway that led to the carports. The townhouses in this section were all single story and had a double-covered carport and a gate leading to a back patio. I spotted Kevin's vehicle in its cubby and waited. On his back gate was a painted arts and crafts sign that read NOT HANDICAPPED, HANDICAPABLE. I waited by the sign. A few minutes later I heard Greg say, "Come on in, Odelia. It's okay." About the same time, the gate to the back of Kevin's place opened and Kevin invited me in.

We stood by the kitchen table just inside the back sliding door. If Kevin had a weapon nearby, I didn't see it.

"I was just on my way out," he told us. He seemed edgy and brittle, with none of his usual confidence. On the table was a duffle bag half filled with clothing. A shaving kit and other clothing were waiting to be packed.

"Where are you going in such a rush?" Greg asked.

"I need to go to my parents. They live in Ojai. It's a family emergency." He looked at Greg, then me, and said, "Hey, isn't Odelia's mom sick?"

"Our family emergency is just as fake as yours, Kevin," Greg confessed.

"Did you call Ann Tanaka before you left the gym today?" I asked, not giving him time to process our lie.

"No, I didn't," he said, a bit too quickly. "Why would I call her?"

"To give her a heads-up that the police will soon know that she was at the tournament when her brother died," Greg said.

"Ann wasn't there," Kevin stressed, looking from me to Greg again. "She was nowhere near there. She was playing tennis that day." His face grew red as he tried to convince us.

"Someone must have lied to the police about her alibi because we have a photo of you and Ann arguing," Greg told him. "The San Diego police have it now."

"That wasn't Ann," Kevin said. "It was . . . it was someone else." He grabbed the clothing still on the table between his two open palms, using his damaged hands like salad

371

tongs, and forced it into the duffle. He did the same with the shaving kit. "Now I have to go. Really, guys, we should all go."

Greg rolled close to him, using his own wheelchair to block Kevin's path. "How are you involved with Tanaka and Miranda's deaths?"

Kevin's eyes popped. "I'm not involved. Not at all. How can you even think that?"

"The woman you were arguing with in San Diego was involved. We believe it's Ann and that she killed both of them."

Kevin shook his head back and forth hard, like a dog shaking off water. "No. Ann would never do a thing like that any more than I would." The passion in his voice was strong and assured.

I moved closer to Kevin. "Are you involved romantically with Ann Tanaka?"

Kevin closed his eyes. A few seconds later, he slowly nodded. "Yes, we've been secretly dating off and on for several years. It started right before Peter took off for Canada. Her mother doesn't approve, so it's tough. She thinks we broke it off a long time ago."

"But what about the other women you're seen with?" I prodded.

"These days they're mostly friends helping me cover up my relationship with Ann." He glanced nervously through the living room and out the front window like he was expecting someone. "Like I said, Ann and I have been off and on in secret for a long time. We broke it off again when Peter returned from Canada."

"I take it he didn't approve either," said Greg.

"Not really. The mother has a problem with me not being Japanese — at least that's what she says. Peter had a problem with his sister being with a gimp." He scoffed. "Strange, huh? He's good enough for the women he dates, but I'm not good enough for his sister." He took several deep breaths before continuing. "I begged her to move in with me when Peter showed up again. He smacked her around. Did you know that? He did it for years."

Greg and I nodded, almost in unison.

"That monster of a mother of hers wouldn't lift a finger to stop it. It wasn't so bad when Peter went to Canada; then Ann only had to deal with her mother treating her like a slave." Another deep breath. "I begged her to come live with me and not look back. I told her I'd protect her."

"Why didn't she?" I asked.

Kevin smacked his dining table with his fist. "Because of the damn money! There's a trust her father set up. She and Peter were

373

to come into the money in just a couple of months."

I stepped forward, curious about an idea that had just occurred to me. "But why couldn't she move in with you until the trust matured?"

Kevin rubbed his hands over his face. "Because the mother controls the trust, and she didn't want Ann leaving her and being happy." He took another deep breath, as if each explanation was a punch to his gut. "There's a morals clause of some kind in the trust," he told us. "If Mrs. Tanaka feels either child is behaving in a way to bring shame on the family, she can extend the maturity of the trust by five years."

"If that was the case, why wasn't Peter penalized?" Greg asked. "He's done all kinds of things to shame the Tanaka name, including blackmail and drug charges."

"Because, honey," I told Greg as the pieces fell together for me, "that's her hold on him. I'm thinking it's probably why he came back to California. After she bailed his butt out on the Canadian drug charge, she probably told him he had to come back or forfeit the trust for five years."

Kevin was nodding. "That's pretty close to what's going on. The way I understand it, she would have done anything to keep

Peter close to her. I wouldn't even put it past Mrs. Tanaka to enforce the clause anyway. Meanwhile, Ann has been towing the line, playing the dutiful daughter, trying to get to her next birthday and to the money. I've told her over and over that I don't care about the money; we'll be just fine without it. But she feels it's all she has left of her father. She feels she's earned it in some sick way and is refusing to leave home without it."

"Ann told us pretty much the same thing," Greg said. I could see from his face that it was falling together for him too. "She said she was going to leave as soon as she came into her inheritance."

"Yes," Kevin confirmed. "She was leaving Southern California. In a few months I would follow, and we'd get married." For the first time, a small smile crossed his lips. "My parents love Ann. They can't wait to welcome her into the family."

"So it was Mrs. Tanaka who killed Peter and Miranda." I said it not as a question but as a statement.

"I honestly don't know," Kevin told us. "But I wouldn't put it past the old witch. Ann told me that Peter was leaving town as soon as he got his inheritance, too. Even though he smacked Ann around, he was also close to her." He looked at us with disgust. "It's sick, I know."

"Did you know that Peter Tanaka was blackmailing Miranda Henderson about being a call girl?" Greg asked.

"Not until this past week," he told us. "When I asked Ann about it, she said she knew but didn't want to tell me, knowing Rocky was a friend of mine. She was also worried that her brother would go after me if he thought I knew. Even though we were friends, he could be pretty vindictive. He was particularly mad about not getting back on the Lunatics." He sighed. "As for Rocky and Miranda, I knew they'd had some problems, but nothing as bad as it turned out to be."

Greg rolled his chair back to allow Kevin more movement. Kevin moved his wheelchair deeper into the living room so he could keep watch out the window. Like most homes where a resident is in a chair, it was uncluttered, with wide spaces in which to navigate. We followed, and I took a seat on the edge of the sofa, perching carefully instead of getting comfortable just in case I needed to move quickly.

"How did you come across June Tanaka at the tournament?" Greg asked Kevin.

"It was a fluke, really," he explained, still

nervously glancing out the front window.

"Is Ann on her way here?" I asked, noticing how antsy he was.

"Yes," Kevin admitted. He looked at me. "You're right. I did call her after I heard about the photo of me with her mother. I told her it was just a matter of time before her mother was hauled away by the cops and to get out of the house now because there's no telling what that crazy woman would do once cornered. She finally agreed with me and is coming here. Then we're going to my parents' house."

"In Ojai?" I asked.

"Yes."

"Did you know that Mrs. Tanaka killed Peter?" I asked.

He shook his head. "Not right off. When I saw her last Sunday, I'd gone out to my Jeep to get something and she was crossing the parking lot. At first I thought it was Ann and called to her, but when she turned around I saw it was Mrs. Tanaka." He lifted an arm up and swiped at his hair. "I wish I'd never seen her. She came up to me and started yelling at me to stay away from Ann. In fact, she told me she was there specifically to tell me she knew what was going on and for me to leave her daughter alone or else. I really thought that was why she was there, at least until Peter died. But even after he died, I thought it might just be a coincidence because of all the evidence against Miranda. But now I know I was just being a fool. I didn't want to believe someone would kill their own child."

Greg pounded a fist on his knee and nearly shouted. "Why didn't you tell the police about Mrs. Tanaka?"

"Because," Kevin explained, his voice twisted in anguish, "she threatened to hurt Ann if I told anyone that she was there or about our conversation, including Ann." He moved his arms around with uncurbed restlessness. "I didn't tell Ann about it until I called her today. Until now I think Ann always thought Miranda killed Peter."

"Not anymore. I made sure she knew the truth."

All three of us turned to the figure that had slipped silently in through the back door while we were talking in the living room. It was a slender middle-aged woman with black hair, wearing jeans and a gray hooded sweatshirt. She moved like a cat burglar, deliberately and with stealth. In her hands was a gun.

# TWENTY-SEVEN

"Ann's not here, Mrs. Tanaka," Kevin said, turning his wheelchair to face the crazy woman.

"I know that," June Tanaka said. Her lips immediately pressed together into a tight red slash. "I managed to talk some sense into her. She sent me to tell you she's not coming and to leave her alone."

"What have you done to her?" Kevin screamed at her. He rolled forward but stopped short when Mrs. Tanaka leveled the gun at his chest.

"We had a little mother-daughter chat, and mother always knows best."

"Put the gun down, Mrs. Tanaka," Greg told her, inching his chair forward a few inches. "Let's discuss this."

"Stay where you are, Mr. Stevens," Mrs. Tanaka told him, "or I might have to kill your wife as a warning." The gun was now aimed at my chest. I held my breath, then let it out, nice and slow.

"It's clear it was you who slipped into Peter's van and put the cyanide into his water jug," I said, staying put. "But why? You seemed to adore your son."

"Because he was going to leave me again," she explained. "The night before he left for San Diego, I confronted him about his plans. We argued." With her free hand she lifted the front of the sweatshirt to expose a trim belly with several large bruises. They reminded me of Steele's injuries but weren't quite as bad. "I can abide many things, but I will not tolerate this."

"He hit you?" I asked.

"We argued. Then Peter cornered me and started punching. He didn't stop until I hit him over the head with a book I grabbed from a shelf."

"Where was Ann?" asked Kevin

"Not home. Probably out whoring around." She gave Kevin an icy-cold look of accusation. "And even if she was home, I doubt she would have stopped it."

I wanted to feel sympathy for June Tanaka but was having trouble mustering any. She'd created the monster that was Peter Tanaka, and she had let him slap Ann around for years. I wondered if the irony had occurred to Mrs. Tanaka that she had been attacked by her beloved house pet that she'd personally trained.

"But why did you have to kill Miranda Henderson?" asked Greg. "She did nothing to you."

"That wasn't the plan," she explained, lowering her sweatshirt. "After I left Peter's van, I crouched behind a car and watched and listened as the Henderson woman and Peter met." She cackled. "I almost ran into that dimwit whose wife plays rugby. He was also spying on them but gave up after a few minutes." She continued to hold the gun steady on me. "Miranda handed Peter an envelope, then helped him refill his sports bottles while they talked — actually, argued. She told Peter she was leaving town and this would be her last payment. He said he would go to her husband, and she told him she didn't care anymore. Frankly, I didn't know if she was stupid or simple, helping her blackmailer like that with his chores, but what better fool to take the fall? Especially after leaving her fingerprints all over the place."

"But why kill her if you'd already set her up?" I asked, pushing for answers.

"Same reason I threatened to hurt Ann if Kevin talked: she saw me," Mrs. Tanaka explained. "Miranda didn't see me in the van but near it and soon enough after I left the poison to be suspicious and tell the police after Peter died. I couldn't have that." She edged closer to us all, moving the gun from me to Kevin. "While everyone was in the gym watching the game, I went back to Peter's van and got his gun."

"Keys." Greg said the word in a simple sharp tone. "You had Peter's extra keys."

"Of course. I knew where he kept the spares for both his van and the vault in his van and made good use of them." She paused and took a deep breath, almost a cleansing yoga breath. After, a small, peaceful smile crossed her lips. The woman had clearly popped a mental wheelie.

"I saw Miranda go to her husband's van after she left Peter, so I knew which one it was. Before I could approach her, she went inside to watch the game. I waited, not sure what to do but knowing I had to do something. Then everything fell in place." Another peaceful smile. "Miranda conveniently came rushing out of the gym, crying hysterically, and hopped into the van. While she fumbled to get it going, I jumped into the passenger's side with the gun and told her to drive. She had no idea it would be her last trip until it happened." Mrs. Tanaka paused and pursed her red lips. "Pretty but not a very bright girl. It's almost ludicrous to think that vain, flighty thing was smart enough to plan a murder."

"You must have had an accomplice," Greg said to her. "How did you get back to where you parked your own car?"

Mrs. Tanaka shook her head. "You underestimate me, Mr. Stevens. I'm in pretty good shape. Although my bruises made it more difficult, I simply jogged a short ways to where I could catch a cab back to where I left my car. Which, by the way, was nowhere near the gymnasium but in another part of Balboa Park."

It was becoming clear it was a standoff — three of us but only one of her. The gun tipped the scales in her favor. She could have easily nailed all three of us with three quick blasts before any of us reached her. The men were in wheelchairs and I was slow on my feet. We stood before her like ducks in a carnival shooting gallery just waiting to be picked off so she could claim a prize. We had to stall and hope Martinez was on his way and hadn't just made Kevin a tic on his calendar for follow-up tomorrow.

"I don't get it," I said, spreading my hands out in front of me. "How did someone like you get hold of cyanide, anyway? It's not like it's on sale at Target, two for five dollars." I used the same sarcastic line Steele had used on me and hoped it didn't cause her to start shooting. What I hoped it would do was appeal to her obvious need to be in control and smarter than everyone else. Kevin stared at me with wide eyes, sure I'd signed his death warrant. What I could have told him and didn't was that his death was a sure thing if we didn't do something drastic.

When I saw a smirk cross June Tanaka's face, I knew I'd bought us some time — probably not much but some. "It's amazing what you have laying around the house after years and years," she said to me, "even cyanide. My late husband was a jeweler. He utilized it quite often in his work. Of course, now jewelers don't, but years ago they did quite often. Some even died from exposure to it in the workplace." She winked at me. I noticed she wasn't gripping the gun as tightly now that she was in a chatty and bragging mood. I hoped Greg noticed that too.

"Your husband," I said, continuing with the topic. "Did he die of cyanide exposure?"

She gave a shrug. "It happens, even to those who are careful."

At that point my cell phone rang.

"What's that?" Mrs. Tanaka asked.

"It's my cell phone," I told her. "It's in my pocket."

"Let it ring," she told me.

"People will be expecting us," Greg told her, picking up on my stall tactics. "They're probably wondering where we are."

"Let them wonder," she said.

"If I don't answer," I said, "they will know something's wrong. I always answer my phone."

"They'll find out soon enough on the evening news." Again she graced us with a small smile. My blood stopped flowing, and I felt my head would explode from the backup.

She waved the gun at me. "You — you're coming with me."

I pointed a finger at myself. "Me? You're taking me hostage?"

"More for insurance."

Greg edged forward a little. "Please, Mrs. Tanaka, take me instead."

"Sorry, Mr. Stevens, but from my experience wheelchairs aren't convenient for getaways." She looked at me. "Dump that phone and come over here, and don't try anything or I'll shoot your husband dead in front of your eyes."

Slowly I pulled my phone out of my

pocket and dropped it to the wood floor. It landed with a clunk. Then, with a quick glance at Greg, I started walking slowly toward June Tanaka. To get to her I had to pass Kevin, who was positioned closest to her. I approached Mrs. Tanaka like a woman heading for the electric chair, walking that long last mile instead of a few yards. Kevin stared at me, frightened, tight jawed, and wild-eyed. I begged him with my eyes not to do anything stupid. I even shook my head the teeniest, tiniest bit trying to get my point across. Whatever went down, him playing hero right now might only make it worse.

Unfortunately, he didn't get the memo.

Like Mrs. Tanaka said, wheelchairs aren't convenient for getaways. While they could be fast on the hardwood floor of a gymnasium or on smooth pavement, they took time to gain momentum, especially if the person in it doesn't have full use of his hands. Using his wrists and forearms, Kevin rolled his chair at Mrs. Tanaka as hard as he could. What he did have in his favor was the element of surprise. With her focus on me and Greg and on getting out of the place with me as insurance, she'd almost forgotten about Kevin or had dismissed him as not being a threat.

Just before I passed him, Kevin bumped

me out of the way and headed for June Tanaka, plowing into her like she was an opponent on the rugby court. She didn't go down completely but was knocked off-balance as he clipped her legs with his chair. As he passed her, Kevin wrapped his powerful arms around her torso and hung on, trying to wrestle her to the ground. She was right. She was in good shape and stronger than she looked. Her right hand, the one with the gun, wiggled free and gestured wildly in the struggle, looking to take aim at something.

"Get the gun, Odelia," shouted Greg.

Even before the words were out of my husband's mouth, I lunged after the tangle of metal and flesh that was Kevin and Mrs. Tanaka. Kicking one of her legs from under her, I gave Kevin the leverage he needed to drop the woman onto the floor. I threw myself on top of her, trying to pin her, and grabbed at her gun hand.

Under me June Tanaka was a madwoman possessed by the devil, writhing, kicking, and screaming with unexpected strength. The whole place was alive with screams and shouts — loud enough, I hoped, to bring help. Kevin and Greg surrounded us, trying to help. Mrs. Tanaka got off a powerful and lucky jab with a sharp knee that landed in my soft middle, causing me to double up. She wiggled away from me and kicked again, this time with a foot, knocking the wind out of me. I rolled off her, gasping for air. Then her foot came down in my face, but instead of hitting me square in the middle, it glanced off the side of my nose and left cheek, scraping the skin and making me scream in pain. She aimed the gun at me, but before she could pull the trigger, Greg launched himself at her from his wheelchair, pulling her down to the floor again. They rolled around until he was on top of her, using his powerful upper body strength to subdue her. She screeched and flailed. Kevin was rolling his chair into the melee, trying to use the wheels to strike her, but with little success.

I struggled to get to my feet or at least to my knees to help. Blood was gushing from my nose. I swiped at it with the back of one hand and gathered myself for the next attack. I looked in time to see Greg make a grab for the gun still clutched in Mrs. Tanaka's hand as if welded there permanently. And that's when I heard the shots. There were two of them.

Everything went silent, like in a slow-motion movie sequence. One of the shots had gone wild and hit the flat screen TV on the wall, shattering it. The other had hit flesh. I watched in horror as my darling husband — my life — grabbed his chest and fell off of the madwoman.

A scream rose in my throat like burning bile — a single word scorching its way upward like a firestorm, expelled in horror and disbelief. *"Greg!"*

# TWENTY-EIGHT

Today is Wednesday — the day of the joint funeral for Rocky and Miranda Henderson, but I didn't go. Instead I was at Hoag Hospital studying the newborns on the other side of the nursery window. In the front was Bubba, a lovely baby boy, rosy and pink, weighing in at seven pounds and some change. His official name was Parker Thornton McHugh — a big moniker for a kid to live up to. The original Parker Thornton was Jolene's grandfather, a judge from Minnesota who'd passed away two years earlier.

The circle of life, *hakuna matata,* and all that crap.

"Cute kid," said a familiar voice behind me.

I turned to see Steele standing about two feet away. He was dressed in one of his expensive suits, not the sweats I'd last seen him wearing. His face was still faintly discolored but almost back to normal. He was walking straight but not yet working out in the gym or running. He was back to work, although I wasn't. From the kindness in his eyes, I could tell he didn't mind. My own face was taking its turn at imitating a gargoyle. Scraped and bruised from Mrs. Tanaka's kick, it was tender, but the nose wasn't broken. It was the second time in a year that I'd taken a bad blow to the face, and my sturdy short nose had held strong again.

I turned back to look at the babies. "Are you and Michelle going to have one of these one day?"

"Who knows?" he answered with a shrug. "Do you think the world is ready for another Mike Steele?"

I chuckled softly. "Sure, as long as the little guy comes with a warning label on his backside."

Steele put a hand gently on my shoulder. "The police want to ask you more questions, Grey. You up to it?"

"Yeah, why not." I'd already been questioned for three days straight by the San Diego police, the Huntington Beach police, and deputies from the Los Angeles location that serviced Altadena.

"You look about to drop," Steele noted. "I

can tell them you'll do it later, after you've rested."

I shrugged. "Now, later — makes no difference. I can't sleep anyway."

In a rare show of affection, Steele drew me into him and held me tight. He smelled good, like fine soap and good wool. "Let's go upstairs. That's where they're waiting."

When Steele and I entered the waiting room, Dev was there with Detective Martinez. They both got up and approached me. "I know you've been through the mill, Ms. Grey," Martinez said to me.

"Mrs. Stevens," I corrected him, staring him in the eye. "My name is Mrs. Gregory Stevens."

"Of course, Mrs. Stevens." He paused. "I'd like to go over just a few more things regarding the case."

"Can you give me a few minutes first?" I asked him.

He looked at his watch, obviously in a rush to be done with me, but said, "Sure. I'll be right here when you're ready."

"Come on, Bill," said Dev. "Let me buy you a cup of lousy hospital coffee." Without waiting for an answer, Dev steered the detective toward the elevator.

When Dev glanced back at me, I gave him a small smile of thanks, then moved forward, heading down the hall to a hospital room I'd come to know as home. Steele came with me, keeping his hand on the small of my back for support.

When I entered the room, Renee Stevens looked up. In her hand was a plastic cup with a straw. She held it out to me, her eyes red and drooping. "Would you like to do this, dear?" Like me, she'd had almost no sleep since Sunday. Greg's father was in a corner, asleep in a stiff chair. The poor guy was going to have a backache when he awoke.

I nodded and took the cup, positioning the straw close to Greg's mouth so he could take a drink. He shook his head. "I have two good hands, sweetheart. I can hold it myself." His voice was weak but even. He looked from me to his mother. "You two need to stop treating me like I'm an invalid. The doctor told you I'm going to be okay."

Yes, Greg would be okay in time. The bullet had hit him on the right side of his chest, nicking a lung and causing it to collapse, but the bullet did no other major damage, and they were able to retrieve it during surgery. A miracle, especially when you consider how close Greg had been to the gun when it went off.

After I'd screamed, I'd fallen on him, trying to staunch the bleeding with my hands. His blood, as precious to me as my own — no, *more* precious to me than my own — was coming out of him at an alarming rate.

"Hang on, honey," I had told him, tears streaming down my battered face. "Hang on."

"I'm okay," he wheezed. "Really." He winced with pain and went pale.

"No," I screamed. "No, you will not leave me! I forbid it!"

"Everyone leaves — don't you know that, you silly woman?"

I looked up. The comment had come from June Tanaka. She had gotten to her feet and trained the gun back on Kevin, lest he try something again.

Without thinking, I lunged at her, gun or no gun. I didn't care about my safety. I didn't care about anything but the good man on the floor with a bullet in his chest. I had to get him help but couldn't as long as Mrs. Tanaka was in control. I aimed for her legs, hoping to topple her again. She jumped back, laughing, and aimed the gun directly at my head.

"No!" Kevin yelled. He surged forward, trying to ram her again. The movement made her take her eyes off of me for an instant. It was all I needed. She couldn't cover both of us in movement. I tackled her to the ground. The gun went off, the bullet hitting the wall well above Kevin's head, then fell from her hand. I climbed on top of her. Grabbing her hair, I slammed her head into the wood floor over and over.

Someone pulled me off of her. I was breathing hard and half crazed. Then I remembered Greg. Shaking off the hands that held me, I crawled over to him and cradled his head in my arms. He opened his eyes, looked into mine, and whispered, "You look like hell, sweetheart."

"Wait till you see the other guy," I whispered back before dissolving into a hot mess.

The hands that had dragged me off of June Tanaka belonged to Dev Frye. He'd been called by Martinez, who was worried Greg and I would get into trouble hanging around Kevin's place. He'd given the address to Dev, who was a lot closer, so he could check it out and make sure we behaved. Had we minded our own business, Kevin Spelling would most certainly be as dead as Ann. She'd been found in the Tanaka residence with a bullet in her brain.

June Tanaka is sitting in jail with multiple charges of murder and attempted murder hanging over her head. I'm not sure what will happen to her. Steele and Seth both think she'll be incarcerated somewhere for the criminally insane. Kevin, heartbroken and devastated by the loss of Ann, quit the Lunatics for the season. He visited Greg yesterday and told us he had decided to sell his townhouse and move to Arizona or Texas, both places where there were active quad rugby teams.

A noise from the corner alerted us that Greg's dad was awake. "Odelia," Ron said, clearing his throat. "You're back. Did you see your friend's baby?"

I nodded but didn't take my eyes off of Greg. "I sure did. He's beautiful."

Steele gestured to the Stevenses. "Come on, folks. Let me take you to lunch. There are some lovely places nearby."

Renee looked at us, then smiled at Steele. "I think that would be a lovely idea, Mike. Thank you." She turned to me. "Would you like us to bring you back something, dear?"

"Sure," I said, still not looking at them. "Steele knows what I like."

"A burger for me, please," joked Greg. "Extra cheese and onions."

Ron Stevens patted his son's shoulder with affection before they left. "Soon enough, son. Don't rush it."

"Where's Grace?" Greg asked.

"She and Clark are at our house, getting

some rest and taking care of the animals. They'll be back later. Seth and Zee are having us all over for dinner tonight."

"After that," Greg said, "I want you to go home and get some rest yourself. That's an order."

"We'll see." I left the bed and walked over to the bank of flowers lining the counter that ran against the wall. "These are new," I said, fingering the petals of a beautiful lily arrangement.

"Those came while you were out," he said. "And don't change the subject."

I opened the card. It said simply: *Get well soon! Love, S & W.* I knew it wasn't from Smith & Wesson. "It's from Sybil and Willie," I told Greg.

A nurse walked in while I was admiring the arrangement. In her hands was another large vase of flowers. "Room for one more?" she asked cheerfully. As I turned sharply, she shut the door behind her.

"Elaine?" I asked with shock.

The arrangement moved to the side to reveal the face of Elaine Powers. "Bet you didn't know I was the Florence Nightingale type, did you?"

Greg tried to sit up. "Elaine Powers?" he asked, just as surprised as I was.

She put the flowers down on a small table

and went to Greg. "Don't trouble yourself, sport. I just wanted to meet you and see how you were doing for myself. But you'll have to excuse me if I say hello and scoot. I noticed Detective Frye hovering nearby. Not to mention Mike Steele, who can identify me."

I stepped forward. "Did Carlos and his mother get to their destination?"

"They sure did. They are now snug as two bugs in the bosom of their family." She narrowed her eyes at me. "You didn't mention them, did you?"

I crossed my heart. "Not a peep. We found a way around it."

"Good." She smiled. "Now I best shove off." She pointed a finger at Greg. "You stay on the mend. You have to take care of my girl here."

"You bet," he said, giving her a small grin and salute.

Before she could protest, I wrapped my chubby arms around Elaine's neck and gave her a tight hug. "Thanks for coming by, Elaine. Thanks for everything."

She disentangled herself from me and stepped toward the door, opening it. Her face was flushed. "You take care of yourself, Dottie. You hear?"

# ACKNOWLEDGMENTS

To the usual suspects: my agent, Whitney Lee; my editors at Midnight Ink, Terri Bischoff and Rebecca Zins; and everyone else at Midnight Ink/Llewellyn Worldwide who had a hand in making this book, and all those before it, a reality.

Special acknowledgment to the United States Quad Rugby Association, especially Dan McCauley and Team Sharp Edge. You guys rock!

For more information about quad rugby, visit the USQRA website at http://usqra.org, and check out the documentary *Murderball*.

# ABOUT THE AUTHOR

Like the character Odelia Grey, **Sue Ann Jaffarian** is a middle-aged, plus-size paralegal. In addition to the Odelia Grey mystery series, she is the author of the paranormal Ghost of Granny Apples mystery series and the Madison Rose Vampire mystery series. Sue Ann is also nationally sought after as a motivational and humorous speaker. She lives and works in Los Angeles, California.

Other titles in the Odelia Grey series include *Too Big to Miss* (2006), *The Curse of the Holy Pail* (2007), *Thugs and Kisses* (2008), *Booby Trap* (2009), *Corpse on the Cob* (2010), *Twice As Dead* (2011), *Hide & Snoop* (2012), and *Secondhand Stiff* (2013). Visit Sue Ann on the Internet at
WWW.SUEANNJAFFARIAN.COM
*and*
WWW.SUEANNJAFFARIAN.BLOGSPOT.COM